THE CHORISTER

and other Jewish stories

To David,

Best Wishes,

Mark

6/11/2011

Also by Mark Harris

The Shtetl and other Jewish stories

Mark Harris

THE CHORISTER
and other Jewish stories

Matador
5 Weir Road
Kibworth Beauchamp
Leicester LE8 0LQ, UK
Tel: (+44) 116 279 2299 / 2277
Email: books@troubador.co.uk
Web: www.troubador.co.uk/matador

ISBN 978 1848766 792

British Library Cataloguing in Publication Data.
A catalogue record for this book is available from the British Library.

Typeset in 11pt Bembo by Troubador Publishing Ltd, Leicester, UK

Matador is an imprint of Troubador Publishing Ltd

Printed in Great Britain by the MPG Books Group, Bodmin and King's Lynn

For my fellow choristers everywhere

"Sing unto Him, sing praises unto Him ..."
(Psalm 105)

"Halleluyah! Sing to Hashem a new song ..."
(Psalm 149)

Contents

Preface

What is love? It is a fascinating question. Love can mean different things to different people in different circumstances. After all and whatever it may represent, love is just a word and, as such, is misused and abused, devalued and undervalued in the vernacular of today's zeitgeist or toyed with in yet another game of semantics. Maybe we need to invent a new word (or words) to reflect what we think we mean, or intend, by the concept today. In the meantime, we can embrace only the love we have before us.

We can understand that human love is bound up inextricably with emotions, even though they may be intellect-led. In consequence, perhaps we need to accept that it is not a subject that lends itself readily to scientific study, scrutiny, exactitude, analysis, measurement or calibration. It seems to follow that love's existential yet mystical essence and complexities are rather more suited to philosophical consideration. How therefore can we, with any substantive degree of confidence or assurance, delineate romantic love (true love?), passion (a passion?), infatuation and heightened physical attraction or desire?

Is love something that can be known, recognised or comprehended only when it actually strikes us, like a spiritual and sacred revelation or (mythically speaking) Cupid's arrow, then surges into every fibre of our being like the blood of life through veins and arteries? But the idea of love at first sight could be a doubtful proposition if the emotion flows in fact from the intellect. If you have to think about it first … well.

We should not underestimate the difficulty of describing or defining precisely something that is abstract; even if it is widespread and familiar, but which might be readily identified only when felt. Our observations, and not just from the popular media, inform us that love can be permanent or transient or may never get to first base: love can be betrayed, love can be forbidden, love can be incipient or unrequited, love can become its antonym, love can wither and die more swiftly than a sublime flower shrivels to nothingness. But love can also be endless, everlasting … eternal.

In the end, we may be compelled to throw up our hands in frustration at our puny and futile attempts to find a universally acceptable definition of love for all or any cultures and for all or any period or time; or to compile an inventory of the multifarious situations in which love, in its many forms, may arise. Could be love defies meaningful definition; and, perhaps, for good reason. Elucidating love may be dangerous; it might expose the intellect to doubt, distrust, scepticism or misgivings about feelings otherwise accepted as genuine.

Be that as it may, from a broad perspective the love hypothesis does seem to prompt, even provoke, many definitions or interpretations and a variety of dimensions, not least that of love and predestination. The possibility of preordination, the idea that a love was meant to be, raises many questions about love's intellectual legitimacy or validity.

The reciprocated and intense emotion of deep affection for another person may be distinguishable from, but not necessarily of an inferior quality to, intense adoration coupled with a physical yearning. Both of these intense experiences are undoubtedly eligible to be construed as love (though some may seek to describe the platonic emotion as love and its romantic counterpart as being in love). But establishing any requisite degree of intensity or preoccupation, the threshold of which may necessarily fluctuate between individuals, could well be bewilderingly problematic.

Equally qualified conceivably to be termed love, though ostensibly of another magnitude, are the deep-rooted feelings to which a panoply of possible relationships may give rise, whether within the family scenario or in the area of close friendships or otherwise. Yet the idea of love as an emotion, whether heartfelt, soul based or (according to the cynically and unromantically inclined) mundanely sourced to some chemical reaction in the brain, is perhaps not to be confined to close or intimate, inter-personal human relations.

It does seem that we have to deny the human capacity to love to the animal world, where any affection manifested inter-creature in the wild, or by a domestic pet to its owner, is regarded or treated as mere instinctive behaviour devoid of intelligent rationale, even in the instances of certain species mating for life. Such conduct seems to fall substantially short of what some might express or construe as the emotional instinct of Homo sapiens. In contemplating the essential meaning of human love, however, we are encouraged by the lexicons to bring into the interpretative equation feelings, surpassing mere affection, that a person is capable of possessing for the inanimate or intangible (perhaps in support of a cause), as well as for the animate but non-human. This genre of love seems limitless in its potential diversity and would extend, by way of illustration, to the artist, sculptor, composer, musician, actor, dancer, singer, writer and author and such impassioned pleasure-givers' passionately dedicated and involved viewers, listeners or readers.

Music, art and literature figure prominently among the multiplicity of cultural pursuits. Indeed, and merely by way of example, an individual's love for singing (including singing about love itself) can seem, arguably, as powerful, emotionally meaningful and deeply satisfying as the love of one human being for another. But can such a category of love exist only below a level of intensity amounting to true love? The sometimes almost fanatically ardent passion that can be felt apparently for a particular sport (The Beautiful Game?), whether as a spectator aficionado or a participant player, exemplifies a deep, loyal and focused feeling that could possibly constitute and encompass the perception of love.

And then surmounting all there is a supreme love, a love that exists in a human being for the Divine. In the words of the Shema prayer: *You shall love Hashem with all your heart, with all your soul and with all your might*, a love that may be expressed in singing and song …

The Chorister

HARVEY THE elderly chorister couldn't find the dark blue velvet bag containing his tallis, the white woollen, four-fringed and black-striped prayer shawl. He slowly bent his gaunt frame and peered with dark sunken eyes into the shadowy depths of the large, freestanding wooden cupboard. The decades-old, cumbersome and musty piece of furniture imposed itself at one end of the choir stalls, an elongated, neon-strip lit room overlooking the spacious interior of the high-vaulted and traditional Orthodox synagogue.

The white silk-lined, dark blue tallis holder just wasn't there, definitely not in its usual position alongside the similar but not identical, velvety tallis bags of his fellow choristers. This is very strange, Harvey mused, straightening up again. When not in use, the soft receptacle with its embroidered gold Magen David, like its two or three predecessors, had rested in the same place on the broad shelf for more than fifty years. A half-century was the extraordinary length of time that Harvey had been a loyal and dedicated member of the shul's male choir. He'd joined, with his life-long friend Morry, at the not so tender age of thirty-one. The octogenarian chorister paused for a moment to remember the warm and amiable encouragement that had prompted his choral enlistment.

"Shekoach! You've got a fine tenor voice, Harvey," the now late Chazan Diamond had praised the young family man soon after his first melodiously rendered recitation in the synagogue, since his barmitzvah, of a Haftorah, the weekly Sabbath reading from the Prophets. "You should sing with our choir."

"I don't know," Harvey had responded half-heartedly, at the same time waving to his beaming wife Cissie who was leaning over the rail of the ladies' gallery. Indeed, it was their tenth wedding anniversary that had spurred Harvey to ask the shul's Warden some weeks beforehand for Maftir that Shabbos. "I used to sing in my local synagogue in London's East End as a boy chorister. But that was a long time ago, chazan. I'm not at all sure that I can accurately recollect the tunes now."

"It doesn't matter, Harvey, you'll soon pick them up again … and dear old Boris the choirmaster will help you, of course," Cantor Diamond advised with his characteristically sincere and winning smile, whilst stroking his neat grey-flecked goatee beard.

"Singing is a lot like riding a bicycle. Once you've learned the Shabbos melodies, and however long the time gap, you never really forget. They're in your head, if not your heart and soul, for ever. You're a young man with a superb voice, Harvey … and too modest if you ask me, which you didn't. Why not give it a try? And tell your friend Morry I think he's an excellent tenor, too."

The following week, though somewhat apprehensively, Harvey and his best pal had taken their seats alongside new chorister colleagues in the choir room high above the Aron HaKodesh, in which were kept the beautifully mantled and silver accoutred sacred Torah scrolls of the Mosaic Law. But not before a thankfully successful weeknight audition with Boris, the ancient and grizzled conductor now sadly pronging his tuning fork and waving his arms for that great heavenly chorus in the sky.

Where the hell is my tallis bag? Harvey realised instantly that he shouldn't be using the word for that infernal nether place, even thinking it (as he was) and especially not on a Shabbos morning in the holy house of worship. He'd always accepted that he wasn't particularly frum; but rather what was now termed "Modern Orthodox", whatever that rather flexible tag, attributed to the moveable feast of religious observance between Ultra Orthodox and Reform Judaism, meant precisely. But how could he and his darling Cissie have enjoyed travelling the world over so many years without sometimes having to ride on Shabbos or eat so-called permissible meals, such as fish with fins and scales and vegetarian, in the manifestly non-kosher restaurants on board winter cruise liners, activities a strictly adherent Jew would condemn as against Halachah?

Harvey arched his body and counted mentally the number of tallis bags arranged neatly beside each other on the lengthy shelf. He reached the quotient nine plus the very large one belonging to the late Boris' successor, the witty and affable Henry. That bag was big enough to also contain a copy of the renowned "Blue Book", comprising liturgical scores for Shabbos and festival services written by the greatest Jewish composers of synagogue music. But where's my bag and tallis? Harvey asked himself anxiously. Who would want to take them? The old chorister adjusted a black kippah atop the few remaining grey strands on his bony head. Dull eyes scanned the cupboard's lower shelves, which held small heaps of disused and dusty black-bound prayer books, many of them in pathetically poor condition with broken bindings and spines or oozing loose pages, as well as untidy piles of foolscap manila envelopes containing choral sheet music. Now growing more than minimally concerned, Harvey once again totted up the collection of velvet tallis holders, noting how impossibly insubstantial their smooth supple material, of various colours and designs, felt on the tip of his long and arthritically twisted right index finger.

All the bags he'd previously added up were still present and correct: Melvin's, Harry's, Tony's, his close friend Morry's, Manny's, Dave's, Gerry's, Alan's, Martin's and music master Henry's. All of them were there … except for his own. No one would want to steal a tallis, would they? Harvey asked himself while shaking his head incredulously. Surely nobody could thieve such things and from a place right above the Holy Ark and the eternal flame, glinting ruby-like in its silver lantern casing. That's impossible. It just wouldn't be done. Yet where was the bag? Harvey raised a curved, thin and unsteady hand to his deeply lined forehead, as if his fingers were about to touch the past. The bag had never been mislaid before … never ever, not in decades. Somehow, and despite his admitted lack of rigorous piety, the apparent disappearance of the prayer shawl seemed to the old chorister like an essential part of his spiritual credo had gone absent without leave.

Harvey wracked his brain and clearly recalled replacing his tallis bag in the cupboard after the service had ended the previous Shabbos. He sighed in a kind of breathless way that seemed peculiar momentarily. This is very worrying, he considered. The vanished articles were of immense sentimental value to him. Cissie had purchased the tallis and its bag in Jerusalem a couple of years back on one of their regular visits to Israel. On that occasion the trip was to mark their diamond wedding anniversary.

"But I don't need a new tallis," Harvey remembered pleading with his beloved spouse.

"I say you do … so you do!" Cissie had reacted crisply and mordantly, grasping her husband's arm as if it belonged to an errant schoolboy and virtually dragging him into the shop on Ben Yehuda. "The one you've got now has had the kishkes taken out of it … you know what I'm saying, darling? If I wash it just one more time the thing will disintegrate. Be a mensch, Harvey. It's time for a new one, and that's that! It's my treat for our anniversary, so stop moaning and groaning. Got it?"

A metaphorical, two-word white flag of surrender to his other half had been raised instantly.

"Yes, dear," Harvey had murmured meekly but mock-submissively, knowing that he knew that Cissie knew that he was absolutely delighted with her lovely thought and very useful gift.

No sooner had they exited the Judaica emporium, an Aladdin's Cave of silver bechers, menorahs, chanuciahs, Seder plates, tallisim, kippahs, challah cloths and learned religious tomes, than Harvey had planted a loving wet kiss on each of his wife's plump and rosy cheeks.

As he rested now against the cupboard in the choir stalls, the aged chorister reminisced that Cissie and he had shared more than sixty years of a wonderful marriage, well against the grain of the modern matrimonial condition. A smile further creased his sallow visage. Who could've asked for more? Well, there was just one thing, his thoughts scrolled almost unbidden. He supposed their sex life could've been better, maybe a tad more adventurous in the bedroom. Unfortunately, he ruminated, Cissie had adopted a rather reticent and inhibited attitude in that connection, unwilling to even consider engaging in the sort of exploratory activities that they might've enjoyed. Yes, there had been some frustrations, Harvey sighed inwardly, especially after the children came into the world. Ah well, the chorister speculated, perhaps he and Cissie had been born into the wrong generation for that kind of tomfoolery.

But only Harvey knew how much he adored his Cissie. Unquestionably, he would sacrifice his life for her. Whatever had been missing for him in the marital bed had been fully compensated for elsewhere in their married life. Cissie had been a wonderful friend and companion, a marvellous mother to two excellent sons, both successful lawyers with families of their own, and was today a glowingly prideful bubbeh to five grandchildren and three great-grandchildren ... so far. And she's still a terrific chef, too! Even now, Harvey could almost taste her prize-winning chicken soup, lokshen and kneidlach. He lowered his eyes, suddenly overcome with sadness. Oddly, his emotions failed to give birth to the tear pearls he'd expected to form. But one thing was for certain ... he loved his life partner more than words could describe.

Cissie would be dreadfully upset if he'd lost his tallis and its tastefully worked bag. Lost them? No, he hadn't lost them! They just weren't in their usual place between Morry's and Melvin's bags. Harvey could hear Chazan Feldman's pleasant lyrical tenor voice rising from the bimah as he made good progress through the early part of Shacharis, the morning service. The elderly singer was always the first into the choir stalls on Shabbos. Being a poor sleeper for as long as he could remember, it wasn't a problematic achievement. Before the choir arrived en masse, he would invariably set out their chairs in two rows, first and second tenors to the front, basses and the now lone baritone, Manny, in the rear. But it looked like the synagogue's shy but amiable and longstanding Gentile caretaker Bill had done that job this week, as from time to time he did.

If before Shabbos came in on Friday night, Henry phoned Harvey with information about the planned music for the following day's service, as he generally did, the faithful and committed chorister would remove copies of the selected liturgical items from their carefully labelled envelopes in the storage cupboard and distribute them onto the seats in the choir room before his fellow singers turned up for duty. But so far as Harvey was aware, Henry hadn't called the previous afternoon after his usual music discussions with the cantor.

It's possible that Henry had forgotten, Harvey reflected. He'd done that occasionally. Ah well, the conductor was getting on a bit, too. Must be at least in his mid-seventies the chorister estimated. And after all, his mind train went on, the average age of the choir today was probably seventy or so. Most of its members had been trilling for decades, practically all of them dear friends in addition to being choral comrades. Mind you, Harvey pondered, the intimate familiarity meant that there'd been the sporadic, almost inevitable, broiges amongst a few of the men over the years. For several months the choristers involved hadn't spoken to each other, often not even a passing acknowledgement. It was a bit pathetic, really; though it wasn't too difficult to upset the over-sensitive, Harvey knew that well enough. Regrettably, it had happened between Morry and himself a few years back. Though, as was invariably the case in these trying matters, neither of them could recall now what had caused the temporary rift in the first place.

Anyway, Harvey acknowledged happily to himself, all that nonsense had satisfactorily blown over now, thank the Almighty. That's the thing about a close group of stubbornly independent-minded and stiff-necked Jewish men growing older and grumpier, he'd concluded sagely. But it was so difficult to attract boys, teenagers and young men into the shul, unless they came from frum families, let alone into the choir which sadly didn't seem to appeal to the very Orthodox youngsters. Harvey sighed to himself at the troubling development over recent times. Not even his two great-grandsons were interested; though he'd tried his best to persuade and encourage them. They possessed quite nice little voices, particularly the older one who'd been barmitzvah in the synagogue recently.

"You're very lucky, Craig," Harvey had complimented him, after the young man had rendered his Torah reading quite delightfully. "Hashem has given you a sweet soprano voice and it hasn't broken yet. Hopefully, it never will. Wouldn't you like to sing in the shul choir? We could do with some new young blood."

"No thanks," the teenager had replied dismissively.

"Tell me why not?" Harvey had persisted though rather despondently.

"I go out on Saturdays with my friends."

"Are any of your pals good singers, like you?"

"Pals …?"

"Friends, Craig … friends …"

"Yeah, I suppose."

"Well, why not ask them to come along to the synagogue choir with you? Then you'll all be together on Saturday mornings, eh?"

"Nice try, but we're all into hip-hop … rap," Craig said, rhythmically jiggling his body. "I don't think that's much like the music you sing in the synagogue, innit?"

"What's rap, Craig? And what's *in it*?"

"What's *in it*? Nothing for you," the boy had quipped cutely in reply.

Harvey remembered shaking his head with depressing resignation, as his cheeky great-grandson grinned manically like Wonderland's Cheshire Cat. There was so much brilliant Jewish liturgical music in the world, so many great Jewish composers from the early part of the twentieth century, writers like Alman, Rosenblatt, Lewandowski and Kahn, so much inspiring chazanut and so many exquisitely melodic choral compositions. But what can you do with kids nowadays? Give them a computer or a TV to stick their little heads into and they're as ecstatic as rabbis on Simchat Torah. Perhaps not the most apt simile, the chorister thought remorsefully. He leaned against the brooding brown cupboard, which over the years had almost taken on a personality of its own, and scratched his narrow bony nose. Nowadays, he felt, teenage boys were interested only in girls, soccer, mobile phones, lurid computer games and … Huh, what was it Craig mentioned? Oh yes … rap, whatever that mishegass involved. It was absolutely hopeless. Without recruiting new young choristers, Harvey had often lamented, the wonderfully harmonic synagogue liturgy would just fade away and die, just like its present choral aficionados. What a great pity, what a terrible waste he sighed to the air.

The chorister turned away from the shelves, resolved to take up the question of his missing tallis with Henry and the lads as soon as they arrived. Lads …? Harvey chortled to himself. That's a good one! Bloody old men like me, and most of them krenkers … also like me, he was afraid to note. What with heart problems, waterworks up the spout and prostate worries, insulin dependency and hip joint replacements it was quite a medical merry-go-round. Sad for the elderly singer to recollect, but the choir had lost a couple of its time-honoured members in recent years. Malcolm, a sorely missed baritone, had passed away a year or more back. Harvey remembered the man with great affection, a good and kind person who'd go out of his way to help anyone in need. His stone setting had taken place a few months ago and the suburban burial ground had been crowded with relatives and his many friends and acquaintances. Poor Malcolm … Harvey recalled visiting him at the hospital the day before his dear fellow chorister had died. Tragically, the dying choir member had notched up an innings of only seventy years, definitely not regarded as past the sell-by-date today. He could still hear the last faltering words they'd exchanged before Harvey had knowingly whispered his final farewell to him. Poignantly, Malcolm had been bravely resigned to his fate, his imminent departure from this world.

"G-Give my love to the boys, Harvey," he'd said in his soft-spoken way, forcing the shadow of a smile to his wan, hollow cheeks as he lay propped against the pillows of his curtain-screened bed in the small ward.

"I will, old son," Harvey had replied, struggling to retain the moisture gathering behind his eyes like water held back by a fragile dam.

"N-Not so much of the old, I'm only seventy."

Choked with emotion, Harvey had pressed his thin lips together until they hurt, devastated to witness a man of one-time stature and strength now reduced to an emaciated weakling.

"Yeah" was all he could find to say to his friend and fellow chorister, fighting for a final few hours on Earth.

"D-Don't get all morose on me, Harvey. D-Doesn't the Bible or the Psalms say that, if we're good, we're entitled to three score years and ten on this planet? It l-looks like I made the grade then. M-Maybe my Maker suddenly needs an experienced cabbie up there … the ultimate fare, eh?"

Harvey had smiled faintly: "Yeah," he'd repeated, nodding slowly.

"I-I'm glad you will be making your second barmitzvah," Malcolm had said quietly.

"Don't worry Malcolm, so will you my very dear friend," his visitor had lied.

The dying man had looked down reflectively at the clinically white bedclothes, doubtless cognisant that they were practically his shroud.

"I really don't think I will."

Harvey recalled lifting one of the fading man's deathly pale hands as gently and compassionately as he could.

"But you will," Malcolm had repeated.

"Who knows? It's nearly a couple of years yet."

"T-The Almighty knows."

"Yeah …"

Soon after leaving the hospital building, Harvey recalled to mind, he'd burst into uncontrollable sobbing. In fact, he'd needed to be assisted by a passing uniformed nurse to a nearby wooden bench. The kindly and understanding young black woman had remained with him until he'd managed to recover his composure. Unsurprisingly to Harvey, his friend's levoyah was held a couple of days later. He'd assisted Malcolm's widow Millie to locate her late husband's large woollen tallis, the garment in which the cadaver of a Jewish man is customarily wrapped before its interment.

Anyhow, the boys might know what had happened to his own beautiful prayer shawl, Harvey hoped as his thoughts returned to the present. Perhaps one of the choristers had taken it home by mistake. That must be a distinct probability. After all, tallisim do require careful washing from time to time. He walked slowly past the two ranks of chairs, and the choirmaster's antique music stand that faced them, towards the net curtain covered, decorative iron grille that overlooked the synagogue's spacious interior. From this position, he could stare down into the capacious well of the lofty-roofed shul. Just like Henry did when taking music cues from the cantor.

Harvey focused his attention on Chazan Feldman who stood in front of his reading desk on the lamp-illuminated bimah looking east to the Holy Ark and Jerusalem. Garbed in his shapeless, black cantor's gown and bearing a high-plumped, black kippah the reader, his elongated black and grey speckled moustache quivering like a hummingbird's wings, rocked to and fro in tempo with his increasingly spirited davening.

Perpendicularly beneath the old chorister, and out of his direct line of vision to the right, the tall, slim and luxuriantly black-bearded Rabbi Bronsky would be praying equally reverently, seated in his high-backed, black leather upholstered and well-padded seat flush with the eastern wall and facing the congregation.

On the four flanking sides of the square-shaped, electric lamp-lit bimah stood the rows of wooden pews of the male members of the kehillah, now beginning to fill their positions for the service. The synagogue's president, treasurer and other honorary officers were prestigiously ensconced in their boxed seats built into the front of the reading dais and also facing eastwards. The ladies' gallery with its four tiered rows of pews as yet with just a handful of women occupying their places, ranged loftily around three sides of the shul more or less on the same level as the choir stalls.

Ah the choir stalls, Harvey sighed looking around with a pensive affection. Many times he'd attempted to calculate the number of hours spent in the oblong room with his fellow choristers. But it was an impossible sum to assess exactly, even for a chartered accountant albeit long retired. All he could conclude with any assurance was that he'd devoted a goodly segment of his life, a substantial amount of time that had not for one moment been regretted. The lifelong, exhilarating theme of Jewish choral music had undoubtedly enhanced his life, especially its spiritual element; and at least to the extent that the chorister had pursued this existential part of his being. He loved singing the liturgy so much.

Standing shoulder to shoulder with his friends of many years and awaiting Henry's cue to begin singing, he'd recognised frequently that trilling the inspirational compositions of the Shabbos music from Ayn Komochah, through the Mussaf Kedushah to Adon Olam at the termination of the morning service had helped him genuinely and honestly to express the sincerity of his personal faith, his own innate and intimate belief in the Almighty. And that way of worshipping Hashem the Creator of the universe, to whom he spoke every night before retiring to his bed and Cissie's warm comforting embrace, had somehow reinforced his firm theological philosophy that the numerous rewarding years as a chorister had served to enrich the soul that would one day return to its Maker.

Alone in the choir room but expecting his colleagues to arrive at any moment now, Harvey sat down on one of the chairs and remembered debating his deeply rooted, religious sentiments with Morry a few weeks earlier. They were relaxing one morning in Harvey's conservatory, each sunk into florally cushioned and comfortable wicker armchairs, nursing hot drinks and gazing, a touch soporifically, through the now statutory double-glazed patio doors at the skeletal winter trees in the suburban semi's back garden.

"You okay, Harvey?" Morry had suddenly enquired of his best friend.

His fellow chorister had looked up from the steaming mug of tea grasped in his slightly shaking hands.

"What?" he'd responded but in a vague kind of way.

"I said do you feel all right?"

"Why do you ask?"

"Well, I've been thinking you've been looking a bit pasty of late. And you had to sit down during the Kedushah last Shabbos. You've never done that before. Henry was very concerned about you, as all the boys were. Is there anything wrong, Harvey? I hope you don't mind me meddling?"

"Nothing's especially awry, aside from my usual physical ailments. I did feel a bit dizzy last Saturday morning, that's true. I came over quite funny all of a sudden. I keep popping my heart pills etcetera, just like Cissie does bless her. You know, when we're ambling along the High Street together we sound like a pair of baby rattles!"

Morry's features had displayed moderate amusement at the mild jest.

"Is your consultant content with you after last summer's little glitch?"

Harvey had placed his mug on the glass-topped coffee table. "Yes, he seems to be. I saw him about a month ago. My GP keeps a wary eye on me, too. But look Morry, they know and I know that there's always the risk of an abrupt, traumatic failure. What can you do? There are no guarantees at our age, are there? But tell me, do you know what the greatest surprise is in life, in anyone's life?"

"So you tell me."

"It's getting old, yes ... getting old. You know, you look into the bathroom mirror one morning and barely recognise the person staring back at you."

"Harvey, my friend ... you're a philosopher. Like Plato and Aristotle. But let me say this. If you're getting old at least it means you're still in the land of the living. It's more than can be said for some of our late mutual friends."

"Yeah, I suppose you're right, Morry."

"Will you be singing with us next Shabbos?" Morry had asked solicitously.

"Just try to stop me. And if you see Henry, tell him not to be worried on my health account. I won't let him down. Never have done, you know that."

"Sure Harvey, but we've been very concerned about your wellbeing."

"Well thanks for that, but please don't be. I'm fine. I'll only give up the choir when I kick the proverbial bucket, not before. And even then, I'll return to haunt you all."

Morry had grinned at his great friend.

"Not that you haven't haunted us with your singing for some time now."

Harvey had rolled his eyes skywards.

"Oh, do tell me when to laugh Morry. Yes, that was very funny."

Morry had frowned.

"Actually, I think it was."

Harvey's pale drawn face had folded into a watery smile at the gentle ribbing.

"Yeah, I suppose you're right."

"It means a lot to you, Harvey, doesn't it?"

"What does?"

"Choral singing …"

"Yeah, I know what you mean," Harvey had interjected.

"Probably more than it does to me," Morry had continued. "Even though I've been singing for as long as you have. Certainly I enjoy being with the choir on Shabbos, the Yomim Noraim and the festivals. I've always enjoyed it, of course, particularly the camaraderie. Ever since Chazan Diamond, may the Almighty rest his dear soul, urged us to join up all those years ago. But, somehow, I believe it goes much deeper for you,

Harvey. Am I right or am I right?"

The corners of Harvey's mouth had curved upwards almost imperceptibly.

"With the greatest respect, Morry, I think you're right. I really do feel that singing in shul touches something profound, mystical and holy within me. Maybe that something is my eternal soul, I don't know. But I do believe we possess a soul that will return to Hashem when we pass away. In any case, I hold strongly to the notion that the musical translation of our prayers uplifts a mysterious part of my being. I just love singing … I love it with all my heart and all my soul. This is very difficult to explain, but choral music gives me tremendous satisfaction. I know it sounds like mumbo jumbo to some people. Though I'm sure you know where I'm coming from, Morry, eh?"

The attentive friend had bridged the short gap between their garden room chairs with an outstretched arm and drummed his podgy fingers on the liver-spotted back of Harvey's hand.

"Yes, my dear friend," he'd murmured, nodding slowly and deliberately. "I believe that I do. But shouldn't loving something with all your heart and all your soul be reserved for the Almighty … or your own dear Cissie?"

Harvey could hear familiar voices on the stairway leading to the choir stalls. Ah, the boys were arriving. He stood up and walked across the room. He peered into the synagogue through the net curtaining. There were almost a hundred worshippers present, more men than women as usual. But number-wise, the congregation was well down on that of even a few years ago. Well that was to be expected, the chorister judged. The community was ageing, its golden age had past. Younger members were getting married and moving out of the area.

He'd always held firmly to the view that a community, like a human being, had a certain life-cycle. It was created, it evolved and developed and gradually aged until, eventually, it evaporated like your breath on a freezing day. That had happened to London's Jewish East End where he'd been born and brought up. And where his brethren, whose parents or grandparents like his came from Poland or Russia, had been replaced by new immigrants seeking the good life in this most tolerant of countries.

The old chorister's leaden eyes roamed the ladies' gallery. All at once they stopped roving. Harvey could scarcely comprehend the image they were registering and transmitting to his brain. In the second tiered row directly ahead, on the opposite side of the synagogue and seated just behind the rebbetzin, he was astonished to see his wife. Cissie rarely came to shul nowadays, other than on Rosh Hashanah, Yom Kippur and perhaps the occasional festival; and of course for simchas like chupahs or bar- and batmitzvahs. But why was she here today? And why was she sitting so hunched up, with her head almost resting on her chest? And what was her widowed younger sister Evelyn from Hendon doing here, sitting beside his wife? And why was he asking himself so many questions? Cissie did attend shul on Shabbos sometimes. And since her husband Cyril had passed away a couple of years ago, Evelyn occasionally stayed with them over the weekend. Harvey imagined he'd forgotten his dear wife had mentioned that his sister-in-law was coming over. So what was new, then?

Just at that moment, the opening of the door to the choir stalls distracted Harvey from his quizzical observations. He turned quickly towards the familiar sound of the squeaky handle being twisted and observed Morry entering followed closely by Henry and Manny. He could hear the other choristers laboriously climbing the steps as he called "Good Shabbos, Morry!" to the front-runner. Odd, Harvey wondered, but the expression of the Sabbath greeting seemed to exist more in his head than the room. God forbid that his hearing was becoming affected, too; though it was possible he was starting a head cold. The chorister knew he almost predictably acquired a nasty one as winter progressed, despite the annual flu jab from his doctor safeguarding him against any more serious viruses. It seemed fairly obvious that his close friend hadn't heard the salutation.

Morry extracted his tallis from its velvet bag, kissed it, draped it around his head and shoulders, bowed and intoned the requisite bracha. But when looking up and in Harvey's direction, it seemed as if he was ignoring his best friend's presence. Bewildered, Harvey tried again: "Good Shabbos, Morry!" That's strange, he reflected. There was no reaction at all from his fellow chorister. Not even a courtesy nod, let alone a verbal replication of the customary salutation. Maybe it was Morry who was going deaf, God forbid! So Harvey transferred his attention to the choirmaster. "Good Shabbos, Henry!" he called. But there wasn't even the barest acknowledgement from the conductor, who appeared to be gazing straight through the elderly chorister. No, don't tell me, Harvey surmised his shoulders sagging, the broiges has returned with a vengeance. But why was this? No, it really can't be. We all parted company in the best of spirits last Shabbos morning. So what's going on here? Harvey quizzed himself feeling an involuntary shiver rush through him like ice cold water.

Harvey raised his head, detecting a change of key in the chazan's voice. This heralded the Mourner's Kaddish, a prayer faithfully in praise of the Almighty recited by those recently bereaved of a parent or other close relative. Soon the choir would be accompanying the cantor in singing the passages that led to the removal of a Sefer Torah from the Aron HaKodesh and its honoured parade around the shul to the bimah. There, after the scroll's mantle, breastplate, rimonim and yad had been removed, the synagogue's minister would leyn, with a special nussach, that week's sedra or portion of the Five Books of Moses from the unrolled manuscript parchment spread out on the reading desk.

The chorister of fifty years standing, almost literally he would doubtless jest, gazed down at Rabbi Bronsky as the minister ascended the steps of the bimah. As if compelled to do so, Harvey's dark-hooded eyes ranged across the men's pews, which formed an ordered arrangement surrounding the platform. Harvey could hear the subdued banter of his fellow singers now assembling into their respective choral positions behind him. Then an astonishing thing happened. Harvey felt as if he was gulping and swallowing hard. Would a mirror held in front of his face have revealed a mask of disbelief and amazement? What's going on here? What is going on here? The question automatically reprised itself emphatically in his confused head. What were his two sons doing in shul? Both of them lived in Hertfordshire and hadn't warned that they would be visiting this weekend. The mask stared bewildered through the nets, its ears straining to hear the prayer rising from below. W-Why are my sons beginning to recite the Kaddish?

Harvey turned to witness the choir rising from their chairs, heads up, alert and focusing attentively on Henry's raised hands poised to conduct them immediately after the mourner's prayer ended. The old chorister sensed there was something wrong with the seating arrangements. In an instant, it struck him. One of the chairs was missing … his chair, which was normally positioned between Morry's and Tony's. Suddenly he realised, with an all-consuming and shocking dread, why his seat hadn't been set out by the caretaker. Bill knew and now Harvey knew. In a shattering moment, he understood everything: why tears wouldn't form in his eyes, why neither Morry nor Henry had responded to his Shabbos greeting, why not a single one of the boys had acknowledged him, why Cissie was so obviously overcome, why his sons were chanting the prayer for a departed loved one … and why he hadn't been able to find his precious tallis.

Madagascar

I DON'T know whether you've ever considered this. But where you live at any particular time may be determined by one or more of so many different factors: your ancestry, your occupation, your education, your personal interests, your historical, economic, climatic or environmental circumstances, your family or other associations, your level of morality even, your external pressures, your ruling government, your amazing good luck or tragic misfortune or, indeed, your chronological age.

My beloved octogenarian, widowed mother lives in a residential home on the leafy edge of an ancient university city. Never in a million years when growing up in London's Jewish East End would my Mum have imagined that she might spend the winter of her years in a world-renowned centre of academia. My mildly physically incapable but thankfully compos mentis mater has a commodiously amenable en suite room in a lovely old, but relevantly 21st century modernised, Victorian mansion. The building's surrounded by luxuriant topiary gardens and boasts an impressive staff-resident ratio. "Why am I living here?" she asked me not long after I'd managed to get her transferred from a care home in North London's suburbia, where she'd resided fairly happily and comfortably for quite a lengthy period. I had to confess that her move was due to purely selfish reasons on my part.

I'm the only child of her long and, so far as I'm aware, joyful and loving marriage to my non-Jewish father and (maybe disappointingly for Mum) an entrenched bachelor disinterested in any shape or form of intimate personal entanglements. Don't ask me why. I just don't know. I reckon that it's part and parcel of my chemistry. I suppose the Almighty made me like this. Yes, I do have some faith but not in any organised religious way, if you know what I mean. After retiring from a relatively successful career in banking, I came to live in this sublime city of venerable and scholarly colleges. I've known and visited the town since my twenties; though I'd graduated with an economics degree from the apparently lesser academic heights of London University. Some grammar school friends, who'd aspired to become undergraduates here, occasionally invited me to stay with them for the weekend. I'll always remember those long, languorous, banter-filled summer days picnicking out of a bulging food and wine hamper, and stretched out on the lovingly tended, sun-dappled riverside college lawns.

I love my mother dearly and wanted to be able to visit her as frequently as possible in my retirement. You see, I don't drive. And being with Mum regularly would've proved impracticable had I not arranged for her transfer from the capital. Admittedly, it was a serious though fortunately non-traumatic upheaval, at least not for me. Mum's former care home manager and I convinced her eventually of the undoubted advantages of being geographically near to me. My mother has been resident at High Trees for several months now. I believed that the settling-in period had passed quite well. But I couldn't really be sure of that. At times, my darling mother can be exasperatingly secretive, and sometimes ambiguous or inconsistent, about her innermost feelings. But I'd been virtually confident that she was faring reasonably well in her new abode.

On one of my Sunday afternoon visits a couple of months back, as Mum and I sat close together in the warm June sunshine on the terrace overlooking the imposing house's captivatingly manicured rear garden, she turned to me. Smiling sweetly, she remarked: "I think I might like it here, Harry." For me, my mother's characteristic and very Jewish kind of grudging understatement was as good an indication of her current contentment as I could ever have hoped to receive. On the other hand, it might've constituted an impliedly conditional announcement. I recomposed some errant wisps of fine silver hair encroaching on mother's brow, then held one of her knobbly rheumatic hands and stroked it as gently as might a butterfly's wings.

Some of the other residents, not otherwise resting or napping in their rooms or within the cool shady lounge, relaxed like us in comfy cushioned, wickerwork chairs on the broad and sun-splashed patio. The flag-stoned terrace was separated from the attractively landscaped grounds by a "milk bottle" balustrade and some stone steps leading down from a wide gap in the middle of the low decorative partition. Beyond the garden's far wall, wheat fields spread out to the horizon like an ocean of calm encircling the residence. And above the lustrous arable farmland a vast, open blue sky was sprinkled with skimming, air floating, diving and soaring birds.

A few of the well-matured folk reclined eyes closed and dozing in their sun-burnished, chrome finished wheelchairs. Like many of her fellow residents, mostly women unsurprisingly, Mum drifted off into slumber from time to time, lulled by the sun's radiating and soothing warmth. The powerful solar embrace was certainly conducive to sleep; and, spasmodically, I needed consciously and forcefully to resist the gravitational pull of my own eyelids. But I noticed also that members of staff, youngish men and women for the most part, were continually endeavouring to engage their elderly charges in conversation. Colourful parasols had been erected on solid wood stands to protect the residents from direct exposure to the brilliant sunlight; and possibly also to help prompt positive reactions to the carers' efforts in procuring their concentration.

I'd spoken briefly to Matron (the house manager liked to be addressed by this title) on my arrival that day, as I generally did just to enquire in passing how Mum was progressing Miss Cumberton, who may've supervised in a hospital at some time in the past, is a charming and highly efficient woman, middle-aged, tall and stately in appearance with striking auburn hair habitually pulled taut at the back of her head into an anachronistic bun. As usual, we sat in her homely yet meticulously organised office on the ground floor, a large room besieged by a host of framed colour photographs of the dogs and cats she'd once owned and that had left her for animal heaven. I shared a fondness for such domestic pets, which I'd mentioned to the spinster, though I've never actually kept one.

"I'm very pleased with your mother's initial progress here," Matron told me with the merest hint of a smile, whilst referring to some papers in a ring-binder file on her desk. She was wearing an almost conventional light blue twin set and tweed skirt. "But, as I constantly advise relatives, the threat of senility, dementia, Alzheimer's and other chronic degenerative problems of the aged is a real concern for us here at High Trees. We try hard to stimulate the minds of our residents in various ways and as much as we can. Happily, we've got the dedicated staff and the resources to enable us to accomplish this including, as you know, bringing in musical and other entertainment. And, as I also recommend, it's extremely helpful if visiting relatives and friends could assist by reminiscing with the residents. It's so very important to keep their memories, and thus their minds, alive and functioning." I was about to interpose a thought, but it was one that the house manager all but anticipated. "Of course," she continued, "I appreciate it's difficult on occasions, especially on a hot and sunny afternoon like today, when all our residents want to do is sleep." At that, and recalling other days, I think I must've coloured slightly. As we stood up to go our separate ways in the mansion, she added earnestly: "And who can blame them?"

I was particularly mindful of Matron's earlier words as I lightly prodded Mum from another little foray into the land of Nod.

"Tea's here, Mum … wake up."

Thankfully, the arrival of hot beverages and cake, brought out from the kitchen and placed on wooden tables by the cheerful young staff, served to instil some moderately fresh energy into mother; and, I noticed, into most of the other elderly residents on the terrace.

"Shall I be mother?" I asked whimsically.

Mum frowned at me.

"Okay, but it's a pity you're not a father," she groaned sardonically and a trifle despairingly.

Yes, I acknowledged, she's well and truly back on track. Good old Mum! She was mockingly lucid and as bright as a button again.

Absolutely marvellous how the first thing to enter her brain after temporary unconsciousness is my deficiency, if that's the right technical term, in the paternity department; and, implicitly, my denial to her of grandchildren. Is my mother Jewish or is my mother Jewish? I poured two cups of tea from the large white porcelain pot and handed her a matching plate with a wedge of Victoria Sponge. Momentarily, an idea that the tempting jam and cream confection would shut her up flitted across my brain. But, at once, I regretted the fleeting, ill-considered and insensitive notion. I love my mother dearly and, bearing in mind Miss Cumberton's pearls of wisdom, I didn't want to deny her the freedom to express any pent-up feelings, however much they might hurt or discomfort me. Truth to tell, I could maybe understand where my mother was coming from. I suppose that's what made it harder for me sometimes. I glanced at her and, all of a sudden and despite her florally colourful summer dress, she looked so pitifully diminutive, grey and wrinkled that I couldn't help biting my lower lip.

A short while later, Mum handed me back the plate with the slice of cake only half eaten. In exchange, I passed her the cup of tea and urged her to be careful with it. Despite her gnarled fingers, she's pleasingly able to hold the edge of a saucer quite firmly with one hand and to grip the handle of a cup fairly safely with the other.

"Cheers!" I declared playfully, before sipping from my cup of piping liquid. "This will cool you down, Mum."

She shrugged her slightly hunched shoulders before slowly raising the cup's rim to her newly reddened lips, doubtless painted caringly by one of the home's companionable personnel. After taking a little of her beverage, mother said:

"Cheers? What are you talking about, Harry? You've never had an alcoholic drink in your life."

Mum was quite correct, right on the ball and as bitingly acerbic as ever. Aside from being boringly devoid of any other mortal vices I'm utterly, and often embarrassingly, teetotal. I'd never imbibed at university, even declining to partake of the cheap picnic vino bought in by my undergraduate chums. My mother is fully aware of my sobriety, of course. I really must make an effort not to underestimate the woman's continuing potential for inner perception and caustic comment. What else does that canny soul comprehend about me? Perhaps there are things that I don't understand, or care to accept, about myself. What's wrong with me? Better maybe if I dwelt on a desert island somewhere. But then again, as I think one philosopher once put it, no man is an island. Or so I believed. Mum returned her cup and saucer to me.

"I've had enough," she sighed, although I noticed that she'd scarcely drained a third of the content.

I replaced the fine china items on the table as she whispered:

"See that man over there … the one in the wheelchair?"

I glanced in the direction Mum was indicating with a small, dismissive flourish of her hand. Three residents on the sun trap of a patio were so installed. Two were women. The man was sitting under a red, white and blue striped parasol.

Despite the circle of shadow beneath the bulbous dome of the summer umbrella, I noted that he looked about ten years older than my mother. Statistically, this would've placed him in his mid-nineties. I had to admire the fact that, in spite of his significantly advanced age, the old man was engaged in what I can describe only as an animated conversation with a member of staff, a pretty blonde assistant maybe in her mid-twenties. Then I corrected myself. Why had I harboured any doubt that an individual nonagenarian might possess the cerebral capability to converse articulately and intelligently? Perhaps Matron's recurrently expressed fears for, and warnings about, her aged and incapacitated charges were having an unbalanced affect on my character assessments.

Medical and scientific advances in recent years have meant that so many more people, men as well as women according to the life assurance actuaries, are experiencing extraordinarily long lives. And it's a longevity marked in numerous instances by a remarkably retained mental alertness and ability. For sure, Her Majesty is despatching an increasingly hefty post of special birthday cards to centenarians each year. Conversely, however, my observations could've been widely off beam and, indeed, quite wrong. It was possible that the old man's hand and arm movements were more erratic and uncontrolled than directed and appropriate. I couldn't really hear what he was saying; I'd merely witnessed the opening and closing of his mouth. For all I knew, he could've been speaking total gibberish; and his carer might well have been humouring him.

I'd been staring at the old man for so long that I'd almost forgotten why I was doing it.

"Harry … Harry?"

It was my mother's barely audible voice but it broke the spell that had focused my attention on the occupant of the mobile chair. I turned to face her.

"Why are you whispering, Mum?" I whispered without awareness. "Why are we whispering?" I repeated, this time in a more or less normal volume.

She pressed a vertical yet crinkly finger tightly against her lips, slightly smudging their bright if not gaudy redness in the process.

"Shush, Harry ... I don't want him to hear me."

I stared at her blankly.

"Who are you talking about, mother?"

She shook her head as if I was being deliberately obtuse and obstructive.

"I pointed him out to you, Harry," she responded irritably. "It's Fred, of course ... the man in the wheelchair. He scares me."

I peered again at the ancient gentleman, who was covered with what appeared to be a tartan blanket.

"How could you possibly be frightened of him, Mum? He looks pretty docile and harmless to me. What could he do to you in his condition?"

My mother stirred awkwardly in her seat. I adjusted the debatably over-plump cushion in an effort to make her more comfortable.

"Well I am," she insisted with a firm finality, her sadly lacklustre eyes revealing some worrying trepidation as she spoke to me, now in her normal tone of voice.

"We were talking about alcohol just before," she reminded me. "Well ... Fred drinks alcohol ... whisky, I think. I don't know. But I've seen him ... every evening. And the staff ... they don't try to stop him."

I couldn't resist a modest chuckle. But I gagged my mouth with a cupped palm lest Mum think, accurately as it happens, that I was laughing at her.

"So what's wrong with Fred having a little tipple of a night? I think he's probably old enough."

I realised immediately that I shouldn't have been so flippant.

"Don't be clever, Harry," came the instant and astringent reprimand. I was suddenly feeling very hot, and it wasn't only from the strong sunshine.

"No, Mum … maybe at his time of life Fred should be allowed to do whatever he wants, so long as he doesn't hurt anyone else. I'm sure, as you say, that Matron and the staff know about his regular nightcap or two or even three. But, doubtless, they take the same enlightened view that I do."

Mother shook her head slowly; but by her evident failure to produce an immediate reply I could see that she was conceding the point, albeit reluctantly.

Then, out of nowhere, Mum resumed her attack.

"He speaks with a strange accent," she said. "I'm sure his real name's Frederick and that he's German I don't like Germans, Harry."

I could grasp a little more benevolently what my mother was now saying. She'd lost some distant Polish family during the Nazi Holocaust and I could readily understand her emotional stance, feelings shared by many Jews. I grasped Mum's hands, I hoped with tenderness, and held them.

"But there's something else about him," she murmured, somewhat dauntingly I thought. "It's something that really frightens me."

I stroked her fingers, not wanting her to be troubled or

distressed in any way in her new home.

"I thought you said you were happy at High Trees. I'll talk to Miss Cumberton about the matter next time I come here."

"No, don't do that!" Mum pleaded leaning towards me anxiously, almost conspiratorially. "Please don't tell her. Please, Harry."

I placed a hand on my mother's shoulder.

"Okay," I agreed. "But tell me, Mum, what's wrong?"

It seemed like she was about to burst into tears. I was becoming concerned, to say the least. And my expression may've unfortunately reflected the fact that I was being economical with the truth about not approaching Miss Cumberton. But Mum's perception remained unflawed and undisturbed; though I was somewhat ambivalent about that.

"I said, don't tell Matron," she urged sotto voce.

Hesitantly, I nodded a still unmeant assent.

"Tell me, Mum. What has Fred said or done to make you so alarmed and unhappy?"

Mother looked frostily askance at the ostensibly innocuous old man in the wheelchair and then turned back to me.

"I think he knows that I'm Jewish," she said quietly. "Perhaps he asked Matron and she told him, I don't know. Anyway, Fred talks to everyone else in the house. He chats to all the people here who are capable of carrying on a conversation. He knows I'm capable of having a chat, but he has never said a word to me … except for one."

"And what's that one word, Mum?" I requested with growing curiosity.

"He keeps on saying the word sorry to me," she replied, a distant look in her watery eyes. Whenever I walk past him or he passes me in his wheelchair, he says … he says, in his German accent … he says, sorry."

Mum was obviously becoming affected by what she was telling me, her breathing was noticeably heavier. She would probably need to take a couple of pills soon. I tried to be reassuring.

"I'm sure that Fred … or Frederick doesn't mean you any harm, Mum," I began. "Don't you think he might've realised that you're Jewish because of the Star of David you wear?"

I pointed to the gold symbol of Judaism at the end of a slender necklace chain of the same bright yellow metal. I detected the barest acceptance of a mistake moving over her face, like the sun's summer shadow advancing across a field.

"And, in fact, if he does know that you're Jewish, and you're right in thinking that he's German in origin, then isn't it possible that Fred could be filled with a remorseful reticence towards you for the heinous crimes committed by the Nazis during the Holocaust? As you know, Mum, six million Jews were murdered during the war. If I'm right in my analysis, I don't think you've got anything to worry about."

A lanky, fresh-faced member of staff I hadn't seen before started clearing away our used tea crockery and cutlery.

"Was everything okay?" he asked politely, noting Mum's half-consumed cake. I detected an Irish lilt in the guy's voice.

"Yes, thanks," I said. "Whereabouts in the Emerald Isle do you hail from?"

The young man began stacking the cups and saucers onto a large round, polished steel tray he was carrying.

"Cork," he replied with a pleasant smile. "That's in the Republic. Do you know the town?"

I gazed up at the lofty assistant silhouetted against the sun's rays and shielded my eyes from the glare with a crooked arm.

"Yes," I said. "I've visited once … many years ago. I recollect a picturesque and congenial place."

As the genial young guy moved away towards the open French doors leading into the house, I noted that Mum was displaying her thoughtful face.

"Penny for them, Mum," I offered.

"I was thinking about Sean," she said kind of dreamily.

"Who's Sean?" I asked without thinking properly.

"You know," she went on. "That handsome Irish chap who took away the tea things just now."

I asked Mum whether he was a new recruit to the house.

"No," she answered. "Sean has been here since before I arrived. He's a really nice fellow. Now and again, he stops for some chitchat with me. If only I was forty years younger …"

And the rest, I thought uncharitably; though I was rather amazed, even intrigued, by mother's romantic notions.

"I like him a lot," she continued, "even if he spends quite a bit of time with that Fred bloke."

I devoted a little time to wondering about her comment.

"Well, maybe the old man's mind needs to be stimulated more than some of the other residents here," I suggested. "Other residents like you, I'm pleased to say."

I may've imagined a little twinkle in Mum's otherwise dull eyes. Or maybe I hadn't imagined it.

"I wouldn't complain if he stimulated me a bit more," she said softly.

No, I really hadn't imagined the tiny sparkle. Mother was becoming wholly incorrigible; and, as they say, seemingly growing old disgracefully. But at that moment, and quite suddenly, I felt inexplicably depressed and melancholy. A short while later I left Mum with her uninformed and oddly expressed apprehensions, her dislike bordering on virtual hatred for Fred and her vaguely distasteful infatuation, bordering on adulation, for Sean. I bought a skinny latte at Caffè Nero in the town and returned to my flat feeling strangely fatigued.

I often take a stroll along the willow-edged river to the footbridge about a mile downstream from town. On the way, I pass the lock where graceful mute swans, waddling Mallard and those annoyingly anonymous white ducks with orange bills sometimes gather, upturning their glistening feathered bodies in the shallow, tranquil water or pecking at the grassy bank-side. It's a placid, peaceful, serene, verging on the sublime, scene that appeals greatly to me, especially when absorbed against the rushing sounds of the frothy stream at the weir adjoining the lock gates. Stately flat-bottomed punts glide by, filled with interested or possibly torpid tourist cargoes and manoeuvred expertly by knowledgeable, pole-wielding chauffeurs-cum-boatmen. And the university rowing teams, with male and female crews straining at the oars, skim and pleat the river surface as they speed past.

On the morning after I'd heard my mother going on about Fred (and of course Sean) I was walking along the riverside path, threading my way between prams pushed by new Mums or Dads and trying to avoid trampling cute little dogs on threateningly stretchy leads. As I sauntered in the sunshine I speculated on the reasons why the old man persisted in saying the solitary word *sorry* to my mother, yet shunning any social contact with her. Was she right about the Jewish connection?

Maybe she was. Fred was apparently of German national origin, and he was apparently somewhere in his mid-nineties. If that was so, he would've been born in 1915 or thereabouts, during the First World War. Clearly I didn't have a clue when he'd set foot in England. But in 1939, when Great Britain declared war on Hitler's Third Reich after its unprovoked invasion of Poland, Fred was probably in his mid-twenties. My next brain wave obliged me to sit down on one of the wooden benches at the side of the pathway; and at the edge of an expansive area of cattle speckled meadows sloping gradually to the river. Waterfowl emerged dripping from the reeds and hurriedly, comically, ungainly but tenaciously navigated the inclined grassy verge and quacked expectantly around my feet, beyond question hoping for some tasty morsels of bread.

What if Fred had been a Nazi? What if he'd been a member of the dreaded SS and had become a willing perpetrator of the Holocaust? As I'd recalled for Mum, millions of Jews had perished in the killing frenzy, massive numbers in the gas chambers of Auschwitz-Birkenau and other death camps. What if Fred's a war criminal, guilty of genocide and other crimes against humanity? What if he'd managed to conceal his identity when applying to become a naturalised citizen of the United Kingdom, assuming he legally possessed that status? I gulped hard as ducks of various species, now joined by several hungry pigeons, took it turnabout to daringly drum their beaks on my thankfully protective trainers. My fertile mind was pulling way ahead of my knowledge of the facts.

I'd read in the newspapers that even old and ailing Nazis were still being hunted down and prosecuted, more than sixty years after the end of the Second World War. To me, that was right. Not one of the surviving and vile murderers should ever be allowed to rest peacefully at night. We owed the justice of that inexorable and entirely justified pursuit to our Shoah martyrs. Let the courts decide whether or not these captured old men are fit to plead or to stand trial. Any sentence on conviction is, in a way, irrelevant. It's justice being seen to be done. In any event, it was a promise if not a warning to any potential future war criminals. I stood up sharply from the bench, inadvertently scattering the diverse bird life now investing my feet and lower legs, determined to discover what I could about Fred's … or Frederick's history. My jumbled thoughts, ideas and questions could've been totally off beam. Perhaps the man had been against the Nazis and fled from Germany, or possibly Austria, well before the war began. Maybe he'd even assisted our armed forces or secret intelligence services during the six-year conflict. And perchance, I could obtain something proprietary from my local pharmacist to cure an over-active imagination gland!

By the time I got back home that day I'd resolved to speak with Matron about Fred and his notionally innocent, but nonetheless mildly questionable, behaviour towards my mother. I knew this would contradict the promise I'd made to Mum about not informing Miss Cumberton of her, in my humble opinion, likely irrational fears. But naturally I was concerned for my mother's wellbeing, whether or not her problematic qualms and suspicions were kosher. Before my next visit to High Trees, however, I'd changed my mind. Instead of approaching the house manager I decided to have a friendly chat with Sean. By doing so, I would not only keep my vow to Mum but also, possibly, I might be better able to elicit casually some useful information on Fred from Sean than Matron. Miss Cumberton was more likely to officially plead data protection.

The following sunny Sunday afternoon, after talking to Mum and hearing again her moaning diatribe against Fred, I buttonholed the young care worker after tea on the terrace. Earlier, Sean had been engaged in what seemed to evidence a lively interaction with the old man, whose wheelchair was in its customary position tight up against the balustrade. It was almost as if he wanted to be as close as possible to the lush green grounds at the rear of the mansion. I led Sean down the steps into the landscaped area, around the expertly and beautifully tended hedge sculptures and through the sunken rose garden to the high railings mounted on the low boundary wall. We stopped and I peered through the tall iron posts to the fields pushing out to the horizon.

"Lovely view isn't it, Sean?" I said cheerily.

He nodded, eyebrows raised and speculating no doubt on why I'd brought him to this spot and where my mundane opening remark was leading.

"I'll not beat about the bush," I went on. "I've got to say that I'm becoming rather fascinated by Fred. I don't really know why … I just have. You seem to have developed a very commendable rapport with the old man, if I may say so. Physical difficulties aside, he appears to be extremely alert for his great age. Is that indeed the case? And do you know anything about his background?"

Sean looked at me closely for a few moments, like he was examining a handful of pills he was on the point of dispensing to one of his charges, struggling I think to discern my motivation. Clearly he wasn't at all sure of the situation.

"It's true that Fred is remarkably astute for his years," the young man responded amiably enough. "All he has told me of his history is that he came to this country from West Germany in the early 1950s. And that previously he'd worked for the occupation authorities as a translator in the post-war British sector of Berlin. Oh yes, and that he'd married an English nurse working in the divided city. I believe she died quite a long time ago. But I do remember Fred telling me, sadly, that they'd not had any children. I know he has lived at High Trees for a number of years now. Matron would know more precisely. Since I've been here he hasn't had a single visitor, so far as I'm aware that is. It's really quite poignant, though maybe not so unexpected. Any relatives or friends are likely to have predeceased him some time ago. Well, that's about it, I think."

Of course I didn't know whether Sean had disclosed all he knew about Fred. But, somehow, I felt fairly confident that he was giving me everything he had. After all, the details he'd provided weren't really confidential. And having in mind the eldest house resident's sociable personality, the few facts I'd now collected about him were probably well known around the home, except of course to Mum. Sean and I exchanged a few more words, now about the care assistant's daily work; and then, together, we made our way back to the sun-drenched patio. Late that night, lying in bed half-listening to a classical music programme on Radio 3 but for the most part thinking about my mother's almost obsessive concerns about the old German, I knew what I needed to do at the next convenient opportunity.

A couple of weeks later a chance presented itself. Matron had telephoned one weekday morning to notify me that my mother wasn't feeling very well, but said it was nothing to worry about. She'd summoned the doctor who'd diagnosed nothing more than a mild throat infection and had prescribed some antibiotics. But I went immediately to see Mum who was resting on the bed in her first floor room. She was pleased to see me but, understandably, reluctant to talk because of the soreness. I left her on the brink of sleep and returned downstairs to the communal lounge. One of the staff kindly asked whether I would like a hot or cold drink. I nodded, requested a milky coffee and sat in one of the chunkily upholstered armchairs. The smiling young woman returned with the steaming beverage and set it down on a low table beside me. I thanked her and she went off to perform her normal duties. As I sipped the hot liquid, I noticed only one other individual in the spacious and elegantly furnished room. It was Fred.

He was sitting in his wheelchair close to the French windows. I could just make out the old man's cranium, with its few curly strands of white hair, rising above the back of his mobile seat. I got up and walked towards him. As I came alongside I could see that, with a faraway look in his eyes, he was staring through the glass doors into the garden beyond the terrace. It was like he was anxious to be outside, as proximate to the exotically moulded hedges, tall shady trees and colourful cornucopia of summer flowers as he could get. Probably there hadn't been any members of staff available to take him onto the patio at that time.

"Hello," I said fairly jauntily.

The old man looked up and a glimmer of recognition slipped across his puffy round and sickly roseate face. He didn't seem unduly startled by my sudden greeting. Perhaps he'd been studiously following my silent approach in the window's reflection. Fred was wearing a plain light-blue dressing gown. Up close I could sense there wasn't much bodily substance beneath the loosely tied, flannel garment. Then his darkly deep-set, beady and wary eyes revealed that he knew exactly who I was. He turned away and gazed through the window again without uttering a word. I pulled up a nearby, high-backed seat and sat down beside the wheelchair.

"Why don't you talk to my mother, like you do with the other residents and the staff here?" I asked quietly. "And Fred, why do you keep saying sorry to her?"

He remained quite still, said nothing and continued looking into the glass.

"Please Fred," I implored him, yet again in a restrained manner. "My mother's getting very distressed about it. I'm sure you wouldn't want that, Fred. I'd be very grateful if you could explain your conduct towards her."

I appreciated that here was a man well into his nineties. I didn't relish the idea of badgering or upsetting him in any way. Although I'd seen him from afar in apparently enthusiastic discussions with his carers, at this minimal distance Fred appeared wretchedly degraded by age and maybe also by some serious underlying illness.

"Sorry," he said out of the blue, taking me by surprise. He'd turned his florid spongiform face to look directly at me. And the eyes, those tell-tale eyes, now mirrored his single word, spoken with clarity but a Central European accent.

"I'm truly sorry," he stated meaningfully. "Sorry … there I go again," he repeated with a faint smile. "You're right, of course. I don't wish your mother to be troubled or distressed by me. I'm sorry … about saying sorry … to your mother."

It sounded as if Fred genuinely meant what he was saying, but he seemed to be saying it in an ingratiating manner.

"Sorry but I can't seem to stop saying sorry now ... sorry." He shook his head in disdain, presumably at himself. Was it my imagination again, or was Fred actually purporting to display an ironically un-Teutonic sense of humour?

"I really don't want to talk about it," the old man went on, shaking his head. "I haven't spoken about it to anyone. But maybe, after all's said and done, I do owe you an explanation for my actions."

I nodded in confirmation and he continued.

"Your mother is Jewish. I think that I've correctly assumed that from the amulet or talisman she wears."

I nodded again.

"Therefore you are Jewish. And from my ailing heart I would like, in turn, to say sorry to you."

I raised my hand and rubbed my forehead in a self-conscious, nervy reaction to what Fred was saying.

"Please believe me when I tell you in all sincerity that I'm not anti-Semitic and never have been. Of course, as a German, I know about the Holocaust of the Jews in Europe during the war. And I hang my head in shame. The word *sorry* cannot remotely reflect my feelings and my abhorrence of the evil perpetrated on your people by my people. But it's the only word that I'm capable of offering to your Jewish mother, and now to you."

He paused for a moment or two and turned to peer again through the French doors. During the brief interlude in our conversation I wondered whether Fred's apology was general or, as I was beginning to suspect, more specifically related to something he personally had done in connection with my people.

"But why don't you speak to my Mum?" I enquired. "Perhaps she would try to understand."

The old man pondered my reprised enquiry for a brief while, then swivelled awkwardly and possibly painfully what remained of his vulnerable and skeletal frame.

"Regrettably, and with great respect, I don't think she would ever understand," he responded facing me again, "and I can appreciate that. I just feel that I don't deserve to speak with your mother. And, frankly, why would she wish to speak with me?"

I have to note that Fred was starting to acutely intrigue me now. And I was inquisitive enough to press him further, despite his advanced age and whatever his medical diagnosis.

"So please Fred, explain yourself to me."

What he related over the next several minutes surpassed my knowledge and, indeed, my imagination.

"It all happened so long ago now," he started. "I was a young man in Nazi Germany. My family was nominally Lutheran, but not particularly pious or political for that matter. Like millions of our fellow citizens in the Third Reich we were caught up … no, trapped in hideous times and had irrevocably relinquished any power to change things. To get ahead in life you needed to join groups and bodies that would, in other circumstances, have been anathema. Yes, I was a member of the Hitler Youth. Peer pressure from my school friends made membership inevitable. But even the present Pope was a member! I went to university in Munich and graduated top in my year with a history degree. This was a few years before the war started. I joined the Civil Service and became a fast-tracked junior official at the Foreign

Office in Berlin. As I gradually proved my worth and was given accelerated promotion, I would often attend meetings and conferences along with the senior administrators advising the German Foreign Minister Joachim von Ribbentrop. And frequently, I was a member of his delegation on overseas assignments."

Despite myself, I was riveted by what Fred was telling me. I'd read many books about Nazi Germany but to hear firsthand from an eyewitness was something else altogether.

"Of course I'd be lying if I told you that I didn't know about the persecution of the Jews," the old man added. "Yes, I'd witnessed or heard about the boycotts, the anti-Semitic propaganda, the seizure of Jewish businesses and the assaults. I knew that thousands of Jews had been forced to leave Germany with little of what they'd owned. Hitler wanted the nation Judenfrei ... free of Jews. He didn't care where they went. He just wanted them to disappear, for ever. But you see, there were many potential receiving countries that refused to take Jewish immigrants or refugees beyond a limited quota ... or, indeed, at all."

I could see tears gathering in Fred's eyes. I thought he was about to become emotional. Nevertheless, I wanted to hear more from him.

"Y-You must believe me," he urged, his voice breaking slightly, "when I say that, as the war developed, I knew nothing of the death camps or the gas chambers. So many euphemisms were adopted for what was really happening to the Jews in Germany, Poland and other conquered and occupied countries. And maybe like the Jews themselves I naively believed, perhaps was desperate to believe, that resettlement in the east meant what it seemed literally to say. I was stupid of course to trust anything the Nazi hierarchy propagated. But earlier in the war I'd been working with others on a plan for the mass emigration of European Jews ... to Madagascar."

I hadn't expected this revelation and it sent a jolt through my nervous system. The notion of Jews being transported to an island in the Indian Ocean struck me as so astonishingly perverse. But then again, I thought instantly, Fred was talking about a Nazi project here. The old man acknowledged my shock and amazement.

"You've obviously never heard of the Madagascar Plan," he went on. "But it was quite a serious idea, at least for a time. If my memory serves me right I seem to recall hearing that Himmler, the chief of the SS, had advocated the scheme to Hitler. The Führer must've been impressed with the strategy of confining Jews to a remote isle off the south-east coast of Africa. Actually it wasn't a novel concept. I think that a Frenchman first mentioned such an arrangement more than a hundred years ago. And I discovered that even the pre-war Polish government had gone so far as to send a commission to Madagascar to study and report back on the feasibility of compulsorily despatching thousands of Jews to that distant place."

Again Fred paused in his morbidly fascinating narration. The effort of both speaking and recollection may've tired him. I glanced surreptitiously at my wristwatch, knowing that it was fast approaching the lunch hour and that the old man would probably want to leave me soon to enter the dining room. But it did appear that he was fighting to summon up sufficient reserves for a further bout of memory recall. Maybe I wasn't entirely startled to hear what Fred was telling me, though I was waiting to know about his own part in the Madagascar Plan.

"Minister von Ribbentrop ordered Franz Rademacher to formulate a set of proposals," he told me, his breathing growing noticeably variable. "As you may know, Madagascar was a French colony. After the blitzkrieg defeat of France in 1940, the projected forced emigration of Jews to the island had been revived …"

I interrupted, pointing vaguely at Fred's heaving chest.

"Okay, but what was your personal involvement in all of this?"

He lowered his eyes.

"I was seconded to Rademacher's team in order to work up the proposition. From a philosophical viewpoint, and I suppose to salve my own conscience, I concluded it would be better for four million Jews to govern themselves in a far off tropical island than to continue subject to persecution in Europe …"

"You're talking about a remote swampy island ridden by disease and barely able to support its native population, not a tropical paradise," I interjected. "Surely the idea would've been that the Jews be abandoned there to starve to death and rot away. The predictable outcome would've been no different to their ultimate extermination in the Nazi gas chambers of Auschwitz and Treblinka."

I could readily discern that Fred was uneasy at my barbed comments and I was strangely glad about this. He sighed deeply and was silent for a few minutes, gawking into the garden. I could hear feeble shuffling movements and the frail scraping and thudding of Zimmer frames in the corridor outside the lounge; and I suspected that the other residents were filing into the dining room for lunch.

"So what were your proposed arrangements for the Madagascar-bound Jews, Fred?"

He looked up at me balefully and I could see watery pearls resting on his swollen, marshmallow-soft cheeks.

"F-France was to hand over the island to Germany," he continued. "The French settlers would be expelled and replaced by the Jews. The plan was that they would operate under a form of self-governing system but subject to a German police governor. The complete operation would've been financed by selling off confiscated Jewish property."

I could hardly credit Fred's story but I was certain it would be verifiable. I'd Google "Madagascar Plan" next time I logged onto the Internet.

"So tell me, Fred, why wasn't this wonderfully scatter-brained but horrific prospect ever implemented?"

The old man wiped some oozing drool from his mouth with the back of a bony white hand.

"We couldn't defeat the British. The RAF ruled the skies and Hitler was terrified of British naval power. Then Allied forces recaptured Madagascar and the scheme was discarded. Our redundant team shut up shop, so to speak. In retrospect, I really believe that the failure of the project led directly to what became known as the final solution of the Jewish problem."

I wasn't really interested in Fred's views on that matter. I pointed at his chest again.

"So what did you do next?"

A faint glimmer of a smile flashed across Fred's features. The old man was, as Sean had described him, sharp and intelligent despite his apparent decrepitude; though, somehow, I felt he possessed a hidden deviousness. I guessed he was about to tell me something that would not necessarily be pleasing.

"I really couldn't take any more," he said, running his slithery tongue along cracked grey lips, now almost free of dribble. "Believe it or not, the work had caused me much despair. I agonised about my role in the so-called evacuation discussions. And I took no comfort from the fact that I was doing what the superiors advised was my duty to Führer and Fatherland. That was no excuse, of course I realised that. I requested a transfer to the Wehrmacht, the German army. After some difficulties I've no need to go into I was deployed as an ordinary soldier, a private you would say, to a regiment in France. Luckily for me, though sometimes I think not, I wasn't sent to the deadly Eastern Front to oppose the advancing Soviet forces. In the autumn of 1944 I was captured, thankfully by British troops, and ferried to England as a prisoner of war to work on a farm in Shropshire. I perfected my English there. So to cut a long story short, as they say, I survived the conflict, was repatriated eventually and served as an interpreter and translator at the occupation HQ in the British zone of Berlin. I fell in love with and married a British nurse. Some years later we settled in London. I became a British national and we opened a small business. My dear wife died several years ago. Unfortunately, the doctors had advised that she couldn't bear children but I'd loved her very much. I retired quite a while back, sold my company and, after a lengthy and debilitating illness, the physical wreckage you now see before you came to reside at High Trees. And now, sir, you have my life story in a nutshell. I hope that you're content and that your mother will no longer concern herself about me. However much I would wish to change the past …"

I left Fred before hearing his final words. As I walked beside the river that warm summer afternoon my head was full of the old man's personal history. I stopped near the lock to watch the swans and ducks splashing about in the slowly drifting current. So many thoughts were tumbling around my mind that I couldn't adequately reduce them to rational conclusions. In spite of all my natural instincts, which tugged in a particular direction, I could feel no pity for Fred or any sympathy for the alleged objections of conscience to his wartime work at Nazi Germany's Foreign Ministry. Why should I even be contemplating the principles of humanity towards this person? I felt only an enveloping numbness as I trudged back across the cattle-sprinkled, riverside leas for a coffee in the town centre.

Over several subsequent visits to my mother we spoke about Fred's story as he'd related it to me. In the result she seemed gratifyingly easier in herself, though of course I couldn't be certain she was actually feeling this. But I'd noticed that the old man no longer appeared on the terrace during the long hot afternoons. Indeed, I hadn't seen him anywhere in the house. In the end, I asked Sean about the home's oldest resident. He suggested, oddly I thought, that I should have a word with Matron. On my next trip to see mother I popped into Miss Cumberton's office. After chatting briefly about Mum, I enquired about Fred.

"Very sadly he passed away a few weeks ago," she informed me.

I showed no reaction as she continued.

"It's very strange really. He'd told me a long time ago that his last will and testament was held in the custody of his solicitor in town. Fred had given me the firm's telephone number and asked me to call them immediately after his death, he really emphasised the word immediately, and of course I did. But I was absolutely astounded when I learned from his lawyer where Fred had wished to be buried. I couldn't see the correlation. Fred wasn't a very wealthy man but the sale of his company had made him reasonably comfortable. Apart from the expenses of his residence here at High Trees, he had little of a material nature to spend his money on. His estate was well able to make the apparently bizarre interment arrangements that he'd insisted upon in his will."

I was very curious, if not impatient, to know about the nature of these bizarre arrangements.

"So whereabouts is Fred buried, Matron?"

It was more than apparent to me that Miss Cumberton had no idea about the significance of her next few words.

"Of all places, and you would never guess, Fred is buried in … Madagascar!"

Born in Canada

I WAS born in Canada. No, no, not that vast North American nation sprawling from the northern border of the United States to the Arctic Circle. Had I come into this world in that wonderfully welcoming and peaceful land, which I've visited several times, the psychology and outcome of my wounded life would've been very different.

No, my birthplace was on another continent altogether, but in a place called Canada. It wasn't the name of a country of course ... no, not any country on this Earth. It was more like some evil niche in Hell. How do I know? It's because my mother described it to me in that way. As I grew older, I came to understand that I was actually born in a country. That nation was and is known as Poland. And the location of my wartime origin was the Nazi death camp named Auschwitz Two or Auschwitz-Birkenau, where one million Jews were murdered and burned to ashes. More particularly, the area where my bloody little body emerged into this world was a small part of the abyss labelled Canada. The tag may've been some kind of sick Nazi joke, something to do with a realm of plenty. Here my mother, alongside other young men and women maybe only temporarily spared their own lives, sorted for shipment to Hitler's Reich the money, valuables and other belongings of their Jewish compatriots transported by cattle wagons from across Europe to be gassed and cremated on arrival.

When she felt I was able to comprehend the circumstances of my first shriek of life, my mother never compromised on her vivid and gruesome descriptions, despite my tender years.

"There was blood everywhere … my blood," she would harangue me. "But then again, Auschwitz was awash with Jewish blood, so nothing unusual there then."

With an almost primeval look in her piercing eyes that always terrified me, she raved on about her agony as other slave women helped to deliver me amongst the shocking heaps of boots, shoes and clothing and the pitiful piles of empty suitcases in Canada. It was as if she wanted me also to experience something of the terrible screaming pain she'd experienced. Not only the excruciating hurt I'd caused her physical body by my red and splitting eruption into existence, but also the acute mental torture of her pregnancy spawned by the horrendous environment in which she'd given birth.

"I'm only thirteen!" I shouted back at her, tears welling up in my sore eyes. "Why do you keep on telling me all these horrible things? Please, Mummy, don't tell me about them any more … I wish I'd never been born!"

And I would run upstairs pursued by her guilt-ridden ranting, slam the door of my room, throw myself onto the bed and sob uncontrollably into the pillow. But I couldn't shut out her voice from my head. I could still hear my hysterical mother, like a wild woman growling unnervingly at the foot of the staircase: "And how old do you think I was?"

In fact she was seventeen when she gave birth to me. I don't really need to inform you that I'm her only child. But I began to hate her, my own mother who'd suffered and struggled so much to give me life. And I have to tell you that I myself have sustained many bouts of depression throughout my years, profoundly black periods each of which has left its own edgy legacy of scarring on my mind. I suppose all of this was eminently predictable. However, and perhaps strangely, there came a time in my late teens when I started to see my mother in another way and my attitude softened towards her. Despite what I've been advised, I still don't know why this happened. But at that time, and possibly stemming from some hormonal alterations in my womanly body, I began suddenly to feel a deep empathy for her perpetual and conscious angst.

As I became more comprehensively aware of what it meant to be a survivor and a child of the Holocaust, I even sympathised with my mother for the immeasurable damage to her psyche. For a long while, largely during my student days, she maintained what for me was a reassuring silence about her time in the most notorious of the Nazis' death factories, where human beings were disposed of on an industrial scale. This comforting reticence to talk about the past certainly helped in bringing us closer together, both physically and emotionally. Now occasionally she would kiss me on the cheek, holding my face tenderly in her hands. At first her novel affectionate approaches had usually taken the form of a quick peck on the top of my head as I sat, perhaps studying, by the desk at home.

Day by day I warmed gradually to this new maternal intimacy. And, ultimately, in the calm evenings we would often sit side-by-side on the living room settee and hug each other for a while.

Whether this amounted to love, I just don't know. But I believe that our newfound affinity of heart and mind served to thaw the glacial freeze that for several years had trapped us in our separate icy domains. There was something still missing, however; something that I maybe felt in my soul but could never quite make tangible in my sentient intellect. Until one day a very good friend at college, whose Jewish stepfather had been a survivor of the Nazi concentration camps, asked me for the first time about my own family. We were sitting in the buzzing students' bar nursing pints of ale. Like me, Mike was a second year history undergraduate, though his speciality was modern European and mine was the ancient world. He was quite a good-looking guy, tall and slim with an unruly mop of dark brown curly hair that looked like he'd just got up (which he probably had), and the cutest smile. He was a few years older than me and I really liked him. We'd met at a party thrown by a mutual friend and seemed to share the same wavelength on life. I suppose the common thread of a Holocaust connection prompted some relevant empathy and interest. But there may also have been a reciprocal spark of physical attraction.

Not long afterwards he asked me out on a date, but I told him that I wasn't really into that kind of thing at the time. I just wanted to work hard at my studies, get a good degree and a worthwhile job after university. Mike readily accepted that; but my perception of his reaction hinted at disappointment. Anyway, we saw each other frequently at college for a pleasant chat, an exchange of views on current topics and a drink. Though I think Mike would've liked more, our relationship was strictly platonic. If I'm truly honest with myself could be I felt something too, even if he wasn't Jewish. His mother was a lapsed Catholic. One afternoon between lectures we bumped into each other in the college bar. He treated me to a bottle of lager and we slid into a corner seat.

"You've spoken of your mother but never said anything about your father," Mike said like a bolt from the blue. "Is there any special reason for that?"

At that moment, my facial expression must've changed so dramatically that my companion stood up instantly and took my hands in his grasp.

"Are you okay?" he asked, serious concern in his voice.

I nodded, withdrew my hands from his and gestured him to sit down again, which he did. I remained silent. Mike looked caringly into my eyes.

"Are you sure?" he persisted. "Sorry to say it, but you suddenly looked really peculiar. I hope I didn't say anything out of order."

After a short pause, I found my vocal cords.

"No, Mike, you didn't and I'm fine."

"Are you sure?"

"Really," I replied, trying hard to give him an encouraging smile.

"So what was it then? You seemed to sort of flip when I mentioned your Dad."

Mike was right. I had kind of flipped. Why? Because in the split second of my friend's question it hit me, and amazingly late in the day, that I didn't know who my father was or anything about him. Why had I never asked my mother this rather fundamental question about my paternal origins? Possibly, I'd sublimated the question in view of the appalling situation of my birth or in light of my earlier relationship, or lack of such, with her. But why had she never volunteered anything about him? It might've been due to a kind of guilt complex, something to do with shame or embarrassment. I really didn't know.

It could've been my subconscious just assuming that my father was another Jewish inmate of Auschwitz. And that he'd slaved beside my mother in the hell of Canada and had fallen in love with her despite the enormity of their circumstances, and she with him. It was odds on that he hadn't survived the death camp to be liberated by the Russian army in January 1945. But if that was the case, why hadn't Mum told me of her quite unbelievable romance at some stage, especially in more recent times when our mother-daughter thing had been improving significantly? It's likely she hadn't told me anything, I speculated, precisely because it was all so surreal and incredible.

All I knew was that, in those awful mind-opening moments when Mike had raised the matter, I grasped the nature of the missing link which I'd been incapable of materialising in my brain over the years. If the gap could be filled, if the last piece of the jigsaw could be fitted into place and the picture completed, and if the answer could be given by my mother even after all this time, maybe it would help overcome whatever barrier had been holding me back, restricting and inhibiting the smooth flow of my emotions.

"Sorry, Mike," I apologised, returning to the present. "You're right. I did flip for a second or two. I'm sorry. I must've looked quite odd. I'm really sorry."

Mike offered me one of his cutest smiles.

"No need to be. I don't want to pry but it's something about your Dad, isn't it?"

We were very good mates, Mike and I, so I didn't want to complain that he'd just possibly opened up a whole can load of unpredictable worms, and then hurt his feelings or make him feel bad. Mike was a sensitive and compassionate person; and there was quick acceptance when I explained the thought processes that had swiftly come to mind-numbing fruition after his unexpected query.

"Forgive me for going on a bit, but isn't it strange that your Mum has never mentioned your father?" Mike observed after the rudimentary explanation for my earlier melodramatic display.

I didn't want to talk any more about the subject; and I felt like getting up and walking away. But Mike was a good human being, and I knew he harboured feelings for me. So I stayed put and responded to his genuine solicitude.

"Not necessarily, Mike. As I've tried to say, there could be all sorts of reasons for her not telling me; not the least being that, probably, she has never been able to get over his death in the camp."

"Yeah, I suppose," he said pensively. "But that presupposes he did in fact die in Auschwitz. Maybe your father as well as your mother survived but rapidly, and ostensibly quite sensibly and practicably, came to the conclusion that their sexual appetites and passion as young adults and the likely surprising and unwanted consequence, that's you, didn't provide a firm and stable enough foundation for staying together after being given their freedom."

I shook my head slowly.

"But what if they'd truly and deeply loved each other? I follow what you're trying to say, Mike. But you know it's tough on my fragile emotions to see myself as an unwanted consequence."

My loyal and sincere friend took my hands again.

"I'm really sorry … I've taken this too far. You're right to be upset, even annoyed with me. Well, you know I sometimes say things. I'm an idiot."

"No you're not, Mike. It's just better for me to believe that my mother and father wanted and loved each other; and that despite everything, I was wanted and loved too. I realise it might've been a one-sided relationship. My Mum could've loved my father but he may've been after what he could get … and later merely rejected her and, of course, me. That, as well as everything else, could've affected my mother fairly seriously, at the minimum. All I do know is that she was never married. That much Mum did tell me."

I must've started to cry. Mike held me close and gently so that my head rested on his shoulder. I was genuinely glad for his comfort and solace.

"What I don't understand," he said, "is how your mother's pregnancy was permitted. Surely once it became physically obvious the Nazis would've immediately eliminated her and you, the child she was carrying. At the very least, the bastards would've aborted the foetus or their so-called doctors, like the notorious Mengele, would've performed some dreadful medical experiment on your Mum."

I thought for a moment about the point Mike had raised and it puzzled me, too.

"I really don't know how Mum escaped detection and death

to give me life, or how we managed to survive until liberation. But you're spot on. It does seem astonishing that her existence in that condition should've been allowed to continue. Maybe she was hidden from the sight of her Nazi supervisors."

"I don't think that could've been so easy. Her absence from work details would've been noticed at once by the eagle-eyed SS overseers."

"I guess you're right, Mike. It's a real mystery."

" Will you now ask your Mum about your Dad?"

"I don't know," I answered, taking a tissue from my bag and wiping the moisture from my face. "I'll need to think very carefully about it. Mum's very brittle at the best of times."

My good friend withdrew his arm from my upper back.

"Let me know if you want to talk about this some more. I'm very worried about your wellbeing. Really I am."

"I know Mike, and thanks for that. But please don't be. It's my problem. I don't want to sound churlish or ungrateful, but I'll work it out … on my own. Don't get me wrong, I'm more than happy to have your generous moral support. It's a great help to me, honestly."

Mike stood, quaffed the last of the lager from his bottle then tenderly inclined my chin towards his face.

"Remember," he said, earnestly, "I'm always around if you need me."

I handed him a smile, which he returned with one undoubtedly much warmer and cuter than mine.

Late one Saturday evening a few weeks after my conversation with Mike, I was relaxing with my mother on the settee in the lounge at home. The curtains were drawn and we'd just finished watching a movie on TV. The film was a romantic comedy, not a genre that especially appealed to me. But it was comforting and calming to sit closely beside my Mum and to see her enjoying the programme. I got up to switch off the television and make us a nightcap. When I returned from the kitchen with mugs of hot chocolate, our favourite bedtime beverage, and set them down on the coffee table, I could tell from her benign expression that Mum was still revelling in the picture's storyline. After we'd taken quick sips of our piping drinks, I turned to look at her.

"Did you love my father, Mum?" I asked her point blank.

She placed her chunky cup on the low table in front of us and, as if strangely exhausted, leaned back against the abstract-patterned upholstery of the couch. She closed her eyes and began breathing a little heavily, I thought, her dressing gown rising and falling more noticeably in the chest area. I became apprehensive that I'd chosen the wrong time to ask, what must've been to her, a startling question. My mother sat up straight again and stared directly at me.

"Yes, I did," she replied, oddly matter-of-factly. "I believe that I did love your father."

She'd responded unexpectedly transparently and without any apparent rancour or bitterness. Her commendably even reaction suggested that mother was in such a mood that might be conducive for me to seek further answers.

"But why have you never told me anything about him, Mum … at least who he is, or was?"

She didn't say anything for a few minutes, but simply gazed down at the mug she now grasped in her hands as if warming them on its china surface and somehow preparing herself for impending revelations.

"Because I didn't want to hurt you," she said at last and, I considered, rather enigmatically.

"But Mum, how could it harm me to know about my own father? And, in any case, don't I have the right to know?"

"I suppose you do have such an entitlement," she said, lowering her eyes momentarily. "Maybe I was wrong. But by keeping the knowledge from you I wanted to safeguard you. I wanted to give you protection …"

"Protection ?" I interrupted. "What were you protecting me from?"

My mother put down her drink and stared intently into my eyes. Possibly she saw something of herself reflected in them.

"Perhaps protection from yourself …"

"Sorry, mother, but I don't really understand what you're on about."

She rubbed her forehead in a nervy way and clasped her hands tightly on her lap.

"I–I d–don't know what you want from me," she stammered out, becoming quite agitated.

"I want you to tell me the truth. Please, Mum And don't spare me anything. I'm a big girl now and I want … no, need to know where I come from!"

At once, I regretted my outburst. I had no cause to aggravate her in any way. And I didn't want mother huffing off to her room so that our innovative bonding would take a hit. I began to feel sorry, even pity, for her as I perceived some kind of painful conflict raging in her mind. I noticed teardrop pearls forming up in the corners of her sorrowful eyes. I fetched an open box of tissues from the oak sideboard and handed one to her. Mum grabbed it and dabbed her flushed cheeks. Then she glanced at me, next at her hands and finally at me again.

"I'm not sure where to begin," she said, with a temperate and self-controlled inflection that was in sharp contrast to the severe and intransigent tone of which I'd previously grown accustomed.

"At the risk of being accused of triteness, why don't you start at the beginning, Mum? Then, hopefully, you'll know where you are."

There I was, doing the flippancy act again. I ran teeth along my lower lip and she gave me a penetrating look that, thankfully, only slightly echoed an earlier time. But it had the doubtless deliberate effect of obliging me to feel remorseful.

"I'm sorry, Mum. Please begin where you want to."

She sighed deeply with resignation and took one of my hands in her own.

"When my parents and I arrived cold, fatigued and terrified on the ramp at Auschwitz-Birkenau, Mum and Dad were selected to die in the gas chambers, though they and I were totally unaware of their imminent annihilation. Despite the awful privations we'd suffered as Jews since the war began, and the horrendous cattle wagon journey to the camp, I suppose my youth told in my favour. Also I was reasonably well put together, if you know what I mean, and quite pretty really with long brown hair resting on my shoulders. I was ordered by the officer in charge to join a group that was being formed up on the platform. We were then led away from the track to one of the many slave labour sub-camps that sprawled across the bleak winter landscape. At the end of our march, around two hundred of us young women were separated from the young men and lined up outside some grim-looking long huts or barracks. The block kapo or leader, a miserably ugly looking woman probably in her thirties, manhandled us brutally into order. With her thick cracked lips twisted into a cruel grin, she bellowed that we would be working on road construction. Kapos, I learned subsequently, were themselves camp inmates, frequently criminal prisoners who'd been given certain privileges by the SS and who often behaved even more cruelly than their heartless Nazi masters. Our kapo was starting to spit out instructions about our hair being shaved off, camp clothing and disinfection showers when a thick-set older man approached her from a gate in a lofty perimeter wire fence. His swaggering gait, auxiliary uniform and rigid, ruthless features marked him out as another kapo. He brandished a long and polished wooden stick that he tapped against his high black boots as he conversed with our barrack boss. Then he shrieked at us that ten women were required to work in his section. Without more, he trudged up and down the line of exhausted and frightened youngsters, their heads downcast not knowing whether the job would be better or worse than road building. He chose his slave workers by whipping them hard across their shoulders with his lengthy baton and shouting into their faces, 'Move three paces to the front … now!' I was one of the girls he selected in this way. The amazing thing was that not one of us who'd been chosen uttered a sound as we were smacked across the body, though my soft flesh smarted from the stinging pain. Probably the common thought was that, had we cried out, the sadistic pig would've been capable of beating us mercilessly to death. In that respect we were quite prophetically prescient."

At that juncture in my mother's horrible story I removed my hand from her grasp and wrapped an arm about her shoulders.

She smiled weakly and continued her narrative.

"The ten women were conducted back through the camp to another barrack area, which stood in sight of two sombre grey buildings with tall redbrick chimneys belching black smoke. We discovered very soon that these structures contained gas chambers and crematoria ovens. Naturally we were shocked and heartbroken when we learned later that our parents, siblings and other relatives had been slaughtered there like sheep by the Nazis. But I can tell you that the will to survive for another day of life was so powerful that I would've done anything, well almost anything, to stay alive. We were lodged in a part of the sub-camp called Canada. Don't ask me why. Perhaps it was a nasty jest ... the Nazis loved their malevolent little tricks, like conning the Jews into the gas chambers with the pretence that they were entering water showers. 'Remember where you left your clothes,' the guards would say fairly pleasantly if things were going well as they led the naked Jews to oblivion. Anyway, our task was to sort the possessions left by the dead and which were piled up in the warehouse. We could smell the foul pungent odour of the burning corpses, which were corrupted into smoke billowing from the towering brick stacks. The sooty smog formed menacing dark clouds that drifted above our workplace. It was a constant reminder, if ever we needed one, of our unpredictable destiny."

On the one hand, I wanted my mother to stop speaking now, right away. I didn't care for learning about my father. I couldn't really process any more information. But deep down I needed to know about him. I suppose it was a compelling curiosity that drove my instinct and overwhelmed my sense of weakness and despair. I think mother recognised my ambivalence. She took my arm from her shoulders, kissed me at the temple and held me against her body.

"I know, I know," she whispered softly. "It may be even more difficult for you to hear of all this madness than for me to relate the nightmare as it was. But I can assure you, my darling, it wasn't just a horrible dream for me … it was terrifying everyday reality. And as you reproached me earlier, you've got the right to know and understand everything that happened to me, and therefore you, in that hell hole."

"Please go on, Mum."

She released me from her tender embrace, rested against a cushion, closed moist eyes for a minute or so to recompose herself and let her mind travel back to that distant time of sorrow and torment, a time when she'd rapidly transformed herself from a delicate young lady into a strong woman with a mighty will to survive the savage horrors threatening to overwhelm and swallow her.

"It was in the early days of my work in Canada that the man who was to become your father took an interest in me. Perhaps I should say that, compared with other sections in the complex camp system, our treatment was relatively okay. But I would especially emphasise the word *relatively*. We young women could keep our hair despite what the kapo had threatened; and we were allowed to take showers and to look after our personal hygiene. Although sickeningly macabre, we frequently took advantage of the pitifully small bundles of stale food left behind by the victims. Even if they knew of this, our SS guards seemed to turn the proverbial blind eye … maybe because their own corruption in this section of the camp was rife. Pilfering by the Nazis from the sorted baggage was commonplace, despite sporadic crackdowns from Himmler's headquarters. The SS were supposed to be an honourable phalanx of men; that is, according to their own warped Nazi creed. But what I'm saying is that it may've been easier for me to survive in Canada than anywhere else in the infamous Auschwitz complex. I suppose as a young woman, reasonably well fed and of passably clean appearance, I was still quite feminine and comparatively attractive."

Mum again shut her eyelids for a second or two; and I suspected she was imagining her appearance as she sorted the sad belongings of the recently deceased. I took the opportunity of the brief and silent pause to put another question.

"Were there Jewish young men, as well as women, working in Canada?"

"Yes, of course," my mother replied at once.

"W–was one of them my father?" I enquired hesitantly.

There was another moment of silence.

"No," came back the firm answer.

I tried to recall my Holocaust reading. There were tens of thousands of people of various nationalities, religions, ethnic and other groupings in Auschwitz and its satellite concentration camps apart from Jews, though of course they comprised the vast majority of the inmates, dead and alive. Russian POWs, Polish Gentile intellectuals, gypsies, clerics, Jehovah's Witnesses and many others were enslaved to death in this extensive camp regime in south central Poland.

"Who was he then?" I asked pointedly, staring directly into my mother's glazed eyes.

She turned her face away from my fixed gaze and mumbled something indistinct.

"Sorry? I didn't quite catch what you just said, Mum."

She looked at me, tears trickling down her cheeks.

"He was an SS man, a Nazi."

I was shocked into numbness and stupefaction, and remained speechless for I can't remember how long. It may've been less than a minute, though. I don't really know. But I began struggling inwardly to absorb, digest and make sense of my mother's laconic but devastatingly significant sentence.

"Sorry, what did you just say?" I kind of repeated myself, as if again I hadn't properly heard or couldn't really take in what she'd said.

"I know this must come as something like an atomic explosion to you. But you wanted to know … and now you do. Your father was a Nazi. He was one of the young SS supervisors in Canada."

"How could …?"

Before I could spit out the venom my mother held up her hand, like a policeman in the road halting a motorist for a random drink test.

"Just as I thought," she almost chuckled. "You will never understand. How could you? This is why I never wanted to tell you anything."

I felt like I was being sucked into a whirlpool and hurled around by the maelstrom, fighting for every breath. I didn't know what to do, what to think, what to say. But in my crazed mind there arose two warring protagonists. One demanded I get up, flee the house and leave my mother for ever. The other urged that I stay where I was, hear my mother out and not be ignorantly judgemental. I looked at her closely and instead of being choked with the hate and contempt I expected, having just been informed that Nazi blood ran in my veins, I felt only an enveloping, fathomless and nihilistic wretchedness.

"Do you want me to tell you about him … or not?"

She had pitched the question to me starkly, harshly but fairly, and I needed quickly to resolve my dilemma.

"Yes, tell me," I replied in a carefully but surprisingly measured tone.

She sat back and nodded, largely I think for her own purposes.

"Okay then, I will. Hans was in his mid-twenties, tall and well-built, quite handsome really with short but striking pure blond hair. He sort of took me under his wings, so to speak, soon after my arrival in Canada. He kept on doing little favours for me, like drawing my attention to a food parcel hidden amongst the heaps of clothes and footwear, then walking away hurriedly so that his Nazi comrades wouldn't notice. There were also times when he intervened to prevent our kapo from beating me senseless. He did this in such a way so as not to arouse suspicions or expose his developing interest in me. I would often hear him telling his colleagues that an efficient worker like me shouldn't be eliminated for minor misdemeanours. In a way, I suppose, Hans gradually became a kind of protector or guardian to me. Later, on one hot clammy summer night, he found me in the showers when I should've been confined to my barracks. He told me to get dressed and leave quickly. He could've shot me on the spot. Such atrocities occurred all the time, for any reason or no reason at all. I'd heard a rumour that Hans had killed three young Jewish men. But when I asked him about this he denied it at first then explained that, while patrolling the camp's perimeter, he'd caught them red-handed trying to escape. In fact I'd witnessed him viciously kicking some of my co-workers, even the women … though I'd never actually seen Hans murdering anyone. The way he looked at my face and my body in the shower that sizzling steamy night told me a lot about his feelings for me. Of course I'd heard many rumours about rapes by the SS in the camps, even though sexual relations with Jews were absolutely forbidden by the higher authorities. Admittedly, I'd seen sorely distressed Jewish girls sobbing their hearts out. But what were they going to say or do if they wanted to survive? There wasn't a complaints department, you know. At first I didn't want to get involved with Hans, of course I didn't. And he may've been playing me along to get rid of me. It was yet another possible Nazi ruse. You couldn't forget that his cronies in charge of the crematoria, on the other side of the fence, were destroying thousands of Jews on a daily basis with Zyklon B. How guilty do you think I felt about that and, in consequence, about Hans?"

I knew it was a rhetorical question. But I fought to envision the situation into which my mother had been hurled. There was Hans, a German, a dedicated SS thug who, it appeared, wouldn't think twice about splitting open a young Jew's head with a shovel or randomly shooting slave workers who crossed his path and whose faces displeased him. Yet my mother was trying to convince me that this evil creature was also capable of kindness and caring thoughts for her, a Jewess.

"But, Mum, answer me this. How could Hans reconcile his unusually benevolent behaviour towards you, a Jew, with his Nazi racial credentials? Wasn't it the case that the SS were indoctrinated with the belief that Jews were no better than vermin, tantamount to a virus, a health threat to their Aryan supremacy that required urgently to be eradicated once and for all? And weren't there strictly enforced laws that prevented any form of intimate relations between Germans and Jews? I can't imagine that the SS administering the camps would've been exempt from such legal strictures, the essence of the Nazi credo."

"You're correct, of course," she said. "And it's against that background that I can't really explain why Hans aided me in the many ways he did. Other than to mention that, when he was walking me back to the hut from a work detail late one night, he said that he loved me and that he would try to help me survive until the end of the war."

I just knew that she would tell me something like this at some point. But when she did I felt physically sick and needed to rush to the bathroom to vomit into the lavatory bowl. When I returned shakily to the living room, my thoughts and feelings in turmoil, my mother had filled a glass with water for me. My mouth was as dry as sawdust and I swallowed the cold liquid almost in one huge gulp.

"Come here," she beckoned me to the settee. "Sit down before you collapse."

I slumped into the settee feeling physically drained and emotionally pole-axed.

"Don't think I'm totally unaware of what you must be going through right now," Mum said touching my hand. "I'm sorry to have had to tell you all this. I can see it has come as a dreadful blow to you. But you did insist on knowing everything. And now you do. Please bear in mind that I wasn't living in the actual world. It was an artificial existence in what had become a surreal nightmare. I could've resisted my admirer's gradually evolving advances. Do you know what? Despise and detest me if you must, but I didn't feel that I wanted to resist them. Don't forget, I was a young girl, just seventeen, with few terms of reference of any kind in that indescribable hell-hole, other than the instinctively compulsive desire to live and survive. It may be that what Hans did and what I did had no connect to reality, neither his reality nor mine. All I can honestly say now is that our actions were, in a single word, inexplicable."

I couldn't get my head around the appallingly devilish fact that circulating throughout my corporeal being was an incongruous mixture of Nazi and Jewish blood. I could virtually sense the contamination, the taint, the poisonous pollution as a weird kind of malevolent and palpable manifestation. Seemingly illogical questions spouted from my mind like, what are the long-term implications of this heinous mixed-blood cocktail? Some years later I was to discover that this particular query wasn't so implausibly irrational.

"I take it you didn't want to have, or couldn't have, an abortion?" I asked. My doubtless cold steely eyes added all there was to add to my enquiry.

"Yes, you're right in both senses. And please don't look at me like that."

"But, Mum … how could you give birth to a Nazi's child? And in Auschwitz! I would've killed myself first. What were you thinking?"

My mother turned away for a few moments. "You really don't understand" she said to the air. Then she faced me again. "Nothing was that black or white for me. To abort would've been highly risky. Perhaps I was selfish in a way. I wanted to live. But there was another important reason for me to have the baby.

I didn't want to be like the Nazis. I couldn't commit murder, despite everything. And in spite of the danger to his life, Hans wanted me to give birth. He never really explained why. But look, by that time Germany was losing the war. Hans knew that well enough. The Russian armies were advancing fast on all fronts towards Poland. I suppose my lover felt his death could be imminent. Maybe he yearned to live on in his child, even though it would be half Jewish."

I knew it could take a long time, if ever, for me to fully grasp and comprehend what my mother had told me, and to form a conclusive opinion about her actions. In the meantime, other questions were cascading through my head like a raging torrent over a waterfall.

"But, Mum, how did you propose to conceal your pregnancy from the kapo and the other guards? Surely such a physical state, when it became glowingly apparent, would've amounted to your death warrant?"

"Fortunately, it really wasn't that difficult to hide your growing existence. I was quite a slender girl, and it was winter time for most of the period I was more visibly with child. But I was not too big with you, so I could take larger sizes of clothing from the heaps available to me in Canada. It wasn't that difficult for me to camouflage my condition during the icy months. And apart from a very few trusted girlfriends, and Hans of course, nobody else knew about you. And that's the way we managed to keep it."

"And what did those trusty mates of yours think of your dalliance with a Nazi?"

"They didn't know about that, and naturally I didn't tell them. They merely assumed that the father was a fellow Jew. They had the impression, and I didn't dissuade them from it, that the father could've been one of the three young men taken away and shot for trying to escape. This made the handful privy to my confidence even more sympathetic and anxious to keep the secret."

"But how did you hope to hide the actual birth?"

"Needless to say, we were very fearful about that as my time approached. Labour isn't painless and I could've cried out in agony and given myself away. But something miraculous happened on the very day of your birth."

"What was that?"

"When's your birthday, as if I didn't know? But just say the date."

"I was born in Canada on the twenty-seventh of January 1945. Why?"

"On that very day Russian troops liberated the camp. In fact, one of the gun-slinging female commissars accompanying the tanks and soldiers helped my friends to deliver you. Even she said that you were a miracle baby. But, thankfully, she didn't know all the circumstances."

The next question shot inevitably to the forefront of my consciousness.

"Do you know what happened to Hans?"

My mother drummed her fingers on an arm of the settee.

"Most of the SS guards fled westwards as soon as the leading columns of Soviet forces were spotted approaching the camp. Unlike them, Hans stayed behind until he could observe, from his concealment, that I was safely set up for the birth. I knew where he was hiding and saw him nod in my direction as I was assisted into the barracks after my waters broke. That was the last time I saw your father."

"Do you know whether he survived the war?"

"He didn't."

"How can you be so sure?"

"I heard that his body had been found riddled with bullets close to the camp, near the railway tracks that had carried the cattle trucks packed with Jews. I recall being amazed that Hans, as an athletic young man, hadn't succeeded in getting further away. Maybe, I've often speculated, he was lingering with the idea of discovering whether the birth had been successful, and perhaps also to learn whether the baby, if safely born, was a boy or a girl. This was just a notion that would come to me from time to time."

"What did you think about him, my father, when you knew that he was dead?"

"I would be lying if I said that I'd felt deeply sad and emotional about him. But I'd also not be giving you the complete truth if I said his death meant absolutely nothing to me. As I've tried to explain to you, we existed on another planet in an alien universe. It was a hellish netherworld where the rules of existence were strange if not incomprehensible. If anything, I recollect feeling that love is a peculiar commodity. And that our own world might be a better place if nothing else existed but love. I'm sorry if that doesn't make much sense to you. I'm not entirely certain that it made a lot of sense to me at that juncture."

We said no more to each other that shockingly revelatory night. My mother retired to bed and I remained downstairs for a while reflecting on her last few sentences. For some years, even after Mum had died tragically in a road accident that wasn't her fault, I did endeavour to make sense of what my mother had finally said to me on the evening she'd told me that my father had been a Nazi, a member of the dreaded SS. I'd graduated with honours from university a few weeks before Mum was killed by a drunk driver. She was so proud of me that I wept to observe her pride and pleasure. Eventually, I'd plucked up sufficient courage to tell Mike about my bizarre bloodline. We would sit in the student bar or some other convenient venue debating the whole issue, almost endlessly striving to reach for me some coherent conclusions, some tolerable closure about what had happened in Canada. We gave up trying in the end.

After graduation Mike and I went our separate ways. I secured gainful employment with an international company in its marketing department. Coincidentally, my job took me periodically to Canada … the country, of course. Whenever my airplane landed in Montreal, Toronto, Vancouver or Ottawa, I experienced this peculiar churning sensation in the pit of my stomach. As I lay on my hotel bed after a long and hectically tiring day, I would close my eyes and think about my mother and sometimes about the father I never knew, and another Canada that had existed in another place and another era.

Quite by chance I met Mike again, oddly enough in a hotel bar in Toronto. He'd qualified as a lawyer and frequently travelled abroad for his professional work. We discovered that our homes in England weren't that far apart. Both of us were single and started to see one another fairly regularly. Very soon we began to realise that we'd always been in love with each other, ever since our student days. A year or so later we got married and lived happily in his house, which was rather larger than the one I'd lived in. After a few years we learned that there couldn't be any children. It was my fault, medically speaking, though Mike urged me constantly not to feel the blame and self-reproach that, inevitably, I did. Following diligent, though on my part occasionally bitterly tearful, consideration we decided not to adopt. I suppose our childless circumstances drew us even closer together, if that could've been possible. But even this didn't prevent my recurring depressions, about which Mike had known before we'd become man and wife.

So there were just the two of us. Until one day there was only the one of us. Me. You see we had this blazing row late one night. We didn't normally quarrel and I can't recollect now how or why it happened. But at some point my husband screamed that Hitler should've gassed even more Jews than the six million he had done. While Mike was sleeping I smashed his head in with a heavy table lamp. When I was brought to trial, my lawyers advised seeking a manslaughter verdict on the grounds of diminished responsibility. But I insisted on pleading guilty to murder as charged. The judge sentenced me to life imprisonment for what he described as "a merciless, horrific and inhuman crime". Over many years now, all the prison psychiatrists I've talked with have been very nice men. You know, we used to spend a lot of our time discussing the meaning of love.

The Barmitzvah

"Hello, Ben! Had a good day at school?"

"Yeah I did, Grandpa. We started learning Latin today. Awesome! Want to sit outside on the patio? It's lovely and warm and sunny this afternoon."

"Sure Ben. I must've dozed off here in the conservatory. You know I call this my sleepy armchair?"

"Yeah I do, Grandpa. Sorry if I woke you up How long have you been here?"

"Your Mum called me early this morning. She said I should come over for lunch. Well, it is a big day tomorrow, eh Ben? She just wanted me to be here with her today. She was feeling a bit emotional. Where's your Mum now?"

"She's in the kitchen. Emily's helping her prepare Shabbat dinner. I think it's something you really like tonight, Grandpa."

"How is your sister? I haven't seen her for a couple of weeks."

"Emily's okay. I think she's got herself a new regular boyfriend."

"Oh yes?"

"Mum thinks she's got too much school work to be going out so often. You know she'll be taking her A-levels next year."

"Remind me, Ben. My memory's not what it was. Emily's seventeen, isn't she?"

"Yeah, she's around five years older than me."

"Well you know what Ben, in my day girls of that age were thinking seriously about getting married and settling down."

"Is that when the dinosaurs ruled the Earth, Grandpa?"

"I like it, Ben … but don't be so cheeky!"

"I'll just drop my bag upstairs in my bedroom, grab a can of Coke from the fridge and join you in the garden in a minute."

"Okay, Ben."

"Do you want anything to drink, Grandpa?"

"No I'm fine, thanks … Wait a second. Okay, I think I'll have an orange juice. Thank you, Ben."

★ ★ ★

"Here's your juice, Grandpa. I'll put it down on the little table for you. Thanks for bringing it out to the patio."

"No problem. And thanks for getting me the drink … very thoughtful of you. Sit down and we'll have a nice chat. It's really beautiful out here today. I haven't seen the sky looking so blue for quite a while now. The garden's a real treat to behold. Your Mum's always had green fingers. And you know what, these wooden steamer chairs your Dad bought at the garden centre last summer are really comfortable."

"Yeah, he says they had similar chairs on the Titanic. Did you ever go on that ship, Grandpa?"

"No Ben, I didn't. But what did I tell you about being cheeky? And wipe that smirk off your handsome little face. I may be old, but I'm not that old! Well, that's my story and I'm sticking to it. Anyway, are you looking forward to tomorrow? I certainly am."

"I absolutely am, too, Grandpa. Mum and Dad as well. And sis."

"Well, there isn't a barmitzvah in the family every week, is there Ben?"

"No Grandpa, there isn't."

"I was speaking to Rabbi Finegold at the shul Kiddush last Shabbos."

"What did he say?"

"He's expecting great things, Ben. I'm hoping we can do him proud ... from my mouth to His ears."

"I'm hoping for that, too."

"I'm confident about it, Ben. Everything will be all right on the night, as they say. And we're so lucky to have such a wonderful synagogue, eh?"

"Yeah, I've always loved its stained glass windows with their scenes and characters from the Torah. I've liked looking at them since Dad first took me to shul when I was a little boy. My favourite has always been the one with Noah's Ark. I think the elephants are really cool."

"You know, Rabbi Finegold's a lovely man. He made Emily's batmitzvah something quite special, do you remember?"

"I was only about seven, Grandpa. But yes, I do remember it. And her party was great. I think she even had a boyfriend then. Emily must be sex mad ..."

"Now, Ben ... no call for that kind of language."

"Sorry. I suppose things aren't what they used to be when you were young."

"You're right there, my darling Ben. Times have indeed changed, and not necessarily for the better. Progress isn't always what it's cracked up to be. The world's a very different place compared to what it was when I was a lad. Anyway, nostalgia's not what it used to be either."

"What are the biggest differences do you think, Grandpa?"

"There're just so many things ... so many changes. I hardly know where to begin. Let me think ... right, I'll give you just three. First, the planet has got a lot smaller, what with all this air travel nowadays. And for another thing, we're living in what they call the permissive society. It's a world where practically anything goes. So long as it makes you happy, that's okay. Sounds good, but I'm not sure it is. It affects stability. Do you understand what I'm saying, Ben?"

"Yeah, Grandpa, I think I do ..."

"And then there're all these electronic gadgets and gizmos. From flat screen TVs and Pod things to Sat Navs and mobile phones that seem to be able to do just about everything, except make a decent cup of tea. I know you've got a very smart phone, haven't you Ben? It's a Blueberry, isn't it?"

"I think you mean BlackBerry. But no, I don't have one of those, though Dad pays for me to have a really good mobile. I don't know what I'd do without it."

"In my day, you never missed what you didn't have which, in my case, was most things. Now I'd never said these modern marvels are bad things. But I was curious so I asked Emily to show me a text, if that's what they call it. Your sister had just received one from a girlfriend about a film she'd seen. And do you know what? She had to translate the thing for me, like it was some foreign lingo. I couldn't understand a single word of the text because there were no actual words in it that I could recognise as English. All I could see were numbers for words, strange abbreviations and odd squiggles. I tell you, Ben. These so-called texts are destroying our excellent language ... well, I suppose any language."

"I don't know, Grandpa. Sending texts is just a very quick way of messaging my friends. You know English is one of my best subjects in school."

"I'm not talking about you, Ben. I'm on about those kids who aren't academic. But I've got to say they're very adept with their fingers on the phone buttons ..."

"Keypad, Grandpa."

"Okay, keypad, schmeypad! I stand corrected. I've got a pay-as-you-go phone. But I could never text, even if I wanted to ... not with my rheumatic fingers."

"I don't want to be rude, Grandpa. But can we change the subject, please? We've had this conversation so many times before. Tell me, what sort of presents do you think the guests will bring to the party on Sunday?"

"Well, Ben, when I was barmitzvah around 1940 quite a lot of people brought me actual gifts rather than gelt. Things were very hard in those days. There was a war on for a start. Most of the family didn't have too much money to spare. We were lucky to have a roof over our heads, what with the Blitz and all the bombing in the East End. And there wasn't a big choice in the shops anyway. But I seem to recall getting things like a pen and pencil set, even a simple box camera and a wristwatch from some relatively well off aunts and uncles. Nowadays, who knows? It could be money, so you can buy whatever you want. Doesn't apply here, of course, but for weddings today the couple usually have a gift list at one of the Oxford Street department stores, like John Lewis or House of Fraser … I've never favoured that idea, though."

"What's a gift list?"

"It's a kind of inventory or list of things that the bride and groom would like to have, usually for their new home. Items like bed linen, sets of cutlery, glassware of various kinds, pots and pans and electric appliances for the kitchen … that sort of stuff. Invited guests can go along to the shop or look up the list on the Internet. That's the right expression isn't it? The prices are indicated against each article, so you can choose something for however much you want to spend."

"But why don't you go for the idea, Grandpa? It sounds quite a good one to me. Wouldn't it save time thinking about what to buy and where to buy it? And the bride and groom will get exactly what they want."

"Maybe, Ben. But I don't like it. You see the couple, and anyone else who might be interested or should I say nosey, could easily look up how much you'd decided to spend. Some people could be embarrassed. Of course it's not compulsory to purchase gifts from the list. But a vast majority of those attending the simcha would probably do so."

"Okay."

"By the way, Ben, have you seen your Mum's and Emily's new outfits for the party?"

"No, they wouldn't let me see them."

"I caught a quick glimpse of your Mum's outfit this morning. I went upstairs to the bathroom for the spare pills I keep there, and her bedroom door was slightly ajar. As I passed by I saw her twirling in front of the long mirror. I guessed she was wearing her new dress for the simcha. But she didn't notice me looking at her. S–She … s-she looked so b-beautiful in it … it's … n-no, I w-won't tell you. Y-You'll see soon enough …"

"Don't cry, Grandpa. Why are you crying? Please don't cry."

"I–I'm sorry, Ben. I It's just that your Mum looked so much like … like h-her m-mother … like Grandma did when she was your Mum's age Y-You're a good boy, Ben, holding Grandpa's hand like this. I'm just a silly old man …"

"No you're not. Grandma was a lovely lady. I loved her very much. We were all heartbroken when she passed away …"

"It was three years ago now, Ben. It's hard to believe. We were happily married for over sixty years you know … it's a long time. B–But I adored her, loved her so much for every minute of every hour of those sixty years. I think I loved her even more at the end than at the start. Now I-I m-miss her all the t-time …"

"We know that, Grandpa. And I remember the wicked party we had on your diamond wedding anniversary."

"Wicked?"

"That means fantastic."

"Okay. Yes, it was marvellous, wasn't it? Your Grandma enjoyed it so much, even though she wasn't at all well at the time. I'm so glad she lived long enough t-to … t-to … s-she would've been so proud in shul tomorrow."

"Yes, but do you know what, Grandpa? I really believe she'll be there with us, in spirit."

"She would've been so proud of you, Ben … saying something wonderful like that. You're very grown up, you know.

She always said she was very proud of you, and now you've won a place at the grammar school."

"Please don't cry any more, Grandpa. It's going to be a terrific weekend. I'm sure Grandma would be happy we're all going to enjoy ourselves."

"You've got an old head on young shoulders Ben. I say that in the nicest possible way. And you're quite right, of course. I promise not to be a stupid old fool any more. Don't shake your head like that. Ha-ha, it's not nice you darling boy."

"That's a great smile, Grandpa. Just hold on to it for the next couple of days … and always. Okay?"

"Okay."

"Tell me, Grandpa. What were you doing when you were my age?"

"Now let me think. You know at my age now, three things happen. First, you start to lose your memory. Secondly, you … you … Secondly, you … Sorry, Ben, I can't remember."

"You're grinning, so I know that was a joke. Anyway, I've heard you tell it before and more than once. Tell me really, what did you get up to?"

"Well, my lovely cheeky boy, I went to school and then, along with all the other kids, I went to cheder classes afterwards, four nights a week for two hours each evening and three hours on a Sunday morning. And I still had time to attend my Jewish youth club twice a week. I think there's a cheder at our synagogue but only on a Sunday morning now. Is that correct, Ben?"

"Yeah, but I wouldn't be able to go after school even if there were weekday classes. I've got so much homework to do. Did you have lots of homework from school?"

"Not really … we needed to help out at home. But it was

different in those days at our school in the East End. At least we had a thorough grounding in Hebrew. I know that a lot of Jewish children go to Jewish schools today, and their parents think that's sufficient for their religious as well as secular education. But because of that, it's no wonder that so many shuls have closed their cheders in recent years."

"I understand what you're saying, Grandpa. But none of my friends, whether they go to Jewish secondary schools or to my grammar school, would want or even be able to spend eleven hours a week learning in cheder."

"Your maths is also very good, Ben. But I still think you and your pals are missing out on something worthwhile, maybe something that would be useful later on. You know, I sang with the choir at my synagogue when I was a kid."

"I didn't know that."

"Yes, I was a boy soprano and a soloist, right up to my barmitzvah. I had a sweet melodic voice, if I say so myself. No, I was told that as well. That's why a friend's father, who was a singer, introduced me to his choir master. I was a chorister from the age of about seven. It was really wonderful going to shul on Shabbos. You might say it was awesome. The large synagogue was so brightly lit, the chazan had such a marvellous voice and the Sefer Torahs in the Ark were beautifully mantled. I'd never seen anything like it before. My parents weren't very religious, you see. In a way, it was exciting for me and poles apart from the dismal old tenement where we lived. It became a sort of escape, like the Hollywood musicals and westerns I'd see at the local picture palace or cinema to you, Ben … though the experience in shul wasn't quite the same, of course. And I do think my intensive cheder studies helped me gradually to appreciate the spiritual aspect, as well as to master the liturgical music. Believe it or not, even at my advanced age I've still got quite a reasonable singing voice."

"I do know that, Grandpa. And Grandma used to tell me you liked singing in the bath."

"Now she's gone I don't do that any more."

"Did you have a girlfriend when you were my age?"

"Ha–ha … that's a good one, Ben. No, as a matter of fact I didn't. You see, I was a bit on the shy side when it came to talking with girls. But Grandma went to the same youth club that I'd joined. I think she must've taken a shine to me. Don't ask why. Anyway, when I was a couple of years older than you are now, I used to go to the club's socials on Sunday evenings. But Grandma took the initiative. I'll remember that night for as long as I live. As her friends giggled, she walked across the floor bold as brass and asked me to dance with her. She was so pretty with her long black hair. I couldn't believe what was happening. I even turned round to see if she was speaking to somebody else. Though I was still wet behind the ears, I knew from then on that she was the only girl for me … and t–that o–one day I w–would m–marry her … a–and I d–did."

"That's such a nice story, Grandpa. But you promised not to cry any more."

"Sorry, I'll try not to …"

"Good boy!"

"Ha–ha, you cheeky …"

"Language, Grandpa! You're staying with us tonight, aren't you?"

"Yes, it's a bit closer to shul from here than from my flat."

"Dad told me that he'd taken you to buy a new suit, shirt,

tie and shoes for the occasion. What're they like? I bet you look cool in them."

"Yes, I think with all due modesty I scrub up really well."

"And you've got such an amazingly full head of white hair. It makes you look so much younger. Why aren't you bald like most men your age?"

"Ha-ha! I suppose it's been pure luck really. My father and his father had a lot of hair until late in their lives. So I think it must be genetic."

"Genetic?"

"Hereditary … you know, passed down through the generations."

"Okay. But what about the new gear, then?"

"Gear … what gear? I don't have a car any more."

"I mean your new clothes."

"Oh. They're smashing! The suit's dark blue and double-breasted, with two vents …"

"What's a vent?"

"It's a slit up the back of the jacket. But look here, Ben, I think we'll soon have to get some nifty kind of translation device to talk to each other. Anyhow, the shirt's white of course. The tie has got wide red and dark blue stripes. And it's silk, noch! Naturally, the shoes are black and very shiny. I quite like brogues, so that's what we bought. Your Dad was very generous. Like always, bless him. He must be the best son-in-law in the world. He's a real gutte neshomah, a good soul for non-Yiddish speakers like you. He paid for everything … wouldn't let me cough up for anything. You know we went to one of the best bespoke tailors in the West End?"

"Yeah, Dad told us."

"Happily, I've kept a reasonably trim figure over the years, so we could easily choose from off the peg. That's all down to Grandma ... she made sure we had a healthy diet. What you eat is very important, Ben. Remember that."

"I will, Grandpa. But you'd better watch it! I think you're going to look smarter than Dad and me this weekend."

"I very much doubt that. But it's going to be a really special affair, and I want to look my best."

"I know that Dad will be making a speech at the party. But Mum tells me you want to make one, too. She didn't know whether you should. She thought you might get upset about Grandma and all that ... like you did just before."

"Yes, your Mum had a word with me about that. But I really do want to say something. I'll be all right, you'll see."

"We don't want you to become sad in any way. We want you to enjoy yourself. If you're going to insist on speaking, promise me you won't get distressed and cry. Promise me."

"I promise, Ben."

"Okay, Grandpa, you've got my permission to make a speech."

"Oh thank you, Ben."

"And make it a good one."

"Don't worry your clever little head, I will. I've already written it down."

"Let's see it, then."

"No fear, Ben. I want what I say to be a surprise ..."

"Did you hear that, Grandpa?"

"Hear what?"

"I think Mum's calling you."

"Yes, you're right. There she goes again. I'd better go see what she wants."

"Okay, Grandpa."

"Probably she thinks I ought to go over my Maftir and Haftorah one more time. After all, I'll only have one shot at it in shul tomorrow. I'm eighty-three years old, and you don't have a second barmitzvah more than once in a lifetime. I want to be word and note perfect, so that everyone can be proud of me … especially Grandma."

Love and Hate

THE FINAL long but dying note of the violin strings at the end of the sonata's second movement was too hauntingly sublime; and, therefore, too crushingly poignant and melancholy for the formally uniformed officer to bear. Before the beautiful, soul-touching sound had dissipated in the otherwise cemetery silent but crowded and dimly lit concert hall he'd taken the high-peaked military cap that rested on his lap and placed it, with a practiced exactitude, over his severely tapered and tightly curled blond hair. He knew there would be no applause from the hushed but clearly enraptured audience until after the third and last movement. So before that was initiated by the lime-lighted performers he rose bolt upright, quickly, smartly, soldierly, as if he were reacting to a bellowed command on a parade ground; although he hadn't drilled or marched on one of those squares for some years now.

He moved swiftly, efficiently, unselfconsciously, like a predator on the veldt, from his middle seat to the end of the line, thankful that he'd managed to book a front row place in the orchestra stalls during his last furlough in the city. Had he not exited so rapidly, some of the neighbouring concertgoers might just have noticed his smoothly chiselled features, accentuated by prominent cheek bones and sky blue eyes, contorted now into an alarming grimace. And had he been unfortunate enough to be imbedded somewhere in the centre of the theatre's auditorium, there would've been a trail of bruised knees marking the officer's hasty departure.

Within a minute, no more, his throat and lungs thirsting for air like a gasping fish just hauled aboard a trawler, he'd traversed the wide carpeted area between the first rank of seating and the stage, crossed a broad aisle, hurried through an arched doorway and leapt a flight of stairs (even instantly afterwards unable to recall whether up or down), almost vaulted the ill-illuminated foyer to the astonishment of a few by-standing and liveried staff ("Goodnight, sir!" they'd called after him in nervy unison) and finally pulled up breathlessly in the warm but night-shrouded and distinctly whiffy street. It could've been the smell of death.

In the enveloping darkness a passing policeman glimpsed a tall slim man at the shadowy foot of the theatre's steps. Despite the gloom, he noticed the vaguely silhouetted figure suddenly stoop forward apparently inhaling and exhaling erratically and noisily or perhaps moaning, even sobbing. As the police agent approached nearer to investigate whether he could assist, or maybe to detect and apprehend a possible drunkard or vandal, he obtained an unobstructed view of the man's black tunic and turned to walk away swiftly. Unaware of his recent close observer, the concertgoer straightened his body to recover his strictly conventional poise, wiped his face with the back of his hand, dusted down his uniform quite unnecessarily and sighed intensely.

Gradually attaining his normal self-assured composure the officer headed in the direction of his hotel, where he usually stayed on brief leaves in the city. He still preferred to walk when negotiating its streets at night; though, during the dark hours, even he would lengthen stride in order to reach his destination as speedily as possible. Increasingly, and on each successive rest stay, he would come upon a road or other thoroughfare he thought had existed but no longer did. In such circumstances he would need sometimes to make a time-consuming, and often physically awkward, detour. Little that had been familiar was now recognisable.

Frequently, it was hardly easier for him to find a new route in the daylight than at night. He'd wondered whether he should avoid wearing sunglasses during the day, which may've made it more difficult to discern pedestrian diversion signs or less problematic passages. Nonetheless, he'd concluded fairly promptly that the black-tinted lenses not only protected his eyes from bright sunshine but also helped to conceal, or at least make less self-evident, the raw if not horrifying reality that surrounded him. For that small calming solace he could certainly bear his blinkered racehorse syndrome.

Wearily, the black-booted officer climbed the several entrance steps of his luckily intact hotel and entered the patrician-plush, marbled and chandeliered but barely lit lobby through lofty, glass-panelled revolving doors. The white-haired night porter, sitting idly behind the dignified mahogany reception desk, happily spotted the guest at once and reached up to the wooden, wall-mounted key board. The officer had requested the same room on each of the several occasions he'd stayed here. He was really quite reactionary when it came to hotel accommodation. On earlier visits, and as usual, he would've taken the lift to the third floor. But on his arrival this time the hotel's director had explained, overly apologetically, that the elevator wasn't operational due to the lack of an essential replacement part. The distinguished-looking, but excessively deferential, administrator had offered a room on a lower floor that the officer had declined out of hand; though he'd been obliged, alongside other clients, to occupy the hotel's spacious wine cellar for some uncomfortable hours the previous night.

"Good evening, Herr Doktor, sir …" the old porter croaked but welcomingly, snapping as near to attention as he was capable physically at his age and in the constricted space available to him. "Y-You've …" he went on nervously as the stern guest, in no mood for small talk, grabbed the proffered room key.

Nevertheless, the officer in the black uniform was glad to note that the staff had learned diligently to address him, as he'd instructed, by reference to his title as a medical professional. "Y-You've returned from the concert a little earlier than …" the porter continued hesitantly, guardedly. "I-I hope that everything's all right, Herr Doktor." The officer forced a sardonic grin. "I'm not particularly interested in what you hope for," he spat out, already turning his back on the mortified, motionless old man and moving quickly towards the staircase.

With a powerful effort of renewed vigour he began bounding up the red-runner steps, taking an agile three at a time. He caught only a faint echo of the porter's feebly called "G-Goodnight, Herr Doktor". When he reached the expansive first floor landing with its large, gilt-framed landscape paintings and a pair of finely re-upholstered antique armchairs gracing an elegant alcove, the officer halted abruptly. His treatment of the innocently solicitous hotel retainer had been inexcusable, he considered, and quite out of character. As an officer and a gentleman, he thought immediately about returning downstairs and apologising to the old man for his unwarrantable conduct. But instead he shook his head, totally in acceptance of a fact rather than repentantly. He started upwards again, now at a more controlled pace, one step at a time.

At the same moment, the literally long-standing night porter was resting his aching feet by sitting on a high-legged chair behind the reception desk. As his lower limbs dangled a few centimetres off the carpeted floor, he pondered anxiously the hotel director's recent verbal reminder to all staff. "The officer on the third floor," he'd stated just prior to the regular guest's latest arrival, "is to be treated circumspectly, correctly and sympathetically whatever he may say or however he might react to you." And he'd added, in his profession's routinely milder intonation: "Please remember that it hasn't been a year since the Herr Doktor's wife and young son died." The porter felt confident that not more than a few minutes earlier he'd followed his employer's orders to the letter. Not that he would've had the temerity to act other than profoundly respectfully and compassionately towards the guest, even without specific managerial insistence. But he couldn't prevent himself from shuddering with foreboding at the idea of defending an allegation by the black-uniformed officer of a suspected affront.

In the third floor room the heavy drapes had been drawn

and the large double bed turned down by the chambermaid. The officer turned his key and entered, then closed and locked the door at once. He undressed quickly in the dark, having removed the wide black belt from its loops and placed his holstered Lüger pistol on the bedside cabinet. His nostrils detected a fragrant aroma but he couldn't identify the delicate scent and reckoned that it wafted merely in his imagination. He knew it couldn't have lingered on from any Slav chambermaid. All of a sudden that night, the third and final one of his short leave of absence, he felt utterly weary. Without even carrying out his usual ablutions or donning his sleeping attire, he collapsed naked onto the bedcovers, stretched his fit, athletic body and expelled a deep sigh. Like reverberations of the eternally swashing waves he'd constantly held in his mind as a child living close to the seashore, the final notes of the strings at the recital echoed in his head: glorious yet at the same time exquisitely but excruciatingly agonising. Perhaps, he mused whilst slowly closing his eyelids, it would be like this when a bullet impacts intentionally on the human brain in the infinitesimal moment before oblivion.

Despite his exhaustion (a fatigue, he would doubtless admit, redolent more of bitterness than dwindling energy) the officer struggled ineffectively to acquire even a transient unconsciousness, a few hours of hopefully uninterrupted nothingness. He opened his eyes again, but almost frighteningly and menacingly the blackness filling the room, like a solid of equal dimensions, matched his perception when sightless. He bit his lip. What had he done to deserve it? His thoughts wandered like a caravan in the desert, travelling from one oasis to another in the wilderness of nomadic memories. He recalled the point

in time when he'd fallen in love, the hand-in-hand strolls along
the meandering river of the picturesque old university town, the
wedding in the mountain meadow encircled by close family
and friends, the birth of a handsome blue-eyed and flaxen-
haired son, the little boy's five happy birthday parties. Warm
globules gathered at, and trickled from, the unseen red rims of
the officer's eyes. He clenched fists until fingernails dug sharply,
but curiously without any pain, into his firm flesh. And then he
thought, for the thousandth time, of the forbidden young
woman with whom he was now equivocally obsessed. "Why,
why … why?" he murmured to himself, his heart aching
beyond the bearable.

He considered such feelings a betrayal, a perfidious infidelity
even though his wife was dead; and no less traitorous to the
cause. Not that the officer had sought to lay hands on the
woman, though he could've done so many times. Watching the
nurse in the operating theatre of the hospital for the camp's
special supervisory personnel, following closely her body
contours as she moved, and being impassioned by her pallid but
beautiful face as she worked with him, was enough to instil the
notion of disloyalty to his recently deceased spouse. Not that his
wife had been unattractive: in his eyes she'd been a delight to
look upon, her fine golden hair plaited around a classical head
like that of a Greek goddess.

As he lay on the bed, wholly sapped but unable to summon
up the comforting cushion of restful sleep, the widower
continued to torture himself, recollecting the first amazingly
inspiring days, weeks and months after he'd met his wife-to-be.
They possessed so much in common, ideologically and
philosophically, a shared and heightened sense of the dynamic

and triumphant new national ethos that they adored and hoped to experience long into the future; and of the things they despised and detested, which they believed would be eradicated sooner or later for a better life to come. Both he and his new girlfriend had felt somewhat like the old discoverers and explorers, the conquistadors of the New World. Before them would stretch a sunlit upland, on a wonderfully blank canvas … as soon as their sacred country's problems had been surmounted. In the throes of his nocturnal insomnia, the doctor was surprised to sense his mouth curving into a thin smile. There had been no doubt in his mind. She had captured his soul. And then without any warning, like an assassin in the night, sleep overcame him.

★ ★ ★

Several hundred kilometres to the south-east of the city, in which the officer now slept, a young woman awoke startled from a dreamless slumber. Her heart beat rapidly against her tight rib cage but she didn't move a muscle. All about her in the elongated wooden hut, previously part of an army barracks, she could hear the normal ugly, night-time cacophony of snores, grunts and moans from her sleeping or half-awake co-workers. The warmth of the day, which served to heat the room until dusk, had soon dissipated after darkness descended like a pall over the camp. The woman was cold, despite her coiled foetal position on the upper bunk. Even the expelled breath of the almost one hundred other women and girls penned into the fetid space failed to de-ice it, the tepid exhalations leaking out beneath the single locked door or the cracks in the wood-slatted walls. She shuddered and thought about re-wrapping herself in the threadbare, grey woollen blanket that had slipped over her hips to the lower part of her legs. But the moment passed. The absurdly lightweight cover was, in any case, repulsively dirty and useless as a shield against the chilly atmosphere.

As a matter of hygiene it was a wonder, she'd often reflected, that the camp authority allowed her to work in the hospital for its administrative staff. Although, of course, she needed to undergo a thoroughly cleansing shower each morning before beginning her nursing duties. That was no problem, certainly not; she could hardly wait to feel the jets of warm water gushing over her head and smooth white skin. In her family's adopted country she'd been a qualified theatre nurse, a scarce skill much in demand now in the infirmary where she was forced to work for a gruelling twelve hours every day. It was an added bonus to her overseers that she could understand, speak and write their language fluently. But this wasn't really remarkable; after all, it was her native tongue.

Her qualifications had doubtless ensured her survival. And the moderately nutritious couple of bowls of soupy vegetables, sometimes mixed with a little grisly meat, she was fed during the day helped to keep her reasonably healthy. At times she was able to smuggle some bread, turnips or potatoes into the hut for the other women, who invariably worked physically harder than her and for even longer periods in a sub-camp's smoke-belching, synthetic rubber factories. These fellow inmates weren't in any way jealous of the nurse's work advantages; in fact, she was held in great esteem by the other women. They appreciated she was taking serious risks in bringing them the small amounts of food that were distributed as fairly as possible, especially to the sick and more susceptible.

The nurse turned and turned again, awkwardly and restively, on the hard boards that formed her bed. But she was more than grateful for the womanly layer of firm young flesh that reduced the discomfort to some extent. Her mind wandered back six months to when she'd arrived in the camp after a horrific journey by freight wagon. What a way to experience a twenty-third birthday, she'd mused. She hadn't a clue where her parents and two younger sisters had been taken; they were separated from her on the platform ramp that coal-black but dazzlingly torch-lit, blizzard freezing and dog-howling night. The camp was so extensive, and the sub-camps so numerous, that her family could be located anywhere. She hoped and prayed they were bearing up well and thinking of her.

Then she dwelt on food again, a more consistent and mind-suffusing train of thought. The next meal, if it could be so implausibly termed, would be a watery gruel and a crust of stale bread with a smattering of jam at breakfast, wolfed down before the women were marched off in the thin dawn light through the barbed wire fencing to their various work assignments. As the young nurse realigned her position on the bed, head resting on hands that in turn lay on what passed coarsely for a pillow, her almond eyes wide open, she thought about the poised blond surgeon she generally assisted in the reasonably well-equipped operations room. She'd been allocated to the officer following her arrival, after her nursing credentials had been checked thoroughly and confirmed. From an early point in their working relationship she'd noticed more or less out of the corner of her eye that, from time to time, he was staring at her; though she knew the distraction was never at the expense of a patient.

At least to this nurse's mind, the officer was a cultivated, knowledgeable and highly skilful medic. But his ubiquitous glances reminded her of the boys at high school, or even at college, who'd been too shy, reticent or inhibited to approach or speak with her. She was almost sure that the doctor had not spotted her glimpsing his ever so slightly overlong gapes. Naturally, he would look directly at her when issuing an order about a patient or demanding to be handed a particular surgical instrument. She was compelled to acknowledge that the intense eyeball glances and the working looks didn't possess the same quality; and, for sure, didn't carry the same import or emotional effect. There seemed to be a significant element inherent in the former that was absent from the latter.

But she was confused, even disturbed by the attention; the officer looked at her with eyes that appeared to hold more than curiosity. It wasn't, she pondered, quite like an entomologist staring into a microscope at an insect, which is precisely what she knew her kind would've meant to him. But she had to admit to herself that something strange and inexplicable was happening between them. And there was another thing about the officer. By the time he'd departed on leave a few days earlier she was convinced that he, but he alone, had become aware of her contraband activities. She failed to understand why he hadn't done anything about it, reported her, slapped her, kicked her, whatever ... Why had he turned a blind eye to her albeit modest, food smuggling operation? Why? Maybe he thought she was a good nurse, and that it would be a waste to lose her.

As she wriggled edgily, the nurse remembered that one of the women working in the hospital's kitchen, a middle-aged rotund-faced cook who'd proved to be very cooperative, had mentioned only recently that the doctor's wife had passed away almost a year ago. Settling into a new but equally unsatisfactory position on the hard planks, whilst unavoidably hearing another inmate urinating into the galvanised bucket at the far end of the hut, she wondered why she was recalling the cooking woman's information. It felt to the nurse like she was an adventurer of an earlier epoch, searching some dark continent for the unknown source of a mysterious river. Or maybe, she thought, her mental processes were more akin to that of a scientist, a research psychologist or even a philosopher who was seeking an explanation to comprehend the rationale for certain human conduct.

She sat up suddenly on the unyielding bunk slats and gazed unseeingly into the gloom of the old barrack hut. The stench of fresh pee hung around her nostrils but the young woman barely noticed. Instead of holding a hand against her nose she raised finger tips to her temple. No, she pondered, beginning to tremble if not shudder … it just couldn't be. The instant chilling realisation that had overrun her nocturnal musings bewildered the already perplexed nurse. No, it wasn't remotely possible. It was taboo, prohibited. There were strict rules against it, as well as serious punishments. She had to be wrong, wildly mistaken.

Eventually, a dismissal and a question emerged from her frantically perturbed mind. Those glances, those purportedly casual but overlong looks, didn't amount to ogling. No, the officer's sparkling blue eyes held much more than lascivious admiration. Was it more an intensive yearning, an overwhelming longing? She fell back onto her bed of nails, a deep and irrepressible tiredness overtaking her. Her head felt so heavy, so pendulous. The last thought before she drifted into a fitful sleep was that it would drop straight through the pillow, the bunk and the floor, continuing to plummet until it reached the very fires of hell itself.

The nurse arrived in the hospital at the usual early hour on the morning of her doctor's expected return from leave. She relished the routine shower, splashing water over her nubile body while anticipating a long hard day; but, in an odd way, looking forward to seeing him again. She donned her theatre dress and a white cap that completely covered her short brown hair. At one minute to nine and waiting for the officer's imminent appearance, she stood alongside a junior surgeon in the regulation-sized, clean and well-prepared operating room. The nervous patient was also waiting: a young camp guard with appendicitis lay whimpering apprehensively on a gurney in the grey-tiled, windowless corridor.

Exactly on the hour by the theatre's wall clock, the doctor's sharp footsteps could be heard at the other end of the wide passageway. At ten seconds past the hour he strode into the operating room. Its two occupants were surprised that the officer hadn't yet changed into the white surgeon's gown and still wore his black uniform with its collar's zigzag silver runes and holstered side-arm at the waist-belt. The first thing he did was to smile directly at his nurse, an action he'd never performed before. She hesitated for just a moment then returned the smile to the doctor. Immediately, the officer heard in his head, for the umpteenth time that morning, the final transcendent notes from the concert's divine sonata. Without warning, he lunged and grabbed the young nurse's left forearm. Startled by the sudden assault, she lost her balance and collapsed in a twisting motion to the floor. Still grasping her limb, the surgeon dragged the woman across the room. She screamed shrilly, a screech of pain and panic like that of a small rodent caught in the petrifying clutches of a huge bird of prey. The awful hurt at her shoulder socket was almost unbearable.

Mercilessly, the officer dragged the girl's shrieking form, like a sack of potatoes, along the length of the corridor, through an open doorway and into the radiant daylight. He flung her body onto the earthy ground where she lay painfully crumpled and helpless, her left arm laying at a crazy angle. She looked up at what now seemed to be a black-uniformed stranger hovering above her like a pitiless vulture. Her mind was uncomprehending, unbelieving, silently pleading as the cries of agony gave way to relentless sobbing. But through the curtain of tears the nurse's eyes began to widen with terror as she saw the man reach for the holstered pistol with his right hand. With his left, he forced her into a kneeling position and clenched her left shoulder in a firm, unrelenting and talon-like grip. She turned her face away from him and stared down at the black soil surrounding her, refusing to look into the crazed blue eyes that incongruously matched the tranquil hue of the heavens above them. The near final sensation of the young woman's life on Earth was the gentle caress of a gun barrel kissing the velvet-smooth nape of her neck …

A Dark Matter

SCIENTISTS, I'VE learned, are becoming seriously anxious about their "Big Bang" theory of Creation. Everything we can now see in the observable universe, they've explained, was brought into being from nothing by the mightiest explosion in cosmic history some thirteen billion years ago. With the most powerful of today's telescopes scanning the paradoxical edge yet genesis of creation, astrophysicists are able to look back and perceive the origins of space and time. Despite evidence, contrary to expectation, that the rate of inflation of universal matter appears to be accelerating rather than slowing down, all still seemed inherently ordered throughout the known parameters of existence. Across a hundred thousand light years the billions of galaxies, with their hundreds of billions of suns, continue to perform to their astronomical gravitational forces and the general rules of physics, as they have ever done. But now the boffins are evidently puzzled by certain revealed anomalies that may jeopardise their formulaic mathematical calculations about our universe, its formation and ultimate destiny in the awesomeness of infinity.

A Dark Matter

Dark space is what these professional stargazers call a mysterious element of strangely invisible matter, which they've equally mystifyingly detected, scattered right the way through the cosmos. In an attempt to find the precise composition and resultant implications of this oxymoronically insubstantial substance, scientists around the world are carrying out competitive laboratory-based experiments, even far underground, aimed at capturing, isolating and identifying its elusive components. The first to succeed in this exploratory endeavour will undoubtedly be awarded a Nobel Prize. Nonetheless, there are said to be major obstacles in the way of discovering what could be a significant clue. One of the tantalising problems, we're told, is that the essence of this baffling and all-pervading dark stuff, which could have some significant cosmic effect, apparently possesses the capability of moving through solid objects, including the complex instruments employed in the efforts to comprehend it.

★ ★ ★

A long time ago, my daughter attended a Jewish primary school. She often came skipping home in the afternoons singing or just humming a catchy religious tune which, as a traditionally observant Jew, I adopted rather affectionately. It was trilled by my little girl like a joyful mantra; and, in my mind's eye, I could picture with some amusement the other six-year-olds in her class gleefully chanting the words as their teacher waved her arms up and down to keep the rhythm on track. I can still remember every single syllable of the song's verses. The lively lyrics came to me while I was watching a television documentary about scientists seeking to understand the nature of some ethereal matter that's spread across the universe …

Hashem is here, Hashem is there,
Hashem is truly everywhere.
Up, up, down, down,
Right, left and all around,
Here, there and everywhere …
That's where He can be found.

Hashem the Almighty, the boys and girls sang, is up, down and all around … here, there and everywhere. And it occurred to me that those hubristic men and women in long white coats, busily experimenting in their ambitious subterranean laboratories, might just find the solution to their cosmic quandary in the simple language of a children's song …

"Hi! What can I get you to drink? What drink can I get you, sir?" The repeated question finally penetrated my consciousness; and the realisation dawned that I'd reached the head of the queue at my chosen coffee shop in the town centre. The overworked, pretty female barista looked at me with a whimsically mixed expression of recognition and expectation.

"Huh … sorry," I said. "I must've been daydreaming. At my age that comes quite easily now."

The girl smiled sympathetically. And then I thought … no, wait a minute, what am I saying? Sixty-one isn't that old nowadays.

"I'd like a regular black Americano to drink in, please."

Politely, I declined the invitation to buy a sweet croissant, a large biscotti or a low fat blueberry muffin. Truly, I'm not egocentrically narcissistic; but I do try to resist such fattening temptations, preferring adherence to a Mediterranean-style diet in an effort to maintain a trim figure and, hopefully, a fit body. Whilst the barista attended to the puffing coffee machine, I delved inside my wallet for the café's loyalty card and slapped it face up on the counter. Nine stamped points, one for each coffee purchased, meant the tenth one would be free. I'd still got three vacant spots, so I paid for my drink as the young woman reduced them to two. The spacious ground floor room was unusually crowded and noisy, even for university term-time, so I carried my Americano upstairs where I knew more seating in a quieter ambience would be available.

I spotted a lone vacant armchair beside one of the round wooden coffee tables in the high-ceilinged and spacious first floor area, where several students were working hunched attentively over their laptops and electronic notebooks. Taking hasty possession I put down my hot drink and removed my coat, hanging it over the back of the fading leather seat. Then I crashed into its smooth shiny concavity. As I shifted to get comfortable I found the coffee shop's card still clutched in my hand. And the notion of loyalty, with its implied attributes of allegiance, constancy and fidelity and its negative implications of unfaithfulness and betrayal, slipped unbidden into my head. I reached into my trouser pocket for my wallet. Unexpectedly, the words of my daughter's lively Jewish school song crept stealthily to my lips; and the image of a starry night sky etched itself bewilderingly on my retinas. I stowed away the catalyst for my thoughts endeavouring to grasp a connection between the concept of loyalty, the star-studded heavens and a simple lyric extolling the ubiquitous spirit of the Almighty.

I bent forward, grabbed my coffee and snatched a much-needed mouthful. After replacing the cup on its saucer, I leaned back into an armchair that seemed to mould itself to my body. I closed my eyes, refusing to be sidetracked by the attractive female undergraduates in tight jeans or miniskirts deftly tapping their Qwerty keypads in the vicinity. And I reflected on the good fortune that had finally brought my wife and me to this charming and youthfully atmospheric city on our retirement from London professional life. That morning, as I walked beside the river from our home to the town, I'd felt faintly soporific, like I was nursing a hangover. That's unlikely these days; although I do appreciate a regular glass of whisky, especially the peaty smoky malts from the Western Isles. My light-headedness seemed to have borne itself into the café and into my vague response to the barista. Maybe I had something on my mind.

Whatever it was, if anything, the something hadn't crystallised as yet. After the first swallow I completely forgot about my coffee; and the caffeine in the cup quickly lost that initial, roasted black heat taste that I loved to savour. I did think about returning downstairs to buy a refill but I was too contentedly ensconced. Oddly, the notion of loyalty again interrupted my thoughts and I took time out to consider its possible manifestations. Not so outlandishly perhaps, religious loyalty, allegiance to one's lifetime faith, shot to the apex of my mental register. And I realised, at once, the reason why my daughter's childhood song had played on my tongue after learning of science's uncertainties about the composition of the universe.

But I sublimated that bizarre dark matter as a stream of other loyalty situations flooded through my grey matter: the loyalty of a brave soldier to his comrades, the loyalty of a patriotic citizen to his country, the loyalty of a conscientious worker to his employer, the loyalty of a trustworthy director to his company and its shareholders. And then thoughts of more personal or private loyalties swirled through my head: the loyalty of a man to his convictions, the loyalty of a father to his family … the loyalty of a husband to his wife. And I got to wondering, in a fanciful sort of way. Would it be possible to measure or quantify, even give a performance rating to, the exercise of a loyalty? And why, in any event, would anyone want to implement such an asinine and idiosyncratic exercise? But my eccentric train of thought persisted. What if a spy became a double agent? What if a Jewish man married a Gentile woman but continued to attend a synagogue for worship? What if an infantryman is killed courageously falling on an enemy grenade to protect his fellow troopers knowing, in the instant of his death, that he leaves his wife and young children bereaved at home? Can divided loyalties ever be severally genuine? Can a man ever be true to another human being if that loyalty is in conflict with his innermost feelings?

I attempted hazily to analyse whether the betrayal of one loyalty can ever be justifiably counterbalanced by adherence to another, and in what circumstances. With no forewarning, the earlier ungraspable something on my mind surfaced unpredictably, even menacingly. Like a wartime submarine's conning tower and deck gun breaking through the pounding grey waves, its helmeted crew then firing on a solitary cargo ship. The sudden rattle of china distracted me.

"Have you finished with this, please?"

I looked up to see a smiling young girl in rather fetching,

dark blue work overalls. She was holding onto a large plastic container of dirty crockery and pointing to my half-consumed now lukewarm drink. I nodded hastily, not wishing the something to vanish from my head like a torpedo propelled into the endless ocean of my lost thoughts. But why the heck was I thinking about predatory wolf packs and fiery destruction on the High Seas? The coffee shop assistant picked up my used items, piled them into her receptacle and turned away. Tangled, coffee-injected notions suggested it was time for me to leave, too.

Once into the sun-sprayed side street, I wandered through the entrance gate of the nearest venerable college. The duty porter in his cosily compact lodge nodded me in as a non-tourist when I flashed evidence of my residence in the city. I strolled around the neatly tended grounds, navigating colonnaded courts, circumventing hurrying, earnest-looking students and academics clutching files, folders and worthy books and made my way beside neat and tidy lawns down to the river. Mindful of the centuries of history and learning encompassing me, I stopped on a humped stone footbridge, propped myself against its sturdy balustrade, glanced back at the majestic old buildings redolent of erudition and scholarship then gazed down into the water's placid current.

It was David's story that I'd hidden away in one of my rarely frequented, cerebral recesses. That was the shadowy something stalking me and that I'd been unable, or maybe unwilling, to acknowledge in the coffee shop. Like a horror DVD that a fan of the movie genre might conceal at the back of a wardrobe; frightened to watch it again yet somehow compelled to retrieve and replay the disc occasionally, as if to rediscover what was so very scary about it. Peering into the calm shallows of the willow-edged river had nudged into my awareness the tragic personal story that David had felt able, ultimately, to recount to me when we'd met, for the first time in over thirty years, in this very town of ours.

I'd known David very well as a close and good friend. We'd been contemporary undergraduates at one of London University's eminent colleges; though our study subjects differed widely. He was reading the natural sciences; I was studying economics. David was a charismatic Type-A, politically motivated and active student, predictably voted into the presidency of the Jewish Society in his second year. Our personalities were quite dissimilar. Though don't they say that unlike poles attract? Sure I was more laidback, or possibly taciturn, and maybe somewhat gauche. But we had our traditional Jewish family backgrounds in common, and some other shared cultural interests that somehow bound us together. I'd soon gained from socialising in conjunction with David because he was such a potent magnet for the most attractive and intelligent female students.

After graduating with really decent degrees, we met irregularly at various college reunions. And it seemed that, like me in fact, he was gradually becoming more religious. But again like me, not in any deeply serious way. Certainly, there'd been a few of our fellow Jewish students who'd gravitated to ultra-Orthodoxy and gone on to yeshivah in Israel. But that wasn't our scene. David married fairly young; he was just twenty-three when he fell in love with Susan, a very beautiful and highly talented girl a year younger than her husband. I could readily perceive why my friend had become smitten with her. And how he'd rapidly twigged that she would be his life's soul mate. In truth, they made a fantastic couple. If I'd had to admit it, I was probably more than a bit jealous.

Susan was endowed by nature with a lissom eye-catching figure, fair curly tresses and a flawless complexion. But she also possessed that wonderful social ability to get on famously with anyone she met and liked. The love of David's life was not only great fun to be with but also exceptionally bright, though in an engagingly self-effacing manner. Despite the fact that her many girlfriends included several so-called JPs or "Jewish Princesses", none of their cliquey arrogance had tarnished her own vivacious yet somehow homely and unpretentious personality. I didn't find the right woman for me until almost a decade after I'd served, somewhat diffidently, as David's best man. I can still recall a remarkably glittering affair at the Dorchester Hotel in Park Lane. Perhaps I was a bit of a tardy runner in the romance stakes. Or it could've been that I was confusingly searching for another Susan. In the final analysis, my university mate's worldly charm, his clean-cut handsomeness and thick, dark brown wavy hair doubtless had a significant edge on me. But there was also the fact that I couldn't have afforded to get married earlier, even if I'd wanted.

David's Hampstead-based parents were extremely wealthy. As I stood on the ancient arched college bridge, staring at some mute swans proudly flapping their huge white wings by the river's margin, I recalled that they'd purchased their son and daughter-in-law's first home, a really impressive detached house in Hendon. Originating from a considerably more modest milieu, to say the most, I'd always self-rationalised the ten-year gap between David's and my wedding in terms of a need to save a substantial sum of money before shouldering any matrimonial responsibilities. Before we'd finally lost touch with each other, as invariably occurs with college friendships, David had become a junior academic lecturing at one of the major northern redbrick universities. It wasn't until several months back, and quite by chance, that we'd met again; and in this charming town that my wife and I had now made our home.

Astonishingly after more than three decades, we'd come across one another at my newly favoured coffee shop. It was a warm and sunny Friday morning; I recollect the day clearly, though not for its weather. I was sitting upstairs nurturing my Americano and thumbing superficially through that week's just published issue of the Jewish Chronicle. I was barely taking in the weekly newspaper's bread-and-butter news stories and features on Israel's intractable problems, the scourge of increasing anti-Semitism in Europe and internecine conflicts within Anglo-Jewry. Mine was a rather insouciant mood propitious for easy distraction by the buzzing comings and goings of the café's mostly, but by no means exclusively, student and predominantly female clientele. I'd finished my beverage and was on the point of departure when I registered a tall dark, wavy-haired man of around my age standing nearby. He was holding his coffee and about to seize the single chair parked beside a newly vacated table. In part, my attentiveness stemmed from his familiar appearance; sometimes you see someone you think you know but the context befuddles the recognition factor.

I must've been staring overlong at the man because he suddenly glanced in my direction. Pseudo-mystics aver that if you look for long enough at someone otherwise unaware of your presence, say on the Tube, in a bar, at a park or whatever, sooner or later that person will return the gaze. Stunned disbelief hardly described our mutual acknowledgement. David's face was a classic of shocked surprise. If only my SLR had been handy. I did have a reasonably high pixel camera on my mobile phone. But I was too astonished to even think about using it. My one-time very dear university friend nodded slowly and knowingly. I stood up. Without at least considering the embarrassing possibility of mistaken identity, each of us moved forward in a kind of clumsy lunge, collided lightly in the middle of the large room and hugged one another with affectionate, heart-warming abandon. After so many years we didn't notice, and in any case wouldn't have minded, the likely bemused gawping of our fellow coffee imbibers.

We were so excited to see each other again that David and I were literally, and historically unusually, struck dumb for a minute or so. In the end, I invited him to my table, which had an extra seat, and he sat down quickly. We hadn't yet said a single word when I noticed some tear drops on his still smooth and olive-tinged cheeks. I leaned forward and moved my arm around his broad shoulders, in what I hoped was a masculine rather than a tender gesture, surmising that our startling meeting had prompted an emotional reaction on his part. I felt no less touched by the reunion. At that moment I was feeling poignantly sentimental, too. But perhaps I'm not so quick to display my feelings.

"I'm sorry, David ..." I said abnormally tentatively and softly for me. Undoubtedly, I was now becoming cognisant of the other customers, a few of whom were gazing at the two of us with ill-disguised curiosity. Then I added jokingly, but with what I rather hoped would emerge as a compassionate smile: "We can't go on meeting like this if you're going to behave …"

Weirdly, I couldn't find the words to finish my sentence. David took out a tissue to dab his face and frowned in a curiously downhearted way at what I thought had been my attempt at humour,

"It's nothing to do with that!" he responded, though quite brusquely I felt.

There followed an uncomfortable few seconds of silence before he said: "No, no … it's for me to apologise … for that boorish comment. I'm really delighted to see you again. How long has it been?"

"Thirty or so years, I believe."

"Well at least there's one good thing. We couldn't have changed in appearance too drastically. I'm delighted to say we recognised each other almost instantly."

I nodded but, in spite of David's duly expressed regret, I sensed an undercurrent of uneasiness in his demeanour. I don't know why but this suggested that David was possibly in two minds now about bumping into me. We chatted amiably enough, sipping our coffees and discovering that we'd both taken early retirement: he from his professorial pursuits in this very citadel of learning, me from an accountancy partnership in the City. As the conversation expanded, my provisional idea that David may've felt unsure whether he was actually glad to see me seemed to be confirmed. I couldn't grasp the essential basis for his apparent doubts because, for my part, I was absolutely thrilled to be reunited with him. Fond memories of our halcyon shenanigans at college piled into my head; yet I was envious to note that David had indeed retained his good looks.

I couldn't forget the tears on our initial manly hug. What was that all about? This wasn't like the David I'd known once upon a time. And then he'd sounded … well, churlish if not ever so slightly truculent, quite contrary to the character I'd known back awhile. I couldn't quite get to grips with the man's attitude now. I'm not so naïve as to suppose that people don't alter, that individuals don't evolve over the years. Nothing stays the same for ever. The past is another country and all that. And don't some philosopher-scientists say that the only cosmic constant is change? But I was intrigued about David's present state of mind towards me. Sadly, I was beginning to feel ambiguous, even regretful, about our encounter and despite our once close friendship. I didn't want to probe my one-time friend's motivations; though I could hardly contain an inner compulsion to do so. As things turned out, it proved unnecessary to fight that mind battle any further. David had just drained the remnants of his coffee when it struck me that neither he nor I had asked after our respective spouses.

"I'm sorry, I should've asked you about your wife," I said remorsefully. "How is the gorgeous Susan? Undoubtedly, she's as beautiful and clever as she ever was."

David didn't say anything immediately. Maybe he hadn't heard my question. I did seem to be speaking in a lower, more self-conscious voice than I would normally. Then he asked, somewhat strangely and a mite abstractedly: "Fancy a walk along the river?"

David rose from his seat before I'd had an opportunity to even consider the unexpected invitation.

"Y-Yes, okay," I replied hesitantly, rising from my chair and not a little baffled by my old friend's suggestion. "I don't see why not."

We left the café together and walked through the town centre's cobbled streets and picturesque alleyways towards the river. As if by mutual consent we said nothing to one another. Finally, we traversed the daffodil-strewn park abutting the waterside. It had taken us no more than ten minutes or so to cover the distance from the coffee shop. I've got to confess that there were a couple of instances during our short amble when I wavered on the brink of spouting some lame excuse to wish David a fond farewell. The pretext could've been a suddenly recalled and plausible engagement that would've allowed us to go our separate ways, maybe for ever. But I didn't say anything, perhaps for old time's sake. Or possibly it was due to a hunch that David's sudden invite to stroll beside the river meant that he wanted to tell me something important in a less public location.

Mothers with their raucous and animatedly energetic children were feeding the local waterfowl and, unintentionally, the flocks of scavenging pigeons and gulls at the place where we'd now reached the river. David and I sauntered further along the path beside the inclined grassy verge until we came to a peaceful and more idyllic spot. My companion moved towards a vacant bench and sat down. I joined him and we rested there, wordlessly gazing across the gently rippling water to the quirkily painted, and plant-pot topped, narrow boats moored at the tree-shaded bank opposite us.

David broke the edgy silence, shattering me from my reverie.

"Susan's confined to a wheelchair," he said evenly as he turned to face me.

I reacted like a grenade had exploded nearby, showering me with mind-blowing shrapnel. Stupefaction almost overwhelmed me.

"What!" I exclaimed, only minimally absorbing the horrific announcement. "What did you just say?"

David was starting to cry again as I stared at him with amazement and disbelief.

"M-My wife's confined to a wheelchair," he repeated, making some small effort to restore his composure.

Questions … so many questions deluged my head, all competing for priority.

"How, why, when?" Again, as in the café, I wrapped an arm around David's shoulders while tear droplets glided down his cheeks. In the space of less than a minute everything seemed explained to me, like a Biblical revelation in the wilderness. And I felt dreadful about my earlier impatient posture towards an old and one-time dear and faithful friend.

"David," I said. "We used to be very close. We trusted each other implicitly. We confided in each other. Tell me about Susan. I think you want … no, I think you need to do that."

He wiped his eyes with a tissue, too rigorously as it happened so reddening their surrounds in the process. His lips were pressed together tightly, like floodgates straining to hold back a torrent of sorrow. Then he sighed, so profoundly that I feared he would be unable to take another breath. Mercifully, David's next intake of air produced a tentative recovery from his almost palpable despair.

"Y-Yes, you're right," he said. "I do need to tell you … to tell you everything."

I nodded, wedging myself into a corner of the hard and uncomfortable seat.

"Susan was involved in a horrendous motorway pile-up," he

began. "It's hard to believe that it happened seven years ago now."

I shook my head with incredulous dismay and grasped David's arm. With glazed eyes he continued, informing me that the emergency services needed to cut his wife free from the twisted wreckage that had trapped her in a prison of jagged metal.

"Fortunately she was unconscious, but on life support throughout the agonisingly lengthy rescue operation," he went on. "But they had to work very carefully. After the ambulance had rushed her to hospital, the surgeons fought for hours to save her legs. They managed to do that, thank God, but only just."

Overcome by his painful memories, David stopped talking for a moment or two. I'd been rendered speechless and devastated by the terrible accident he'd described. I couldn't take it all in. It was just too horrible to contemplate. My words *gorgeous Susan* returned to haunt me ... poor darling Susan. And I shuddered to think what a living nightmare my friend had experienced when, as he then recalled, the police had informed him about the crash and the medical advisers had later explained about Susan's spinal injury and the sad prospect of permanent paralysis. What could I say to David? What could I offer him by way of meaningful consolation? How could I form my emotions into syllables and link them into words and sentences that would then be adequate to the task? How I wished that I could've been by his side during that awful period. I was sure he would be able to deduce from the moisture gathering in beads on my face how seriously shaken I was by his distressing news. In fact he prised my hand from his arm and, in turn, gripped mine so tightly that it hurt. We just sat there, tuned in to the same station and virtually immune to our discomfort on the tough seat. Personally, it was with a heavy-hearted remembrance of how full of the joys of life Susan had been in our student days.

Then we began talking again. David related how valiantly his wife had borne news of her paralysis, the months in hospital and the many stabilising operations followed by weeks of convalescence and aching but necessary physiotherapy.

"Susan was absolutely wonderful," he said. "She was so courageous. Even her doctors were astounded by Susan's fortitude and stoically fatalistic acceptance of her situation. I don't know what reserves of strength gave her the will-power to sustain those early years of physical pain, soreness and, of course to her, dire inactivity. At first, I didn't see how she could bear to confront the future. She'd been such a vital and vigorous individual with so many pursuits, charitable endeavours and sporting interests. She'd absolutely adored our regular winter skiing holidays in the Alps. And I have to say that I feared gravely for her continued sanity. But as it turned out, she was a much braver and stronger person than me. I really shouldn't have been so amazed. But what I think also helped enormously, apart from the family, was our shared faith in the Almighty. And our dear rabbi at that time was tremendously supportive. I don't know what I, let alone Susan, would've done without him. Of course I sought further medical opinions, both in this country and abroad. In the desperate hope that someone somewhere could do something more for my wife, maybe with some pioneering surgery …"

I shifted on the firm bench slats. "Did you discover anything?" I asked, without much hopeful expectation that David's search for a cure had been fruitful.

"About four years ago," he went on, "I was given the name of a surgeon in Hamburg. Advice was that he'd been testing a new surgical procedure in the area of Susan's paralysis. I contacted him at once and Dr Schmidt said he would be willing to help, if possible. But Susan didn't want to go to Germany. Some of her father's East European relatives had been murdered by the Nazis. I suppose that I understood her feelings. Naturally, I was very disappointed and upset for her, but I respected my wife's motivation. I didn't press the matter with her."

"Was there any other medical possibility anywhere else?" I enquired, nearly certain that a remedy was sadly unlikely.

"Although we followed up some leads in the States, unfortunately there wasn't a positive outcome," David noted. "I'm afraid that medical science hasn't yet advanced sufficiently to reverse, or even to partially alleviate, Susan's particular spinal problem. Her consultant surgeons have patently done their very best for her. I recognise that, of course. But, as they felt compelled to remind me, she would have to live with the inability to move, or have any control over the lower half of her body, for the rest of her life."

At that, David broke down comprehensively. Sinking forward and holding his face in shaky hands, he began weeping pitifully.

I tried to comfort him. But it was a good ten to fifteen minutes before he was close to some moderate semblance of normality. Throughout that almost unendurable time, doubtless for him and certainly for me, one or two passers-by looked disturbed by the wretched riverside scene we must've presented. Penetrating this terrible bout of sobbing, I suggested to David we walk further along the path to a waterside pub where I'd downed the odd pint of lager. I sensed he needed a stiff alcoholic uplift, probably a double or even a treble whisky. And I told him so. His sobs diminished gradually to a plaintive whimpering. At last, he shrugged his shoulders and agreed, reluctantly, to my tentative proposal and dragged himself up off the bench as I stood up, too. I could barely digest the totally routed appearance of a man I'd once known to be so strong and unshakeable. As we walked along the riverside path, little did I know what further dark matter David was considering disclosing.

We progressed slowly beside the sloping grassy bank; and in response to my gentle enquiries, David felt able to explain how they'd adapted their home and acquired full-time domestic help to make everyday existence relatively easier and more bearable for Susan. And how incredibly speedily she'd attained a positive echo of her former full, joyful and active life, learning the optimum way to perform what would otherwise have been quite simple, personal, everyday tasks.

"It wasn't always easy for her ... or for me, for that matter," he explained, obviously struggling to pull himself together. "There were real impediments, frustrations and obstacles. Some of them proved to be insurmountable. But my wife was magnificent, never surrendering, never giving up the effort to improve her performance. That was Susan all over, of course ... inspiring, determined to master, or at least come to terms with, what fate had decreed for her. And in the midst of everything that was being thrown at her, she held amazingly to her unfailing sense of humour. Memories of the past made it difficult, sometimes impossible, for me to observe Susan wheeling herself around the reorganised ground floor of our house. Believe me, there were times when my wife felt the need to comfort yours truly like a mother might give succour to her sick child."

If only weather-wise, it was evolving into a fine spring day. Most of the waterside hostelry's patrons were sitting alfresco, spread across the quaint eighteenth century inn's walled beer garden, enjoying the balmy sunshine with their favourite drinks. Neither David nor I was in the glowing mood required to sun ourselves; so I found us a quiet cubicle-like corner niche inside, below the old pub's character-full ship's beams. The building had been standing for some three hundred years so we were surrounded by centuries of history and a relaxed atmosphere. I knew the landlord was proud of the pub's prolific boating theme, which he'd developed with numerous paintings, etchings and sepia photographs of various river vessels and small craft that spanned the years in a seeming attempt to completely obscure the dark wood-panelled walls. Oars of different types and sizes, brass compasses, wheelhouse bits and pieces and other seafaring paraphernalia were affixed to any exposed parts of the low-ceilinged saloon's ancient timbers. I wasn't especially fascinated by the nautical artefacts but I'd often found the ambience suitably calming. I sat David down, hoping that this charming and peaceful venue might in turn distract and tranquilise him. I went to the bar counter in the virtually deserted room and ordered two large blended whiskies. The way I was feeling I could've easily demolished both of them in the blink of an eye. But, dutifully, I brought the glasses back untouched to our table and joined David on our thankfully well-cushioned, albeit hardwood seat.

I was slightly taken aback when he raised his chunky glass

and swallowed its entire honey-coloured content in one throat-arching gulp. He closed his eyes, savouring the gut-warming Scottish brew and allowing the fiery uisge beatha, the so-called water of life, to smoothly get on with its soothing internal business. Not wishing to lag behind my old university friend's intake I followed suit immediately, relishing the golden liquid sliding down into every fibre of my body and enjoying the warmly infusing afterglow.

"I really needed that," I sighed; then, smiling broadly, I returned my empty glass to the polished, ship-plank table. "And I expect you did too, David. I'll get us another round."

When I got up to head back to the barman, David looked at me and an unnervingly pleading expression spread across his face like the enveloping umbra of an eclipse. As I waited patiently for service at the bar, I glanced at David. He was staring peculiarly at me, as if trying to recognise someone he wasn't sure he knew. In truth, however, I don't believe he was actually focusing on anything in particular; it appeared like he was looking through a glass darkly, as they say. If I'd had to guess, I would've said that he was fighting inwardly to decide whether to tell me something more. From his deeply anxious features, the effort to resolve the issue appeared to be painful and distressing Returning to our cubby-hole with two further double shots of Scotch I could sense from my old friend's eyes that he'd made a definite and final decision.

This time, we each took a hurried initial sip of the liquor. I gazed at David and he would likely have noticed the benign expectation residing in my eyes.

"You always did have the knack of reading my thoughts," he said. I half expected his mouth to curve into a grin but he merely retained his serious, tense and edgily imploring look.

"So what do you want to tell me, David?" I responded, equally gravely but without any of my erstwhile friend's evident nervousness.

"It's very complicated … it's …" he went on uncertainly, cautiously. "I've told no one, no one, about … You'll probably want to kill me when I tell you … and, in all sincerity, I wish you would. I've frequently considered topping myself in recent times. I really don't deserve to live any more. But you see I'm a weak, cowardly, ghastly person … I just don't have the guts to end it all."

I couldn't take in what I was hearing. What was David talking about? Was he referring to suicide? What the hell was he saying? I was totally mystified by his appalling outburst. Maybe, I reflected, the years of endless sadness, anxiety and concern coping with Susan's condition had finally unhinged the poor man.

"What are you going on about, David? I don't understand."

"No," he countered, throwing up his hands in a despairing gesture. "How could you?"

"Then you must help me to understand. Why would you want to do away with yourself? Is it something about Susan? From what you've told me, I think you've cared for and supported your dear brave wife brilliantly."

Then David shocked me yet again. He laughed stridently, though the sound was more like a hysterical, manic cackle. Providentially, there was no one in the near vicinity to hear such an unsettling, hyena-like noise. I was starting to think that my instant diagnosis of mental or psychological impairment was sadly accurate.

"David, try to control yourself," I urged him in a heightened whisper. "This isn't like you ... not like you at all. In fact, you're scaring the living daylights out of me! I'm really concerned for your wellbeing now. What's the matter, David? What's wrong with you? Please tell me ... I know you want to. What's holding you back? We were very close to each other at one time. You can tell me anything. Perhaps I can help in some way."

A few minutes of silence ensued.

"Okay, I will tell you," he said eventually and quite lucidly, as if he'd made a supreme effort to steady his emotions and steel his resolve. "But I'm afraid you can't help me. No one on this planet can help me now."

I found the change in David's behaviour almost as disquieting, if not upsetting, as his previous weepy state.

"I love my wife dearly," he continued. "More than I can say. I would die for Susan ... that is, if I had the courage."

I shook my head disapprovingly and David went on regardless.

"Before ... before her accident, since we were married of course, Susan and I had enjoyed a full life together ... enjoying each other, you know what I mean, as husband and wife ..."

I nodded, my comprehension slightly preceding his words.

"It's been more than seven years ... Susan's paralysis ... s-she's unable ..."

I stopped him at that point with a firmly raised hand. Naturally, I knew what he was achingly striving to say. He didn't need to spell out the details for me.

"Please, David," I said softly. "You don't have to go on. I know what you're trying to tell me. I really do. I couldn't even imagine what you've been going through ... and, needless to state, the emotional turmoil that must've afflicted your wife and the mother of your children."

En route to the pub David had informed me that they'd had two children, a boy and a girl, both now married with children of their own, though one lived in New York and the other in Jerusalem.

"I understand, David," I said desolately after taking another sip of whisky. "And I can see clearly now why you've been behaving so erratically, so uncharacteristically. Meeting me again has resurrected all your memories of a happier time when Susan was ... I think I'm starting to regret that we've crossed paths today. I'm so sorry David ... our reunion has only caused you grief."

He gave me a strangely quizzical look.

"No, no ... you've got it all wrong," he said with some sense of urgency whilst shaking his head. "You can't possibly comprehend because you don't know anything. It's not about Susan ... as such. This is about me ... what I've done."

Puzzlement hit me in the face but I recovered quickly.

"And what precisely have you done, David?" I asked with emphasis.

"Susan's divorced sister comes to care for her one day a week, Wednesday, actually ..."

"Susan's sister?" I said in a tone possibly laden with suspicion.

David chuckled in a reasonably normal way.

"Don't be stupid," he responded laconically, reading precisely my now regretfully inventive and salacious thoughts.

"Allison's weekly home visits, so to speak, give me some respite and a chance to do things for myself, personal shopping, getting my hair cut and going to some classical recitals given by advanced music students at the colleges here …"

I nodded an acknowledgement. I'd been to one or two of the free concerts myself.

"I'd go to the well-attended, half-hour to forty-five minute performances fairly regularly. You generally see the same people in the audience, week after week. One time, some months back, I spotted a new face. It belonged to an attractive, slender and dark-haired woman I estimated to be in her early fifties. At a number of the following weeks' music venues I noticed her again. In fact her appearance was quite striking. On a few occasions, and in an oblique kind of way, I'd seen her glancing in my direction. From time to time, we nodded smilingly at each other. I supposed this was in recognition of the apparent coincidence that we'd selected the same one of several possible offerings each week; and thus, that we possibly shared a similar taste in classical music. One Wednesday, and for the first time, we found ourselves sitting next to each other. I don't know why … yes, I think I do … but at the end of the Mozart piano recital I mentioned to this woman, to whom I'd never spoken previously, that I was heading off for a coffee. I hesitated for just a moment but then I asked whether she would like to join me. Surprisingly, the lady agreed at once; and we walked to a nearby café, which I knew was favourable for quiet conversation."

I was listening to David quite intently, yet I wasn't entirely sure that I was properly grasping the import of his story. Maybe I just didn't want to grasp it.

"Katie told me that she was a part-time history teacher at a local secondary school … and that she was a widow," David related matter-of-factly. "We enjoyed an interesting chat over our hot drinks; then, after half-an-hour, we said our goodbyes and went our separate ways. I purchased a few personal items in the town and walked home feeling quite light-headed.

I smiled. "Is that it, David? I thought …"

He ignored my interruption.

"That night I lay awake beside my sleeping wife in the bedroom we'd constructed downstairs. I tried hard, really I did, but I just couldn't prevent myself from thinking about Katie. The following Wednesday, after attending the same choice of recital quite by chance, Katie and I had coffee together again … and again, though this time by mutual arrangement, the following week. Of course I'd told my new acquaintance about Susan, and she was very sympathetic. Her husband, apparently a heavy smoker for most of his relatively short life, had died from lung cancer several years back. I was similarly compassionate about her loss; although for some reason or reasons she hinted at but didn't elaborate on, I suspected the marriage hadn't been a particularly happy and fulfilling one for her. We knew there wouldn't be any concerts during the coming few weeks. It was the end of the university term. Katie asked whether I would like to come to her flat for lunch the following Wednesday. I thanked her for the invitation but told her that I couldn't make it. She gave me her mobile number and said I should call or text her if I changed my mind…"

David paused for a few moments. I could almost visualise his brain working some frenetic overtime. Spookily, it was becoming difficult for me to look at him directly. I was fearful, even terrified, of what he might go on to tell me. But in those fleeting seconds of silence I was unable to convince myself that David had changed his mind.

"During the next few days," he continued, "I told myself

over and over again that it would be wrong to have Katie make me lunch in her apartment. So I didn't change my mind."

I clasped my hands together with satisfaction, possibly relief, and nodded slowly. David seemed to note my notionally confirmatory movements.

"Sorry, no … I didn't change my mind about Katie making me a meal at her home. And just to be really clear on the matter, it was nothing to do with Kashrut if that's what you were thinking …"

"No, it wasn't," I interjected.

"But I did phone Katie …" he went on, "… to ask whether she would like to have lunch at a restaurant in a pretty village I knew a few miles outside town. She agreed instantly."

I'm certain David noticed the significant change in my expression. And I thought some water was collecting in the corners of my old chum's eyes.

"I was completely mixed up," he said rubbing his forehead. "Unless you'd experienced what I've been going through emotionally over recent years, I really can't expect you to understand. I'm still a fit and healthy man with normal feelings and needs … needs that, regrettably, couldn't be met. Only the Almighty knows how I tortured myself in the days leading up to seeing Katie again. And I discovered something else. Maybe it was something inside me that had been hidden away there, a separate entity … an invisible man lurking within my own body, loitering somewhere between my heart and my inner self. And that something, whatever it was, possessed the treacherous capacity to be disloyal … to betray faith, soul and everything held dear. Although the ache I felt was almost impossible to bear, I couldn't stop or even control what amounted to the equivalent of riding a runaway train. The evening before my lunch appointment with Katie, I called her and asked whether I could reinstate the earlier invitation to eat at her flat. Again, she agreed at once and sounded very pleased, if not delighted. After our lunch the next day, w-we ... w-we made love on her bed ..."

Tearfully, David now halted his confession. He grabbed a tissue from his coat pocket and dabbed his chin, cheeks and eyes. His glassy pupils focused vaguely on my face. Then he waited ... waited maybe for some kind of sign from me, some comment, some reflection on his actions, the disloyalty to his wife, to his faith, to his God. He waited ... waited for a response to his betrayal, to his unfaithfulness. And he waited ... waited perhaps for my castigation or exculpation. So then I left him waiting ... waiting for the words that he would never hear, at least not from me, on this dark matter.

The Glove

FOR THE remainder of that early spring but cold and moisture-laden day, as I walked the drab and depressing residential streets of the one-time ghetto, I couldn't stop myself thinking about a child's black woollen glove.

I really needed to focus my attention on the old Jewish quarter of this Polish industrial city. That's why I'd flown hundreds of miles, with an overnight stop in Warsaw and a two-hour rail journey through murky and uninspiring countryside, to be in this grim place. Like a flickering century-old silent movie, a strangely pulsating image of the glove lying on the snow-covered ground of the ancient Jewish cemetery played across my mind's eye. My paternal great-grandparents had departed the gritty and increasingly menacing town (menacing for Jews that is) for the alien sanctuary of England in the late 1870s. A mere sixty years before the victorious invading Nazis occupied the country and began the wholesale confinement, persecution and eventual elimination of its Jewish population.

So it seemed to me that my East European ancestors had not only been courageous refugees but also uncannily prescient ones.

But how, I'd wondered, could an unexceptional, discarded or mislaid little glove have overpowered my thought processes? Consequential upon this preoccupation I was tramping, almost but not fully unaware of my surroundings, around the dark, damp-dripping inner courtyards of decaying tenement buildings, meandering through chaotic huddles of market stalls selling basic foodstuffs, cheap plastic goods and jumbled second-hand clothes and trudging past regimented, concrete grey ranks of post-war Stalinist housing blocks. Before my visit I'd read that between 1939 and 1945, when the Soviet army had "liberated" the city, a vast majority of the ghetto's quarter of a million Jews, who'd barely survived death by disease, maltreatment or starvation, had perished in the gas chambers of Chelmno and Auschwitz-Birkenau. But I couldn't understand why an insignificant accessory item of child's clothing could so dramatically overwhelm my thoughts and emotions regarding the tragic enormity that had devastated this Polish town only six decades ago.

That morning on entering the burial ground, which is located in a northern enclave of what had been the ghetto area, I'd not espied any glove. Numerous scattered little mounds of ice, glistening despite a leaden sky, had seized my initial attention. The thawing legacy of a fairly recent snowfall covered narrow gaps and filled shallow hollows between the seemingly endless rows of ageing memorial stones. Nonetheless, the cemetery took on the appearance of a neat and carefully tended park. Beside its lofty, iron-grilled entrance gates I'd read a prominently displayed notice referring to a charitable foundation whose generous funding supported necessary maintenance work.

Walking unhurriedly along the broad, concreted but slightly undulating main aisle I was intrigued by the often-stark contrast in the size and style of the headstones. Classically designed, opulently marbled and dynastic mausoleums of the city's nineteenth century Jewish manufacturers and entrepreneurs dominated the expansive, tree-shaded grounds. These huge and lavish commemorative structures dwarfed the far more modestly endowed memorials of humbler brethren. But such comparisons palled considerably when an umbrageous branch path I was exploring opened onto an unexpected, sky-dominated field of ice-encrusted grassland that was filled with a myriad of minimally-marked graves. These sad and densely grouped burial plots, as a nearby sign indicated, were the final resting places of many thousands of Jews, men, women and children, who'd perished in the wartime ghetto.

I stood for some time rock still and chillingly numbed, even with my coat collar pulled up, staring across the flat, far-reaching expanse of small metal tomb-markers that had been screwed to thin metre-high steel tubes. I struggled to imagine the horrific ghetto existence of those Jews whose Earthly remains now lay buried, many anonymously, in this desperately forlorn parcel of Polish land. It was as I approached the cemetery gates at the end of my self-guided tour that my eyes were attracted to a small black object resting on the off-white ground. I crouched low and, on closer inspection, identified the soggy-looking article as a woollen glove. But I didn't touch it. Whilst steadying myself on the uneven and slippery surface, I guessed the item had belonged to a child of about eight or nine years of age. Standing upright again, I peered instinctively around the immediate vicinity but couldn't see another living soul.

I glanced down at the solitary little hand warmer. Perhaps predictably, the glove had ensnared my innate curiosity. Questions tumbled helter-skelter into my head like collie-harried sheep into a holding pen. Who was the glove's owner? And had it been dropped by accident? Had it been left at this spot for a particular reason? And why would a child have been brought to a cemetery? As a traditional Orthodox Jew I'd long held to the view that youngsters shouldn't be taken to visit such a morbid place, even though Judaism regards it rather mystically as a beth chayim or house of life. There seems time enough when, later in life, a journey to the burial ground will become a melancholy but inevitable necessity for a son or a daughter. Still focusing intently on the glove, I supposed that a child of either gender could've worn it; though I retained a strong impression that it had cosily enfolded the left hand of a little girl.

Late that night I met a woman, actually two women, in a smoky basement jazz club near the Stary Rynek, the old town's fairytale-picturesque main square, with its charmingly restored churches, town hall and medieval merchant houses. Prior to going out in a change to dry, warm but coolly casual clothes topped with an overcoat, first for some dinner, I'd relaxed in my hotel room from the day's lengthy and exhaustive trek. After phoning my wife and reporting my activities of the last few hours, I'd stretched out on the Queen-sized bed and gazed up at the tassel-fringed, lilac shade suspended from an elaborate ceiling rose. Lilac … rose? The semantically floral association oddly conjured up a vivid but out of context picture in my head.

The image was a vignette portraying one of several similarly occupied, and manifestly impoverished, old women I'd observed standing alone at street corners in the drearily oppressive old ghetto district. At the shawl-wrapped woman's feet stood a plastic bucket containing a pathetically few bunches of flowers that she was offering for sale to sallow-featured and equally poorly clothed passers-by. At first, as dull red, passenger-packed trams trundled past, I'd speculated about why any of the pedestrians moving along the wet pavement would spend, as they did, a preciously spare zloty or two on such impractical stems rather than buying extra provisions. It soon struck me that they needed, even yearned maybe, to see a splash of colour, however small, on their tables, mantle-pieces or window sills so as to brighten, at least transiently, their bleak and miserable surrounds. I shifted the plump pillow under my neck, closed my eyes and, instantly, the small black glove made a brief appearance in my mind. But it melted away in a sort of cerebral thaw when I raised my eyelids.

I was more than reasonably content with my spacious, high-vaulted accommodation. The hotel had been designed and furnished in the belle époque tradition with pillared and chandeliered public areas, impressively large and gilt-framed paintings and a magnificently galleried restaurant where I took a first-rate buffet breakfast. Sadly, the harsh or neglectful years of war and occupation, and the socialist realism of a so-called liberating communist regime, had eroded much of the hotel's former glory. The building itself, façade grimed over decades by the city's polluting factories and chimneys, fronted an ironically café-lively and architecturally eclectic thoroughfare, which I could conveniently survey by leaning over my fourth floor Juliet balcony.

Being a dedicated and veteran aficionado of Scotch whisky, especially the mellow honey-coloured Highland malts, it had taken me several trips to Der Heim to acquire what is now an active admiration for the Polish nation's ubiquitous alcoholic beverage. Vodka's sharp and clean-cut yet reassuring bite and manageably intoxicating effect, notably during the hazy early morning hours in an atmospheric nightclub, appeal to my culturally repressed bohemianism. I always purchase a bottle of my favourite distillation, for the hotel room, from a local liquor store soon after arriving in a Polish town. The variety of vodkas on offer is astonishing, as are the relatively low prices for a Western European visitor. A bottle of Zubrowka, infused with a single distinctive blade of bison grass for flavour, is my usual choice from the hundreds of brands available.

It's said that there are two well-defined groups of Poles: those who enjoy a drink and those with abdominal ulcers. Over time I've acquired the knack in avoiding the medics. A shot-glass of vodka demolished in one foul swoop just a couple of hours before a drinking session will do the trick nicely. Before leaving the hotel that evening I'd leaned against the French doors to a virtually illusory balcony with the requisite preparatory glass of Zubrowka gripped in my hand. I stared down at umbrella-wielding workers hurrying home through the drizzle. Once again, and unbidden, my brain overlaid the busy street scene with the depiction of a child's glove. Until the two images, street and glove, actual and unreal, segued into an incomprehensible singularity. I turned back into the room.

Admittedly, I'm not the planet's greatest jazz fan; though I generally enjoyed the Trad Jazz genre during my university days in the mid-1960s. But the point is this, I think. Invariably you'll find a comforting range of age groups in most authentic and respectable jazz venues; and certainly that's the case in Poland. I reckon this isn't so surprising. People of my age were born closer to the twentieth century's golden era of the Blues. In any event I enjoy the relaxed, vodka-savouring ambience of the Polish clubs, where men and women sway rhythmically in harmony with the musicians' soulful offerings.

But let's get something straight. I don't feel my age. And, with all due humility, I don't look it. But a youthful existentialism is not entirely a matter of physical appearance. To my mind, it's also a question of mental attitude. There are so many of my contemporaries who lock themselves into a psychological straitjacket, stereotypically insistent on looking, acting and doing as they believe a person of their age ought to look, act and do, regardless of personal inclination. They join third age clubs, watch too much daytime television and don't go out at night if they can help it, will only venture abroad in secure groups or on cruise liners, don't like walking too far and generally dress like bubbehs and zayders.

It was beyond midnight. I'd been in the underground jazz club for almost an hour. Two attractive brunettes wearing svelte, short black dresses and probably in their forties were perched on stools across from me at the horseshoe-shaped and mirror-backed bar. I'd taken a short break from the heady intimate buzz of the cavernous cellar room, where a steamy jazz quartet was now playing up-tempo.

Uninvited as usual, the little black glove had made yet

another appearance on my retinas, superimposing itself on the group of stage-lit musicians like an overprinted postal stamp. So I escaped to the bar. One of the amiable, bearded bartenders slickly refilled the shot glass I'd placed back on the dark wood counter. I handed him a five zloty note, amounting to a little over one pound sterling, and told him to keep the change. Both women were Polish, self-evidently so by language and looks. Even in London restaurants I can nowadays distinguish a Polish waitress at one hundred paces … well before she takes my order.

Needless to say, but I was likely to be the only Englishman in the club that night. Surprisingly however, and as I soon discovered, I wasn't the only Jew. The two women, too dissimilar to be other than friends I guessed, appeared to be stealing occasional peeks in my direction as they chatted animatedly with each other. I tried not to reveal that I'd noticed their studious glances. Probably, I thought, they'd overheard me order the vodka shots in my falteringly accented and severely limited use of their native tongue. Back in London, incongruous foreigners intrigued me too. I nodded to one of the friendly barmen for another refill; and, in short order, a further slug of the sharp-edged, translucent liquid was sliding comfortably down my welcoming gullet. A fourth shot followed then a fifth. Perhaps I was starting to feel self-conscious at the attention I seemed to be receiving from the other side of the shiny, curving bar-top. I hoped that the alcohol intake would serve to curb my flamboyant imagination's preliminary stirrings. Or at least keep at bay the recurring and now faintly troubling image of the little black glove. But no, the vodka didn't achieve either of these effects. Instead, my alcoholic consumption accomplished something else entirely: the normal thing, in fact. It began to loosen up my fragile inhibitions and, in consequence, my tongue. I leaned across the bar.

"Does anyone speak English?" I enquired to the world-at-large, though my question was aimed truly at the two women sitting directly opposite me. The brunette on the right, perhaps the older and more elegantly attractive of the two, put down the cocktail glass she'd been toying with. She inclined the visible upper half of her body towards me.

"Of course!" she replied crisply in perfect English but with an appealing Polish intonation. "Are you drunk?"

The slight shock of the woman's curtly presented query promptly and effectively brought me to whatever of my senses remained intact.

"No, I'm not drunk," I grinned whilst recovering sangfroid and posture. "Just in need of some understandable conversation, I suppose. My Polish is pretty feeble."

My verbal assailant laughed, pushing away some of her shoulder-length tresses from a smooth-skinned, oval face and classically beautiful features. Her cute-looking but clearly rather shorter and fuller-figured companion, whose pale round face held lingering traces of Slavic ancestry, chuckled at my unfunny response. But it occurred to me that she was merely mimicking her friend rather than comprehending our exchange. So I assumed that her command of the English language was non-existent or, at most, not particularly good. What my interrogator asked me next took me even more unexpectedly.

"Could you join us over here?" she invited. "I want to show you something."

I really wanted to decline the invitation. An image of my wife entered my head. At least, I considered, it made a pleasant change from the glove; though I felt somehow that my levity was misplaced. Once again, my inborn inquisitiveness stepped into the driving seat.

"Okay," I found myself reacting, grabbing the glass holding a sixth vodka shot. I slid off my stool, walked round the bar as bidden and sat myself on the empty perch next to the oval-faced woman. As she greeted me with a smile I could now see clearly that her eyes were of the deepest jade green. It may've been the over-application of jet-black mascara and the dark eye shadow that highlighted them so acutely. I was reminded immediately of Elizabeth Taylor portraying the Egyptian Queen Cleopatra on screen. It's a marvellous mystery how the mind works in the early morning hours.

"You have lovely eyes," I said.

"Thank you," she replied, adopting a coy expression. "But it's probably the vodka."

I must've displayed my confused face.

"I didn't know that drinking vodka could beautify the eyes," I mused aloud.

"No, no!" she cried. "You misunderstand me. What I meant was that your compliment is likely to be the alcohol talking."

I shook my head; and I realised, in an instant, that it may've been my vodka intake that had attracted her and her friend's initial attention.

"Absolutely not," I assured the woman pouting enchantingly at me.

"Okay, perhaps I believe you," she said. "Now let me show you something … by the way, my name's Anna and my friend's name is Marla."

I introduced myself and Marla leaned sideways, resting an

elbow on the edge of the bar so as to see me unhindered by Anna's albeit willowy frame perched between us. From that position she threw me a syrupy smile that stretched across her prominent cheekbones, but she remained silent. Her friend rummaged in a black leather handbag resting on her lap and withdrew a black smart phone. She stabbed nimbly at the tiny keypad on the sophisticated mobile then scrolled through copious folders of digital photos. Stopping at one picture, she tilted the screen at me. It showed the profile of an eye-catching blonde.

"Do you know who this is?" she asked me, with the inevitable tonal edge of an east European speaking in English.

Somewhat bemused I studied the image carefully, absorbing a face that looked familiar. Maybe, I mulled, it's a well-known film star whose name eluded me. Then the smooth feminine features in the photo mutated astonishingly into the form of a child's glove. I blinked rapidly a few times and the glove dissolved, giving way to the head and shoulders portrait of the fair-haired woman. In the bar mirror I caught Anna's reflection staring expectantly at me.

"Well?" she pressed.

I cogitated for a further brief time, becoming increasingly puzzled. But then it came to me, in a flash: "Huh … I think it's you," I blurted finally.

"You're quite right," Anna said with a flicker of satisfaction in her eyes.

I sighed, I thought with relief but I wasn't sure. Nothing seemed real.

"But you're a brunette," I remarked unnecessarily, admiring Anna's cascading and shiny black hair.

"How observant!" she declared, mocking me playfully whilst glancing at her mobile's glowing screen. "But do you think I look sluttish as a blonde?"

I was surprised by Anna's bewitching candour.

"W-Why do you ask?" I questioned, struggling to collect myself.

Her eyes anchored onto mine, as if she desired to launch herself into them and dive deep down into my very soul.

"There are certain men … well, it's just that I wasn't taken very seriously as a blonde," she informed me in a self-pitying kind of way, at the same time studying her long-fingered, exquisitely manicured hands. I gazed at them, too, noticing that she wasn't wearing any rings.

When Anna looked up again I could see that her words had provoked an emotional, if not vulnerable outcome. But why was she involving me in all this? She half-turned to Marla who tenderly placed an arm across her friend's shoulders and whispered something into her ear. I couldn't tell whether Anna was a natural blonde or brunette but didn't dare seek confirmation either way. I wasn't at all sure of the situation I'd landed myself in; though I didn't sense a personal will strong enough to back away from it. Of course I appreciate that, sometimes, an individual feels a compelling need to reveal certain innermost almost secret thoughts and feelings to a total stranger. It's a truism that familiarity breeds contempt. An outsider is more likely to be a sympathetic and non-judgemental listener. But there's always a calculated risk in this behaviour.

I gulped down my sixth vodka and ordered another. With their agreement I called for two more cocktails for my newfound friends. Anna was staring at me, waiting patiently for some sort of reaction to the comment she'd made about herself. And, thanks to the vodka, I felt a distinct obligation to provide one.

"I don't know why you weren't taken seriously as a blonde," I said. "Whether or not a person is taken seriously by others should depend purely on his or her personality or character, not on the colour of their hair. Or any other extraneous factor, for that matter. If I may be so bold, you strike me as being a highly intelligent woman. But my opinion has nothing to do with the tint of your impressive locks. Why should it be discriminatory in that rather absurd way?"

My intentionally tactful but certainly authentic response, which I'd hoped wouldn't be taken as in any manner patronising, seemed to elicit a positive facial reaction from Anna. The barman delivered well-shaken liquid concoctions to the two ladies, and poured a vodka refill for me in a fresh shot glass. I wasn't really totting up my consumption now. Anna appeared appreciably calmer; but her flashing green eyes glinted. She swivelled on her barstool and exchanged a few words with Marla who'd been grinning uncomprehendingly at me during my conversation with her friend.

"Dziękuję," Marla said, aiming the Polish word for "thank you" directly at me.

"My friend has very little English," Anna added quite superfluously. "But she's very glad that you understand, and she thanks you for that."

I wasn't entirely sure what it was that I was supposed to have understood, so I merely gestured an acknowledgement to Marla for her gratitude. Anna lightly touched my forearm.

"Thanks from me also," she murmured.

A short while later Anna disclosed that she was a divorcee. And that Marla was divorced, too. "Broken dreams," I thought I heard Anna mutter with a wispy sigh. Then she revealed that her father was Roman Catholic and that her late mother was Jewish.

"So you are Jewish under Halachah," I noted, not yet able to construe my fellow drinker's motivation for giving me this information

Her face took on a blank expression.

"What?" she said.

"The fact that your mother was Jewish means that you are too, under Jewish law," I explained. Anna rolled her expressive eyes upwards.

"I know that!" she stated with a firm emphasis that rocked me a little. "But how do you know this?"

I informed her that I was Jewish too, and Anna looked amazed.

"I would never have guessed," she said, telling me about the luxuriantly bearded men in big black hats, black curlicue side locks and long black coats that she'd frequently observed walking to the city's only surviving synagogue on a Saturday morning. I opened my mouth to speak but she stopped me, correctly anticipating that I was on the point of elucidating the distinction between an ultra-Orthodox and a traditional Jew. But I explained the difference anyway.

"I know all about such things," she chided me mildly, following up her implied reprimand with a winsome smile. "I've read a lot about Judaism."

Voluntarily, she went on to give me the history of her

confused and complex upbringing. I was starting to feel a genuine pity for Anna who, despite the self-assured persona she projected, was coming across more like a little lost soul. Marla sipped her drink uncomplainingly, maybe feeling lonesome and sidelined because of her inability to participate in the dialogue. As she listened, wrapt in her own private musings, to the jazz group's mournful sounds filtering into the bar area from the performance space, Anna and I talked on. The refreshing openness of our conversation prompted me to mention the little girl's glove that I'd seen in the sprawling Jewish cemetery, and which I couldn't banish from my mind. Interestingly, Anna wondered whether the burial ground's caretaker had a young granddaughter; but she didn't think I was being obsessive, just overly curious. She confided her own fixation for poignant things, like the poor old women selling flowers in the one-time ghetto quarter. As she spoke of this, tears came to her stunning eyes and a chill abseiled down my spine.

At one juncture, Anna abruptly interrupted the flow of our exchange.

"I know you're married," she said. "I've seen your gold wedding ring. But where's your wife?"

At once I felt ill at ease, even guilty at some level, realising suddenly that I'd been sitting very close to the young woman for some fifteen minutes or more. I stumbled over my response.

"U-Unfortunately, my wife couldn't make this trip … s-she was needed at her office."

"I see. So she trusts you then … when you're away from home?"

I hesitated, I don't know why, but it was only for an instant.

Perhaps I was thinking about Anna's relationship breakdown, though she hadn't divulged any details.

"Naturally," I answered, smiling but trying hard to decipher the enigmatic look in the woman's eyes.

She laughed and, I could swear flirtatiously, brushed her fingers against my arm. Then she turned away from me and, taking an askance peep in the bar mirror, I noted that her friend was tugging at Anna's sleeve. Marla said something in a low voice; even though she knew well enough that I wouldn't be able to translate what had been said. Whatever had been whispered so intently, Marla's forceful expression and sideways peek in my direction suggested that her words had possibly concerned me. Anna faced me again.

"I need to go outside with Marla for a while. Will you be here when I get back?"

I was nonplussed but managed to get out a "Y-Yes, of course".

Without more, the two women disappeared into the crowded gloom. I ordered another shot, swung it nimbly down my throat and imagined that I saw a child's black glove hovering above the bar. Was I hallucinating now? I blinked wildly to rid myself of the vision and the article evaporated, to be replaced by Anna's now mind-monopolising question: "Will you be here when I get back?" My fertile imagination was launching itself into warp-drive, accelerating in no time to compute impetus, meaning and potential. I fought psychologically to shake off some alien nonsense seeking to invade my conscience. Involuntarily, I revolved my wedding ring with thumb and forefinger then called for another refill.

Waiting for the women to return I experienced a cloying

headiness. Some minutes later, through the enveloping haze, I glimpsed Anna and Marla on the other side of the bar. They were forging a purposeful path through the buzzing throng towards the smoky fug of the jazz room, from which now floated the sad, sentimental notes of a solo saxophone. Amazingly, the women utterly ignored me, not even casting the briefest of glances in my direction. As I watched them I detected some dark smudging around Anna's eyes. It looked to me like she'd been crying. I wondered what had happened between the two friends out of my sight and hearing. It was only later that I may've come to some understanding.

In the street outside the club, shocked into breathlessness for a moment or so by the freezing night air, I fell into one of the taxi rank's waiting cabs. After a few minutes I was collecting my key from the hotel's reception desk. Once in the room, I collapsed onto the bed without undressing. My last two mind-images, before quickly losing consciousness, were of Anna's mascara-smeared cheeks and a child's black glove. Some hours later, in the final seconds before I awoke lathered in sweat, I experienced a terrifying nightmare. Black-helmeted SS troops were machine-gunning a huddled group of shrieking Jewish women and children in the cobbled courtyard of a rain-drenched ghetto tenement. A frothing red tide swept out from the shadowy arched entrance of the death-darkened building and gurgled down gutter drains into rat-infested sewers.

After showering, shaving and dressing, practically without opening my eyes, I was startled by an intensely bright light. More or less at once, I realised it was the sun streaking in through the French windows. Of course, I hadn't drawn the curtains. I opened the glass doors to my sliver of balcony and looked down into the street. There were plenty of signs that it would be a fine day. Restaurant proprietors were putting out tables and chairs on the broad sidewalks: an infallible signal that the weather forecast was promising. I couldn't confront the buffet breakfast display so I just downed a large, strong black coffee in the café opposite my hotel. As I savoured the hot caffeine a now familiar picture of the glove usurped my psyche again. Immediately, I knew what I needed to do. But before I resolved to do it, I thought I saw Anna walking alone on the other side of the roadway. I wanted to attract the attention of this woman with the long black hair, but I didn't. I was still half-asleep, my identification probably mistaken.

In the mildly warming sunshine I tramped uphill on the stony, tree-lined road until I reached the entrance gates of the Jewish cemetery. The shoulder bag dragged on my back but carrying it was a habit now. My wristwatch told me it was nearly midday. I didn't feel overdressed in my padded rainproof anorak. Poland is very much like England in the unpredictability of its climate, especially during the early days of springtime. So it's always prudent to be prepared for a rapid change in the sky's beneficence when away from any useful shelter.

Once through the gates I searched around. I soon located the glove; it was still lying on the thawing, slushy path where I'd found it the previous day. "Yes!" I exclaimed loudly, a bit like Pythagoras' "Eureka!" exclamation after he'd discovered his theory of displacement while in the bath. I picked up the icy-stiff object, recoiling a little at its cold, woolly dampness on my bare hand. I could hardly believe that this simple winter accessory could've achieved such iconic status in my mind over the preceding twenty-four hours. But I recalled Anna's compelling philosophy. It's easy to become emotionally preoccupied, even fixated, on the poignant. As I contemplated the pathetic little glove resting in my palm, I was startled by rustling sounds close behind me and then a child's voice.

"That's mine," the disembodied voice said quietly but firmly. "That glove belongs to me."

I turned and looked down on a small girl I estimated to be about eight years old. Her unkempt fair hair straggled about a thin pallid face. She was staring at the glove and I noticed that her eyes were a very light blue, though sorrowfully lacking in sparkle. She wore a buttoned-up dark topcoat, the precise colour of which was impossible for me to determine. There appeared to be some worn and dirty areas on the front of the ankle-length and nondescript garment. The unsightly marring could've amounted to wet grass-stained patches, suggesting that the girl may've fallen over very recently.

"Are you all right?" I asked gently, not wishing to frighten the child.

"Yes, I am," she replied remarkably confidently, adding politely: "But could I have my glove back, please?"

She removed a small black object from her coat pocket and held it up as evidence of her entitlement to the hand-wear in my possession. It looked like a matching black glove. I bent down and handed over the other half of the pair.

"Thank you, sir," she said deferentially, bowing her head slightly.

I was surprised that this little girl was communicating with me in English, and with such an articulate delivery. I presumed she'd overheard my monosyllabic declaration on rediscovering her glove. Although that didn't explain how well she spoke my national language. Naturally, I assumed she was Polish. So I speculated rapidly about how and where she'd learned to understand and speak my native tongue so fluently. Even at her young age perhaps she was studying it at junior school. After all, democratic Poland is now a member of the European Union. But I also had in mind that nation's long, strong and continuing relationship with my Polish ancestors' adopted country.

"Where did you learn to speak such good English?" I enquired.

The girl ignored my question, stuffing one glove into each of the side pockets of her coat. I tried again, this time taking a more tangential approach.

"What's your name?" I asked.

The girl turned away and began walking along the main path deeper into the cemetery. I seriously considered calling it a day and leaving. But I was curious if not intrigued to find out more about the little girl and why she was wandering around this sad place. So I followed her. With nobody else about, so far as I could see, I didn't want to intimidate her in any way. The modern sensitivity to any adult/child situation, certainly in the context of strangers, didn't escape me. Doubtless hearing my footfalls on the path's crispy ice patches, the girl glanced over her shoulder at me and stopped in her tracks about ten metres away.

"My name's Anna," she called out. "What's yours?"

Anna. Anna. Anna! Unbelieving, I kept repeating the name to myself. I was completely stunned by the incredible coincidence, my mouth tasting as arid and granular as rough sandpaper. I told the girl my name as I came alongside her.

"Don't be afraid, Anna," I said with as reassuring a tone as I could muster. "But what are you doing here? Is anyone with you?"

"There's no one with me. And I'm not afraid of you, if that's what you mean. You've got a kind face. Anyway, I'm not frightened of anything. I just like walking under the trees. It's very peaceful and quite safe for me ... really. I'm here every day."

Anna began walking again and I maintained my step in time with her diminutive paces.

"Where do you live, Anna?" I ventured.

The girl waved her arm in an arcing motion.

"Over there," she said. "Not far from the wall of the cemetery. Now I've found my glove I'm going home."

"Do you mind if I walk along with you for a while, Anna?"

She shook her head and her dishevelled hair flew around her pale little face.

"No, I don't mind. I know you're not going to hurt me."

"Of course I'm not going to hurt you."

The fact that I was accompanying such a young girl in so deserted and isolated a spot was scaring me even if wasn't disturbing her in any way. I just hoped and prayed that anyone coming along the path, who might know Anna, wouldn't get the wrong impression about my motives. But there was something going on inside my head that impelled me to be with the child. I was content to be led onto a track between some monumental nineteenth century tombs. Everywhere was so quiet and still, not even the faintest sounds of birdsong could be heard. I remembered from perusing a plan of the grounds that a side entrance had been clearly marked. We seemed to be heading in its direction. Ambling along I noticed that the flat heels of Anna's shoes were well worn down and that the uppers were heavily scuffed. There was barely any of the original hue of the footwear remaining visible. I imagined that her family were quite hard-up and possibly resided in one of those dilapidated tenements or grimly decaying, Soviet-style housing estates I'd wandered around the day before.

"You mentioned that it's nice and peaceful in the cemetery. It is. But is that the only reason you like being here, Anna? It's not the kind of place you generally find children playing in or roaming through."

There was a brief interlude before she replied.

"No, it isn't the only reason. There's another one."

I prompted her lightly.

"Yes?" I said.

Anna stopped and gazed up at me, scanning my features as if trying to assess my likely reaction.

"I like being here because I'm Jewish."

I must've looked more than a touch taken aback by the statement.

"You don't look Jewish," I commented. "I'm Jewish too, Anna. But you might've suspected that from my being here."

In her turn, Anna appeared amazed.

"No, I didn't think about that. You don't look Jewish. But many people come here who aren't of our religion."

I nodded slowly several times, impressed with the girl's admirable intelligence.

"Yes, I suppose you're right, Anna."

We moved on again. The route ahead of us was narrowing, the foliage of flanking trees intertwining above us like a leafy roof allowing only fine shafts of sunlight to penetrate. The memorial stones were smaller here, tightly crowded together and copious. It was really cold in the shade. I just about recollected shivering in the sub-zero temperature on staggering from the jazz club earlier that morning. The memory alone sent an icy shiver through my bones. I flinched, pulled up the collar of my anorak and noticed that Anna had slipped the black gloves on her tiny hands.

"Nearly there," she said, staring straight in front of her.

I assumed she meant that we weren't far from the side gate of the cemetery; and therefore quite close to where she lived. But she halted, turning to look up at me.

"Are you proud to be Jewish?" she asked, her dull eyes locking onto mine. "I am."

It was the unexpectedness of the question that nearly threw me off balance. Anna's little upturned face looked so pained and hopeless that I almost felt like crying.

"Y-Yes, I am also very proud to be Jewish, Anna."

I was reluctant to probe her thoughts but I gave way to my curiosity.

"Tell me, Anna. Why does your pride in being Jewish make you look so sad?"

She lowered her head as if in deep meditation. But I took her gesture as a deliberate evasion of my question, maybe quite rightly. She'd swiftly struck me as being intellectually mature, amazingly so for one of such tender years. It was none of my business anyway. There was no good reason for her to respond; but, in the end, she did.

"It's because I can no longer practice my Jewish faith," she murmured; and I glimpsed a shadow of anguish steal across her wan cheeks.

We progressed along the dark, narrow and gravelled track as I struggled to gather my thoughts. I wondered whether the girl came perhaps from a mixed-faith family. I recalled my conversation with her namesake at the jazz club. The older Anna's father hadn't been Jewish. Maybe the little girl's father wasn't Jewish. But, then again, Anna the child had used the words *no longer*, implying that she'd enjoyed at least some upbringing in the Jewish religion. Possibly her mother had been widowed or divorced and had then remarried. Her natural father may've been Jewish but her new Dad isn't. And it's the stepfather that isn't permitting melancholy little Anna to follow her faith and heritage. I chortled inwardly. It seemed like I'd worked it all out.

"Anna," I said, "why can't you practice your Jewish faith any more?"

I felt she was on the point of answering my question when we were flooded with a towering wave of bright warm sunshine. We'd emerged from the gloomy canopy of arboreal greenery and now stood surveying an extensive swathe of rough, ice-flecked grassland. Here were spread out thousands of simply marked graves which, as I recalled from my earlier visit, comprised the final resting places of Jews who'd died in the wartime ghetto. And on the far side of the multitude of burial plots ran the cemetery's perimeter brick wall. I could now make out a wrought iron gate halfway along its dismal length. And I could see, beyond the wall, a phalanx of sombre concrete buildings, the sun's rays rebounding off their miniscule windows.

"We're close to where I live now," Anna remarked to the air as I gazed across the vast sunlit area of open ground laid out before us.

"Yes," I said. "You mentioned it's not far from that wall."

I wanted to remind Anna about replying to my last query but I felt unusually inhibited, even though I was conversing with a child. It seemed pathetic that one so young, who remarkably understood enough to want to be a good Jew, couldn't be one for whatever reason. Out of her earshot, I mumbled to myself, "I'm so sorry, Anna". We started off again, Anna ahead of me, edging cautiously down a slithery grass embankment to negotiate our way between the modest metal grave markers spread across the flat and pathless land. We were just twenty metres or so from the gate when I slipped and flew headlong to the ground. My shoulder bag swung round my body and largely cushioned the fall. But I knocked my right knee on a stone protruding from the hard frosted earth and yelled out at the sharp twinge that jolted my thigh.

Reluctantly but unavoidably I grasped a nearby burial marker, thankful that I hadn't been impaled on it. I dragged myself painfully and with difficulty to a standing position and looked around for Anna, hoping she hadn't fallen too. She was nowhere to be seen. Being several steps in front of me, it was possible she hadn't seen me collapse into an undignified and aching heap. Though surely, if Anna had been reasonably close, she would've heard my piercing scream. Perhaps the girl had been further in advance of me than I'd thought. Probably she'd now exited the grounds and was safely back home. Why should she have felt any obligation to wait and say goodbye to me, a total stranger?

I happened to look down at the marker that I'd luckily missed when plummeting, but which had opportunely assisted me in getting to my feet again. In one crushing instant I sensed what felt like blood draining from my head. My throbbing legs weakened and I crumpled to my knees, bizarrely numb to the agony that buckling movement must've caused me. As I stared incredulously at the face of the rectangular memorial plaque, I could hardly process what my eyes were transmitting to my brain. My skull felt as light as a helium balloon. I read a name etched into the metal marker between a few Hebrew words and two dates, one in 1932 the other in 1943. The name, which I read again and again and again, was … Anna.

Out of the corner of my eye, I spotted a small black object lying nearby on the lightly frosted grass. It was a child's woollen glove …

No Stranger

ICY WINDS born in the swirling Arctic Ocean, nurtured over the freezing white wastelands of Siberia and nourished above the endless Steppes of Mother Russia howled through the huddled dwellings of the shtetl in the Pale of Settlement. Besieged by poverty and the long, dark and bitter northern winter, with its plunging sub-zero temperatures, frenzied blizzards and deep strangling snows, and assailed by rumours of fearful massacres of their kinsfolk by Cossacks in the east, the Jews of Kerechnev slept cold and fitfully in their beds.

The old and the pauperised, the unemployed and the unemployable despaired and starved, froze in their slumbers and would surrender to merciful sleep for all eternity. Others struggled to survive the harsh tragedy of their chilling and bleak existence. Eternally optimistic luftmenschen, with their bulging bags of prayer books, mezuzahs, yarmulkes and amulets, hung about the cobbled marketplace and its narrow side streets ready for any opportunity to earn a few miserable kopeks. Small tradesmen, whose Sabbath candlesticks or other precious heirlooms had been seized for non-payment of the Tsar's onerous taxes, existed on the brink of financial ruin. Humble workers, slaving for endless hours at noisy sewing machines and ill-lit benches, were sick with anxiety that their jobs might be lost and their large extended families deprived of sustenance.

Indignity heaped itself on degradation but, despite everything, life persisted in Kerechnev. Babies were born, boys celebrated their barmitzvah while young men and women were betrothed and married. The shuls, shtiebls and prayer rooms were, on a daily basis, thronged with those in the community whose profound faith in the Almighty for a better world never wavered, never faltered for a single moment in spite of the continuous hardship and suffering. But there were few in the town who didn't pray for some kind of miracle.

Chaim Kotolsky, the well-built and bearded baker, was just about ready to sit down for supper with his family. The nature of his business meant that Chaim was relatively prosperous. He resided in one of the best houses in the shtetl of some two thousand Jewish souls. His wife Feigl, whom he considered to be the most beautiful woman in the town, and their three demure teenaged daughters, Sarah, Rebecca and Esther, were agreeably but modestly clothed as befitting an Orthodox Jewish household. And there was often the luxury of meat or poultry on the dinner table, not only because Saul the butcher was Chaim's brother-in-law. But the baker was a good, kind and generous man, much respected in the kehillah for never forgetting to give tzedakah to those people less fortunate than the members of his own family. He was devout and philanthropic, performing many mitzvahs and acts of chessed towards his fellow man. Every Friday night before Shabbos came in he would give out challahs, without any charge or return whatsoever, to the town's cash-strapped yeshivah bochas and to its weak, sick and destitute. But Chaim himself would never acknowledge that his donations and good deeds amounted to charity in any way. He regarded his largesse not as a charitable distribution but as more of a redistribution of the good fortune with which the Almighty had seen fit to provide him. And so he was loved by the townsfolk and adored by his wife and children.

Chaim, Feigl and the three girls had washed their hands before taking their usual places at the dining table. Paintings of famous rebbes adorned the walls of the solidly well-furnished and wood-floored room. The heavily bearded, pious and learned scholars of the Halachah seemed to be looking down with approval at the homely and traditional Jewish scene and the loving observance of Yiddishkeit. A white linen tablecloth edged with lace was spread across the long table. Prayer books were set out at the head of the table. Around it sat respectful daughters and a beloved spouse who handed the small silver casket of salt to a devoted husband and father on the point of reciting the bracha on breaking bread.

There came a sudden loud knocking on the front door, which was followed by an exchange of anxious glances around the table.

"Who can that be at this late hour?" Feigl addressed her concerned husband.

Chaim shrugged his shoulders then adjusted a black yarmulke on his bushy mane of dark hair and shook his head. He rose from his chair, walked purposefully but with some trepidation out of the room and across the wide carpeted hall.

His wife and daughters peered, with a mixture of worry and curiosity in their eyes, around the doorway of the dining room, its open-hearth fire crackling behind them. The baker secured a heavy iron chain that hung on the wall to the strong wooden street door which he now unlocked, with a key taken from his trouser pocket, and opened a small way before snatching a look outside. Although Chaim was a strong man who feared little save the supreme power of the Almighty, he felt that cautious circumspection was called for when answering to someone unexpected pounding on his door, especially at night.

Flurries of flaky snow hurtled past, unmasking a tall figure standing on the doorstep. A large fur hat, a thin black beard etched white with snowflakes and a ruddy woollen muffler framed the dark handsome face of a young man. Chaim made out clear blue eyes above high cheekbones, the blue almost matching the colour of the stranger's exposed and frozen cheeks. The man appeared warmly dressed, however, in a long though well-weathered overcoat. But the wind was so bitingly chilling that he was slapping both sides of his body with overlapping, thick-gloved hands and stamping up and down in the crunching snowdrift with his black, possibly knee-high boots. His breath formed clouds of steam in the frosty air and found its way through the gap between the slightly ajar street door and its sturdy frame, which boasted a substantial mezuzah, and into the house.

"Can I help you?" Chaim enquired firmly.

"I do hope so, sir," replied the young man, panting with effort in the nightmarish weather. "I've just arrived in town. But I'm a stranger in these parts and a bit lost. And this filthy night isn't helping my navigation. Luckily, I saw your light. I'm looking for a bed for tonight. Do you know of a hostel or a cheap lodging house nearby?"

The middle-aged baker fingered his cupple and gazed beyond the lad into the hellish maelstrom. His wife called out.

"Who is it, Chaim? Hurry up and close the door. You're letting half of Siberia into our nice warm home! And I need to dish up."

Chaim beckoned to the man.

"You'd better come in … quickly now," he said, gesturing to the young man to accept his invitation at once.

The baker released the security chain and opened the door just wide enough for the invited guest to squeeze through with his bulging haversack. Before doing so, the stranger shook the mantle of loose whiteness from his top coat and scraped the undersides of his boots on the stone step. Chaim shut the door quickly and gave the young man some space in the lobby, an area somewhat cooled now by the invasion and occupation of a winter's punitive and howling night. The three sisters had lined up chattering and giggling behind the proud and stately figure of their mother as their father bolted the front door.

"Leave your baggage here for the time being," the baker said, indicating a place beside the hat-stand and below the gilt-framed, oval hall mirror. "Take off those soaking outdoor clothes and come into the warmth. You'll catch your death of pneumonia, may the Almighty forbid it, if you stand in them any longer. We're just about to eat and you must join us of course."

"I-I don't know how to thank you, sir," the stranger responded, hesitant and flustered, having noticed the three coyly smiling young ladies standing by the open door of the dining room. As he removed his snow-sprinkled fur headwear, revealing a small black skullcap, and his overcoat and scarf, disclosing an obviously well-worn dark blue suit, the youngster fought shyly to look everywhere but at the three young women staring at him with such steadfast interest. The baker understood at once the source of his guest's embarrassment and grinned knowingly as he introduced his wife and their beaming offspring. The stranger acknowledged them with the hint of a reticent bow.

"My name is Ephraim," he said. "Ephraim Schinsky. May I please thank you so much for showing me this very thoughtful hospitality. It has been, to say the least, dreadful on the road here today."

"Take off your boots also," Chaim ordered though in a kindly, fatherly fashion.

"Yes sir."

"Esther will bring you my spare pair of slippers. It looks like we have the same size of feet. And please stop calling me sir. We don't stand on ceremony in this establishment."

"Sorry, sir I mean, sorry."

Chaim turned to his youngest daughter, who was almost seventeen. Obediently and without more, Esther bounded up the staircase. Her mother and sisters hastened into the dining room, to set another place at the table for their unexpected visitor, or to the kitchen to bring in steaming bowls of soup and dishes of poultry, potatoes and other vegetables. The youngest girl returned shortly to the two men now exchanging small talk in the hallway. The new arrival seemed to be more at ease as he chatted amiably with her father. Esther handed the dry footwear to Ephraim, her eyes barely raised in diffident admiration of the young man's attractively formed features. For his part, Ephraim couldn't resist an inner sigh which spoke of the understated beauty of the young woman, her soft delicate face a subtle pastel colour from a water colourist's palette, her long brown hair fanning over the shoulders of her slender but feminine figure, her limpid hazel eyes reflecting an almost fragile nature and a demure innocence. Chaim gently stroked Esther's head and glowed with pride as, together, they watched while Ephraim slipped his cold feet into the welcomingly dry footwear. The patriarch of the household grasped the young man's arm.

"Come with me," he said. "You'll doubtless wish to clean up quickly before we eat, which my dear wife is insisting we do at once before the food gets cold."

"Where do you come from, Ephraim?" Chaim asked.

"From a town in the east," was the simple, vague and unhelpful reply.

The family and their guest had been seated around the table for some minutes. Perhaps understandably, the traveller appeared urgently preoccupied with the meal placed before him. His host and hostess gave each other satisfied nods and smiled encouragement at Ephraim to eat his fill. The three girls could scarcely concentrate on their own plates for gazing at the good-looking stranger. And their mother's stern reaction to their behaviour could only fleetingly hinder her daughters' uncharacteristic conduct. Ephraim looked up momentarily and at that very instant happened to be confronted by five pairs of staring eyes, eyes brimful with inquisitiveness. In a flash he absorbed Esther's unassuming loveliness, the less pretty but nonetheless pleasing Sarah and Rebecca and the pride, love and care revealed on their parents' faces. But he almost choked on the sudden realisation of his ostensible fixation on the delicious fare placed before him and the nebulousness of his scantly described origins.

"Y-You must think me both ill-mannered and inattentive," Ephraim spluttered, striving to recover some composure after a short bout of coughing and a slap or two on the back from the baker's chunky hands. "I really wouldn't blame you. But I haven't eaten like this for some time …"

The young man looked across the table.

"The chicken is wonderful, Mrs Kotolsky. And the vegetable soup was …"

"Made by Esther," Feigl interjected, waving her hand in the appropriate direction.

Her youngest daughter's blush brought the colour of a ripe plum to Esther's cheeks. It gave her heart-shaped face a warm inner radiance, like a harbour lamp welcoming home weary fishermen. At once she covered her redness with flattened palms.

"Mama!" she cried, her exclamation slightly muffled by her hands.

Sarah and Rebecca, seated between their mother and sister, hand stifled little chuckles. Chaim shook his head in resignation, rested his bearded chin on intertwined hands, elbows grounded firmly on the table and turned to the visitor.

"Women," he sighed. "But I do love my family very dearly."

"I can certainly see that, Mr Kotolsky, if I may say so," Ephraim felt he should offer.

Chaim's curiosity spoke again.

"So tell me, my friend, where exactly is this place in the east that you mentioned just before?"

Ephraim forked a roast potato, cut it into halves, slowly moved one speared segment around his plate and hesitated for a moment or two. Seemingly transfixed by the appetising cuisine, and without raising his head, he said quietly: "I'd prefer not to talk about my home town," he said enigmatically, raising the fork to his mouth. "I'm sorry ... I don't want to offend in any way."

Chaim exchanged concerned glances with his wife. Turning back to the stranger, who'd begun eating again, he remarked: "I think we may appreciate your reluctance to speak of your home. Some dreadful stories have reached us here from the east. But eat now. You're obviously very hungry."

The guest looked up suddenly again, this time at five caringly empathetic faces ranged around the table. He smiled with gratitude then attended to his dinner. But in an instant, the young man's happy expression changed to a gruesome mask as his ears caught the sudden roar of the rapacious and snarling snow storm beyond the heavy drapes covering the windows. Chaim saw that Ephraim was shivering. He touched the young man's arm and voiced his thoughts.

"You must've had a terrible journey, my son. We're so sorry."

Ephraim nodded gloomily.

During the remainder of the fine repast Chaim used his best endeavours to cheer the unexpected visitor to his home, mainly with some amusing anecdotes about his bakery and its various customers, among whom were several larger-than-life characters. The room was warm and cosy, flames flickered and danced comfortingly in the hearth and the glowing oil lamps gave out a heartening light. Feigl and the girls had heard the tales many times, so they began removing the plates and dishes into the kitchen. When they returned bearing trays laden with cups of lemon tea, a platter of parve sweetmeats and a bowl of apples Chaim was just finishing one of his self-proclaimed repertoire of entertaining yarns.

"So I said to Mr Poliakov the tailor, now take my advice and use your loaf …"

Ephraim bent his head and laughed, then looked up to see Esther's lovely smiling face as she placed a hot cup of tea in front of him. Her cheeks blossomed into the colour of rose petals as their eyes met. Hers reflected pools of adolescent eagerness; his were dark, sensuous and admiring. The transient blush seemed to propel Esther to her place at the opposite end of the table. As she sat down, her sisters whispered to each other then stole quick glances at Ephraim and behaved generally like a couple of schoolgirls. Their mother launched yet another disapproving look at her older daughters who, with lowered eyes, began sipping their citrus drinks quietly. Feigl now gave further attention to her guest.

"Have an apple, Ephraim," she urged. "Fruit's very good for you. Or perhaps you would like a slice of my husband's delicious honey cake?"

The young man shook his head, his face demonstrating a deepening fatigue.

"No thank you, Mrs Kotolsky. The cake looks marvellous but I've eaten so much already I really haven't got any room left for it. You've been so very good to me. And I'm more than indebted to you for your warmth and humanitarian spirit. But tiredness is rapidly creeping up on me now and I must find a bed for the night before it's too late."

Chaim stood up and placed a firm gripping hand on Ephraim's shoulder.

"No question about it, you must stay with us tonight," the host insisted. "You cannot possibly search for accommodation at this late hour and on such an awful night."

Feigl and her daughters nodded sympathetically, Esther maybe with more self-conscious enthusiasm than her sisters.

"But I cannot impose any longer on your kindness," Ephraim responded earnestly, rising from his chair.

Dismay flitted across the youngest girl's soft lips but her father was adamant.

"No buts, my son. How could we allow you to go out into this brutal, freezing night? You will not find lodgings now. And, if we let you go, we would feel responsible for anything that happened to you … may the Almighty forbid it."

"I'll make up the bed in our spare room," Feigl added. "I can assure you, Ephraim, it will be no trouble. We've all enjoyed your company this evening."

The three sisters nodded silently again, straining to conceal their delight, if not excitement, at the prospect of having the young man sleep under the same roof. Ephraim's shoulders visibly sagged, an apparent sign of his surrender to their pleas the family was pleased to note.

"I'm persuaded," he said. "And I cannot thank you enough. I too can hear the blizzard raging through the town. You wouldn't have needed to twist my arm too much."

"Then it's settled," Chaim grinned, clasping his hands together in triumph. "The women will attend to your bedroom straightaway. We can see how exhausted you are. You must get some rest before you collapse with weariness."

As Chaim led Ephraim into the hall, Feigl and the girls rushed upstairs to the second floor to prepare the unused bedroom with fresh linen. The young man retrieved his bag then turned to his host.

"You've been so very considerate to me, Mr Kotolsky, it seems impertinent for me to seek a favour …"

"What is it?" the baker asked with interest, standing ready to do anything reasonably within his power.

The visitor stammered shyly: "I-I w-would very much like to have a bath before going to bed."

"How stupid of me," Chaim said, shaking his head with annoyance at a personal lack of foresight. "Of course you can take a bath after your long journey. I'll bring it to your room then fetch the water when you're ready for it."

Ephraim smiled and nodded with gratefulness.

"Thank you, Mr Kotolsky."

After freshening up the spare room, Feigl and her daughters returned to the kitchen and began washing and drying the used crockery, cutlery and cooking utensils. Chaim left them chatting happily at their tasks while he manhandled the galvanised tin bath to the second floor. When he entered the bedroom he noted that Ephraim had removed his jacket and tie and was laying out some night attire on the double bed with its high white deck. Leaving the sturdy bathing facility in the centre of the simply furnished room, with its single curtained window and old wooden wardrobe standing against the wall, the baker went back downstairs to fetch the hot water.

Ensuring that the water, which was constantly available from the large metal container on the black kitchen stove, was not too hot by adding to it from the cold water bucket, the baker made several journeys to Ephraim's room. On what he estimated would be the final ferrying up the stairs with two heavily laden pails, he found the door to the spare room shut. He couldn't quite remember whether he himself had closed it on his last trip. Chaim rested the weighty buckets on the landing floor and turned the handle, pushing the door slightly. Hearing no sound of objection, he picked up the water carriers and sidled into the room. Immediately, the baker's face registered acute mortification. Right there in front of him, Ephraim stood stark naked in the bath.

"O-Oh, I'm so sorry!" Chaim declared, his cheeks flushing intensely as he stared transfixed with discomfiture at the young man's nude body. "I should've knocked first. But there didn't appear to be sufficient water on my last visit, and you were fully clothed then ..."

Ephraim didn't seem to be half as perturbed, embarrassed and self-conscious as his poor bemused host who, by now, had averted his eyes.

"Don't concern yourself, Mr Kotolsky. I should be apologising to you. I ought to have been sensible enough to lock the door before undressing. But I must thank you for all your trouble. I think there's more than adequate hot water now. And your wife kindly left out a rug, some soap and a towel for me. I'm indebted to you and your family for all your generous and thoughtful assistance."

Chaim had now recovered his equanimity and rapidly set down the two buckets he was still holding.

"I'll leave these here ... just in case," he said, retreating towards the open door.

Before departing the bedroom he wavered for a moment and thought: *You know, Chaim, any man can wear a skullcap but ...* Then he turned to the young man, who was bending at the knees and about to squeeze himself into a sitting position in the tub. Chaim smiled at him and in such a manner, Ephraim felt, that the man's left eye appeared to be winking.

"And by the way," the baker added. "It would be a very sad day indeed if we couldn't help ... a fellow Jew."

Jerusalem Quartet

(1) Going out and coming in

KRISTALLNACHT, THE night of splintered glass, killed my father. No, not directly you understand. Though many Jews were murdered on the streets of Berlin and other German towns that terrible night of shattering panes in November 1938. Nazi mobs rampaged unhindered through the capital city. Synagogues were set ablaze, Jewish shops and businesses looted and burned and their windows smashed to smithereens. Thousands of Jewish men were rounded up and transported to concentration camps. But it was the trauma of that one crystallised night of hell, and the subsequent pressure on Jewish existence in Hitler's Third Reich, that struck fatally at my father's heart. He passed away just before Pesach 1939.

I'd ventured on tiptoe into his bedroom a few days before he died. His ashen, waxy face was like a shadow on the white pillow and said everything there was to say about his mortal condition. Gently, carefully, I snuggled up to him on the bed. I remember feeling the prickly stubble of his chin on my cheeks and forehead.

"Please don't die, Papa," I cried softly.

My father managed to summon sufficient strength to lift a leaden arm from atop the bedclothes. I felt his thin cold fingers on my warm wet face.

"You're a good boy, Alex," he rasped weakly. "Look after your mother and sister."

A deep and agonised sigh emanated from his throat. I began sobbing pitifully and wanted to hug him tightly; but, regretfully, he warned me not to do it. He'd been a wonderful father to me and my sister Fay, who was two years younger than me. I just wished he'd let me show how much I loved him; but I suppose it would have been too painful for my father, physically and maybe emotionally too.

"Don't worry about me," he continued, speaking slowly and in a hoarse whisper. I had to lean in close to his mouth to hear the words and, at the same time, prevent myself from pressing against his feeble body. "For every going out there's a coming in ... every departure leads to an arrival," he murmured. "Like the Exodus of the Children of Israel from Egypt to the Promised Land ..."

The effort of uttering a mere few sentences exhausted him and he sunk into merciful sleep. I was only twelve years old but I had an inkling of what he meant. Father was a good man. Everyone respected him and sought his advice and words of wisdom or, as he insisted, common sense. He wasn't a very religious person, at least not in a conventionally observant sense. But his beliefs were strong, loyally held and constant. He deserved to have faith in an afterlife.

At the end of July 1939, my mother dropped a bombshell. I

was playing a game with Fay in the lovely garden of our large house, which was located in one of Berlin's pleasant leafy suburbs. I suppose we were very lucky to be still residing there at that time. Mutti came running out of the conservatory towards us.

"Both of you have to leave for England next week!" she called out. "I've managed to get train tickets for you on the kinder-transport."

As she approached us I could see that her eyes were pools of moisture.

"But why do we have to go, Mutti?" I asked plaintively; then throwing down, in a fit of pique, the big colourful rubber ball my sister and I had been bouncing around the apple trees beyond the lawn. Fay burst into tears, burying her face in mother's apron.

"It will be much safer for you there, my darlings. I'll join you as soon as I can obtain my visa and exit permit …"

"But when will that be, Mutti?" I pressed anxiously, trying hard to be strong.

Mother knelt down on the recently mown and sweet smelling grass and held my sister and me close to her bosom.

"I don't know exactly, Alex … Uncle Bernstein is working on it right now … soon I hope," she said, kissing both of us on what must've been hot, red and salt-moist cheeks. "Maybe a few weeks, a month or two …"

"Another exodus," I muttered to myself, recalling father's stories about the expulsion of Jews from Spain and Portugal in medieval times and the flight of our people from Russian pogroms in the late nineteenth century.

"What did you say, Alex?" mother enquired.

I shrugged my shoulders and shouted as I ran to collect the ball from the flower bed into which it had rolled.

"I didn't say anything, Mutti."

It was a devastatingly tearful departure at the Hauptbahnhof, one of the city's principal railway stations. Fay and I stood nervous and disorientated on the platform with all the other kinder-transport children destined for England. Around our necks hung stiff cards inscribed with our names and special numbers; and we carried our pathetically small suitcases, just one each, packed with some essential clothes and underwear. In my free sweaty little hand I clutched a brown paper bag with something for us to eat during our long journey by train and ferry boat. I can remember clearly the acrid, burnt coal odour of the huge black steam engine and the reek of grey coke cinders flying off the tracks. We waited patiently, but with a growing apprehension, to board the train. There was a continuous wailing all around us, from the parents as well as their offspring. It was like a house of mourning. The noise emerging from the dense moving knots and huddles of fathers, mothers and children and the stench from the locomotive were dreadful and making me feel really sick. I recollect nursing a nasty headache and the inside of my nose was sore and hurting. Mother was squatting beside us in our constricted space on the platform her arms wrapped about Fay, who was weeping bitterly, seeking though unsuccessfully to comfort both herself and my little sister.

I can recall the sudden shrill, ear-shattering sound of a steam whistle, which for a few moments drowned out the piteous sobbing of parents clinging desperately to their progeny; and the heart-breaking screams of the infants as they were finally forced to climb aboard the carriages. It was packed and stifling inside our compartment. Fay and I fought to find space at a window. Billowing sooty clouds of steam scudded past us, doubtless from the big engine stack, then plumed upwards to the curved and blackened roof canopy of the station. We spotted mother vying to carve a passageway towards us through the milling throng that surged forward like a tide. She was holding a white handkerchief tight to her face, either protecting herself from breathing in the noxious vapours; or, perhaps more likely, in an effort to conceal her anguish. Unable to get close to our window, she waved frantically in our direction as the train began to pull us away with a succession of chugging roars.

Fay and I struggled with the other kids to retain our position by the window, pressing our flushed faces against the smeared and murky glass. I tried to raise my hand in a farewell gesture but it proved impossible in the crush of pushing, crying and pleading youngsters. I saw mother for the final time as, at last, she broke through the mass of adults holding her back and hastened to keep up with the moving train, now slowly but surely gathering speed. Her mouth was open and she was evidently shouting something at us. I strained my eyes in an effort to read her inaudible lips. It seemed to me that she was calling, "I love you … Alex, Fay … I love you both …" Then she disappeared from view as we began to accelerate through the smoky grey mist and out of the terminus.

At that moment I hated my mother. It grieves me now to think that I ever did, or even could. She'd been a marvellously caring, devoted and loving Mutti in extraordinarily difficult and dangerous times. I had many friends in Berlin whose parents had fallen apart in the crisis, totally unable to cope with the terrifying persecution of the Jews and the horrendously unpredictable circumstances of their own existence. But mother was now sending us to an unknown destination and a frightening future in a strange country far away. And in a way she was constraining me, against my will, to betray my father's dying wish. *Look after your mother and sister*, he'd urged me on his death bed.

The Nazis invaded Poland at the beginning of September 1939, just a month or so after our safe arrival in England. The borders of Hitler's Greater Germany were now closed. Fay and I were settled with a Jewish family in North London. Although they were very kind people and took really good care of us it was a difficult period, especially for my sister who sobbed herself to sleep every night calling for her Mutti. I did my best to comfort her but it was nigh on impossible. She was inconsolable. I don't know how but from time to time we received letters from our mother; though there was no return address to which we could write. After the end of 1943, the correspondence dried up and we became terribly concerned for her safety and welfare.

In the summer of 1945, with the defeat of Germany and the end of the war in Europe, we learned through our English guardians and via the International Red Cross that our beloved Mutti had not survived the Holocaust. She'd perished in the notorious Auschwitz-Birkenau death camp in the autumn of 1944, but not in its gas chambers. She'd been forced to slave for her Nazi masters in one of the extensive sub-camps. But in the end, and almost inevitably, mother had succumbed to exhaustion, freezing cold winters and starvation. From the cynically and meticulously maintained camp records, the authorities could tell us the precise day of her death. At least Fay and I could now light Yahrzeit candles, and I could recite in the synagogue the Kaddish memorial prayer for a deceased parent, on the correct date.

★ ★ ★

My darling wife Stella and I made aliyah from England to Israel (yet another exodus?) in the early 1960s. We reside in Tel Aviv and have three children, all married with children of their own. My sister Fay was married late to a very decent, older man who understood her sensibilities. They had just the one child, a son. His name's Gary. He's a successful solicitor and single. Fay and Gary live in North-West London, though my nephew has now left home for an apartment of his own. Sadly, my brother-in-law died a couple of years ago.

Last year, during Chol HaMoed Pesach, I was sitting on a bench in Charles Clore Park on Tel Aviv's glorious seafront. It was a delightful spring morning, warm and lulling, and I was relaxingly observing the sun-sparkling sea break against Old Jaffa. Stella was engaging in some retail therapy in one of those ubiquitous and glitzy new shopping malls. A man, tall and grey-haired like me but with a slight stoop, sat down on the bench. I could sense him staring at me and I was starting to feel a bit uncomfortable. Finally, he spoke.

"I know you," he said in Ivrit with some excitement and more than the suggestion of a Central European accent.

As it transpired, the man had a phenomenal recall, far superior to my own moderate ability. I couldn't place him at first; but he remembered my face from school in Berlin many decades back. This was absolutely incredible and, naturally, amazingly flattering. Though I suppose some people have the talent for recalling the essence of certain facial features from long ago that were captured and preserved somewhere deep in their memory cells. We seemed to get on very well once we'd established our common historical credentials. This all occurred in a whirl of nostalgia that almost rendered me giddily overcome with some poignant, but also some joyless, reminiscences. In just a few minutes we'd exchanged names and abbreviated personal narratives going back to the 1930s. Isaac told me that his own parents had turned down the possibility of his joining the kinder-transport destined for England. And sadly, I learned from him that his entire family had been deported from the Reich on a transport to Auschwitz in 1944.

"My parents were selected immediately for the showers," Isaac informed me sucking in his lips, his cheeks suddenly looking dark and hollow. "I'm sure you know what that meant, Alex."

I nodded my understanding of the euphemism and he continued.

"When I'd descended from the cattle truck onto the platform packed with fellow Jews that hellish floodlit night of barking hounds and guttural orders, I was approached by one of the camp inmates who was wearing what appeared to be striped pyjamas. He and other similarly garbed, zombie-like creatures had been stacking piles of luggage seized from us new arrivals from Germany. He looked scarily at me, and I nearly jumped out of my skin when he grabbed my arm. 'When you get to the ramp and the head of the queue,' he whispered huskily 'tell them you're eighteen and a carpenter by trade.' Then he scurried off to join his work gang by the growing mountain of battered old suitcases."

Isaac paused for a few moments, as if catching his breath; or maybe because it was emotionally problematic to bring to mind the dreadful events he was describing.

"Luckily I was a big lad for my age, which was only fifteen," he went on. "Perhaps my muscular build was the reason why this pitiful prisoner had picked me out of the pitiable horde of humanity tumbling from the filth and foul stink of the animal wagons. I don't know why but I did what the wild-eyed man had urged me. The SS officer in charge of the selection despatched me with a number of other strapping lads to one of the sub-camps where we slaved, and where many of the boys died in the most vile conditions you definitely couldn't imagine. At the beginning of 1945, with the Soviet army advancing rapidly from the east, thousands of us slave workers from the main and satellite camps were forced to march westwards towards Germany in appalling winter weather."

The poor man took out a handkerchief from his trouser pocket and wiped his watering eyes. I could barely conjure up in my own head the terrifying images that were doubtless filling his.

"Those too weak to walk," Isaac continued, eyes blurred by his bad memories, "or even to crawl on hands and knees were finished off in an ice-shrouded, roadside ditch with a bullet through the back of the neck ..."

I twitched involuntarily at the horrors I'd been fortunate to escape, even assuming I would've outlasted the camps.

"One moonless night I managed to evade our vicious guards and fled into the forest. I'd been planning my escape for some days. Realisation had dawned that unless I took what was clearly a perilous risk, I'd probably end up dead very soon. I only just managed to survive ... please don't ask me how. And, subsequently, I joined up with a partisan group of Jews and communists. After the end of the war, I found myself shunted into a refugee camp near Vienna. A year or so later, having made some useful contacts, I was smuggled into Italy. Ultimately, I arrived on the shores of our homeland on a blockade-runner. I was just in time to help fight the Arabs in our War of Independence."

To say the least, it was a harrowing story; but equally an enthralling one. At one point, Isaac rolled up his shirtsleeve to reveal the concentration camp number tattooed on his forearm.

"We're both survivors, Alex," he said, "you and me ... survivors!"

I begged to differ. "No, Isaac," I reacted sharply. "You are the true survivor. You survived Auschwitz, the death march, the guerrilla fighting in the forests and the hazardous journey to the Promised Land. Even during the Luftwaffe's Blitz on London, Fay and I were evacuated to the peaceful countryside in northern England!"

I didn't tell my newfound friend, at least not then, about the tugging vacuum, the awful chasm, I still experience deep within my being. It's a sensation of utter emptiness, a black hole of nothingness because I never went through the hellish nightmare that Isaac had experienced during the war. Suddenly, I was alarmed to see my companion clutch his stomach. He got up quickly and announced quietly that he needed to go to a toilet, but that there was no urgency.

"Is it the matzot?" I asked, hoping his immediate problem

had no more sinister basis. "Some say they carry the curse of the Pharaohs!"

"No, no … it's not the matzot," Isaac replied, wincing and evidently in some pain. "It's my guts … a legacy of …"

I stood up, quite concerned, and held out an open hand.

"Can I help you?" I offered.

"No … thanks, Alex, I'll be all right … really. I get this trouble occasionally. Sorry, but I have to dash now …"

We exchanged telephone numbers hurriedly and said our hasty goodbyes. Without further delay, Isaac walked away quickly across the grass in the direction of the Dan Hotel.

Isaac lives in Jerusalem with his wife Hannah and daughter Emunah, who's a librarian in the city and a single young lady. We've become very good friends in the last twelve months, often visiting each other's homes. Over that time Stella and I have gradually come to the notion that Emunah should get together with Gary. My wife and I are moving to Jerusalem next year, hopefully before Pesach. Yet another going out and coming in, I suppose. This time I know Papa will be very pleased.

(2) Next year in Jerusalem

THE EL-AL 747-400 crossed the Mediterranean coast of Israel above a shimmering white Tel Aviv and descended towards Ben Gurion. Gary shifted in his window seat and switched off the mini-screen in the seatback facing him. The "Fasten Seatbelt" signs pinged overhead and he smartly clunk-clicked.

He was a nervous flyer and as usual on take-off and landing, the most potentially dangerous of airplane manoeuvres, Gary began sweating profusely. The aircraft's huge winged fuselage banked gently for its final approach to the international airport. But, this time, it wasn't actually the jumbo jet's airborne proximity to the ground that was the real cause of the lawyer's trepidation. It was the fact that he was soon to meet, for the first time, the girl of his dreams. At least that's what his Israeli Uncle Alex had promised him during numerous telephone calls to London. In the last few moments before touching down safely with just a minor bounce on the runway, Gary recalled Uncle Alex's incessant bombardment leading to a lengthy description of the blessings of matrimony.

"You're in your forties with a marvellous career … a successful solicitor, noch! But you've got no steady girlfriend, Gary. What's the matter? What's wrong with you? I take it you're not …"

The interruption was instant.

"No, Uncle Alex, I'm not gay!"

Gary knew that his uncle genuinely harboured the best of intentions; and he'd frequently considered that his mother's brother was indeed a shining example of wedded bliss. He'd married Stella, a Mancunian, a year or so before they'd made aliyah in the 1960s. And they'd raised three Sabra children during a stormy and uncertain period in the State of Israel's problematic history. But Gary didn't relish hearing a regular diatribe, similar to that his widowed mother Fay had been spouting. Having his own apartment in Hendon had afforded him some semblance of peace and independence. But he couldn't cut his Mum's telephone line (or could he? Gary had sometimes fantasised). Nor could he justifiably refuse to stay over with his widowed mother in Golders Green during Shabbat. Nowadays, even the Finchley law firm's senior partner was wont to inject words like nuchus into discussions with his associate. And in the middle of work meetings about commercial leases, High Court writs or witness subpoenas!

As the giant Boeing taxied along the tarmac after a relatively smooth landing, Gary breathed a deep sigh of relief and recalled his telephone conversation with Uncle Alex the previous month.

"Look Gary, if I could shlep all the way to Manchester on the train to meet my future wife, you can fly to Israel to meet

Emunah. Besides, it's summer time. And Fay tells me you've been working very hard these days and really need a holiday with some guaranteed sun. So let's hear it for a trip to Israel, eh?"

Whilst forcing himself to listen to his uncle, Gary had slumped further into his new leather sofa.

"Who says that Emunah is going to be my future wife anyway? In the first place, I know next to nothing about her … and I've never set eyes on the woman. And besides all that, she's never seen me! Bit of a leap of faith, uncle."

The solicitor heard Uncle Alex sigh into his mouthpiece.

"Your memory must be failing you, Gary. Didn't I send you a photograph of Emunah? Do you remember that?"

His nephew's unseen expression had displayed severe signs of irritability.

"My memory's excellent. Can't say that about the photo! It could've been taken on the Titanic … after it sank and at the black bottom of the Atlantic Ocean, where you can see zilch!"

Gary made out a stifled chuckle at the other end of the line.

"I'm telling you, Emunah's a shayner madel … and from an exceptional family, too. Her parents are very dear friends of ours."

"But you've told me so little about her, uncle."

There was that telltale sigh again.

"What more do you need to know? She's thirty-five, of medium height with long black hair and works in a library in Jerusalem. I've told you all this already."

By now the target of Cupid Alex's bow and arrow had grown distinctly restive.

"The picture was useless, uncle. I really don't know what she looks like."

"Are looks that important to you, Gary? If so, I think you should take …"

"No, of course not," the youngish man had intervened apologetically. "Appearance isn't everything, I know that. But I'd sent you a very sharp image of me to pass on to Emunah. I certainly expected more than a fuzzy snapshot in return. It just makes me a bit suspicious, you know. After all, I am a lawyer."

Gary thought he could hear avuncular fingernails scratching a hard pate.

"Listen to me, please," Alex had begged his nephew. "You're my sister's only child. Would I mislead you?"

The solicitor had rested his head against the settee and stared at the ceiling.

"With all due respect, but in a word, my answer is in the affirmative!"

Uncle Alex had countered instantly.

"O ye of little faith, now look! Emunah is no Julia Roberts. But believe me, she's a very attractive and intelligent young woman."

Somewhat guiltily, Gary had mimicked his Uncle Alex's language and intonation but regretted it immediately:

"So she's no Julia Roberts, eh? More like Julia Robot, maybe?"

Alex had been ready for that kind of nonsense response. He knew Gary's zany if not warped sense of humour, if that's what it was, well enough.

"From what I hear, you're no Tom Cruise yourself. Since we last saw you two years ago, I understand you've developed a noticeable little paunch and that your hairline's receding. Hair loss may be a premature, though not necessarily unnatural, phenomenon at your age. But don't you get any exercise?"

Gary loved his uncle dearly and he knew that his uncle loved him dearly, too. But the youngish lawyer didn't take kindly to this pressured personal attack.

"Don't worry," he'd reacted sardonically, "my brain gets plenty of exercise."

"I'm not talking about your brain, as you well know."

"Look, uncle, I've had plenty of girlfriends. I just haven't found the right one for me ... yet."

Gary had almost predicted the next springboard assault.

"Fay says you're becoming, what do they call it? Ah yes, a nebbish! That's what we used to term a back number in days of yore. It's a man advancing in years who'd done the rounds of those available girls prepared to date him ... once, perhaps twice. It's someone who can't quite break out of the downward spiral of rejection, who begins wearing cardigans knitted by his mother and generally allows his physical appearance and social life to slide in the wrong direction."

A now irate if not enraged nephew shifted awkwardly to the edge of the couch, so that a button flew off his maroon wool cardigan, and thumped the armrest with a tightly clenched fist.

"Uncle Alex," he'd shouted into the phone. "I'm not dead yet!"

★ ★ ★

The old Peugeot 305 edged to the slow lane of the Jerusalem-Tel Aviv motorway beneath a scorching sun that beat down on the arid landscape like a hammer on an anvil. Finally, the car turned off from the busy highway onto a slip road that led to the airport. Emunah shifted in the driving seat and switched off the classical music station on the radio. Nervousness assailed her as the small French runabout joined the traffic en route to Ben Gurion. But it wasn't the sometimes crazy antics of her fellow Israeli motorists that had caused her current apprehension. It was the fact that she was soon to meet, for the first time, the man of her dreams. At least that's what Alex, a good family friend, had promised her about his nephew Gary during numerous telephone calls from his new apartment home in Jerusalem. She couldn't help but bring to mind the man's relentless salvoes, leading to a lengthy recital of the blessings associated with the matrimonial state.

Admittedly, she'd often thought, her parents' friend was certainly a glowing illustration of wedded bliss. He and his wife Stella were lovely genuine people with three fine children who had happy families of their own. Truly it was a domestic success story like that of her own parents, and despite the many difficulties of coming to grips with a paradoxical, continually assailed and often deliberately misunderstood even demonised land. But Emunah could've done without the persistent pressure her parents had been exerting for many years now. Having her own tiny apartment had given her some semblance of peace and independence. But she couldn't cut her parents' phone line (or could she? Emunah had sometimes fantasised) or refuse to go see them on Shabbat. Nowadays even the senior librarian was wont to slip in words like nuchus when talking to her; and in the middle of discussions about book classification systems, digitisation of ancient documents and Internet source materials.

As the Peugeot pulled into a vacant space at the international airport's short-term car park, the young woman remembered her telephone conversation with Alex the previous day.

"Look Emunah, if I could shlep all the way to Manchester by train to meet my future wife, you can drive to Ben Gurion to meet Gary. Besides, your Dad says you could do with a day's break from that stuffy old book depository. Okay?"

Emunah had slumped deeper into the comfortable cushions on her new armchair.

"Who says that your nephew will be my future husband, Alex? I've never met this man, I know next to nothing about him. And it's not a book depository!"

The librarian picked up a snapshot from the glass coffee table, a flat-warming gift from her favourite yet now exasperating unofficial uncle.

"He looks normal enough," she'd noted, virtually damning with faint praise. "But how long ago was it taken? A small passport-type picture doesn't tell me very much."

A rounded chuckle had filled the earpiece.

"I'm telling you," her caller had advocated, "Gary's a fine man, a lawyer as you're aware ... and he's from an excellent family. Don't forget, Emunah, I'm a member of it too."

Alex's favourite, but now inordinately resistant, young lady had reacted swiftly.

"But you've told me so little about him."

A profound sigh had issued from Emunah's receiver.

"What more do you need to know, sweetheart? He's in his youngish forties, of medium height and works as a solicitor in London."

The target of Cupid's bow and arrow had become weary.

"But I don't really know what Gary looks like. As a

professional researcher, it makes me a little suspicious."

The odd noise she'd then heard emitted from the phone's speaker sounded like fingernails scratching an old man's bony head.

"Listen to me, Emunah. You're my very dear friends' only child. Would I mislead you?"

"With the greatest respect Alex, I think the answer must be yes."

He'd responded instantly.

"O ye of little faith, my darling Emunah! Look, Gary is no Tom Cruise. True. But believe me, he's reasonably good looking."

Emunah had then emulated Alex's words but not without a sense of guilt.

"No Tom Cruise, eh? Maybe he's more like a Tom Thumb?"

Alex had primed himself for such a silly assault on his hype: "Know what Emunah, you and Gary have a similar daft sense of humour. Anyway, from what I hear but not to be too unkind, you're no Julia Roberts yourself. Since we last saw you a couple of months back, I understand you've put on a bit of weight here and there. Don't you take any exercise now you've bought yourself a car?"

The librarian recalled her face feeling fiery hot.

"Please don't fret on my behalf. I get plenty of exercise walking along miles of library bookshelves."

Emunah promptly, and intuitively, regretted using that last word.

"I don't want to say it, but best be careful you're not left on one of them."

Her cheeks were almost at the point of spontaneous combustion.

"I've had lots of boyfriends … I just haven't met the right man for me … yet."

Alex had countered at once:

"Just make sure, sweetheart, you don't become what we used to call a back number. After all, you're not getting any younger."

Emunah had moved awkwardly in her sturdy new chair, recalling the odd grey hair or two on her head, then thumped one upholstered side with a bunched fist. "Alex, I'm not dead yet!"

The night after he'd spoken on the telephone to Gary and Emunah, both of whom he loved so very much, Alex had retired to bed asking for a special forgiveness from the Almighty in his prayers. And then, wrapped in his slumbering wife's arms, he wept himself quietly to sleep.

★ ★ ★

Alex had arranged to meet Emunah in the Arrivals Hall at Ben Gurion. When she spotted him, tall and distinguished looking, the young woman ran across the concourse and tapped Alex on the shoulder. As he turned she stretched on her toes and planted a big kiss on his cheek.

"Still friends, then?" he enquired with a sort of bashful, school-boyish grin.

The librarian gave him an affectionate hug. They looked up at the electronic Arrivals monitor as it scrolled to indicate that the El-Al Heathrow flight had just landed on time.

"What do you think, my darling Alex?" Emunah murmured, whilst threading her left arm through his right and squeezing tightly.

Gary retrieved his suitcase from the carousel and made his way through the Customs area to the exit. He was trembling with, to him, a novel mixture of anticipation, excitement and trepidation. At the barrier, Emunah also quivered with a similarly innovative combination of emotions. On entering the bustling Arrivals Hall the London lawyer instantly recognised his waving uncle, who was standing head and shoulders above the patiently waiting family and friends of incoming passengers. The young Israeli noticed the youngish, not bad looking guy returning her lofty companion's greeting with a high hand gesture. In turn, Gary observed a quite attractive young woman standing beside his mother's brother. The solicitor's eyes met those of the librarian. Alex witnessed the promising ocular encounter with a lovely warm feeling caressing his heart.

And he recollected a rainy day in Manchester many years ago. He knew precisely what that kind of meeting of eyes could mean. Very likely, he thought to himself, it was love at first sight …

Gary hugged his uncle and pumped his hand, action displays that Alex had hardly expected in view of their earlier, fraught telephonic conversations. Emunah watched as Alex said something close to his nephew's ear. It sounded to her like, "Do you forgive me for all my relentless harangues?"

Before Gary turned to smile at her, Emunah just about caught his whispered reply.

"What do you think, uncle?"

As Alex formally and beamingly introduced the young people to each other, he could hear in his head quite distinctly the joyful jingle of wedding bells. Even though he knew well enough they would not be ringing at any Jewish marriage ceremony. Observing closely the well-matched couple chatting comfortably together on the way to the car park, the honorary shadchen gazed skywards and despatched a short silent prayer: "Please God we can encourage an early engagement and then a speedy chupah, maybe for next year ... in Jerusalem."

(3) This year in Jerusalem

JERUSALEM IN late springtime is like a fine French wine. Like the wine, the city is well-matured, warming, a gorgeous colour, drenched in Mediterranean sunshine and richly intoxicating. In such a gloriously invigorating setting, the toast L'Chaim! is on everyone's lips. This was especially true at the wedding of Emunah and Gary. The chupah took place in the luxuriant, sub-tropical gardens of one of the radiant Israeli capital's grandest hotels.

Gary's widowed mother Fay, who'd flown in from London the night before the marriage, stood tearfully under a golden canopy that was decorated with a stunning floral arrangement and remembered with love her late husband Sam. Emunah's parents, Isaac the Holocaust survivor and his wife Hannah, gazed with mixed emotions at their only child as she drank from the wine-filled silver becher. Fay's brother Alex, who'd made aliyah with his wife Stella in the 1960s, accompanied his emotion-charged sister as the officiating rabbi intoned the blessings. Alex smiled to himself with a deep satisfaction as the couple kissed each other at the conclusion of the service. He recalled his strenuous, though largely unwelcome, efforts to bring together his solicitor nephew from Hendon and the Jerusalem-based librarian daughter of his and his spouse's best friends.

At the end of his visit to Israel to meet Emunah, Gary had proposed matrimony to her. It really had been a proverbial case of love at first sight when they'd made eye contact at Ben Gurion Airport that brilliant summer's day last year. Despite his earlier feelings of remorse if not shame at the uncompromising tactics he'd adopted to get the two people together, Uncle Alex nonetheless felt now only a sense of triumphant pride at having achieved his longed for success. As she was being driven to the chupah in a chauffeured white limousine, the librarian recalled the difficult conversation with Gary on the evening the London lawyer had asked her to marry him. After she'd prepared, and they'd eaten, what Emunah hoped was a splendid dinner of St Peter's fish with a pepper and aubergine salad in the tiny kitchen of her small Jerusalem hills apartment, they sat together on the settee in the compact, open-plan living area.

"Emunah, please be reasonable ... I can't come to live in Israel," Gary had implored her.

The Israeli had risen and walked into the kitchen space. Gary had followed her.

"You must also try to understand," she'd said, her eyes watering. "I'm a Sabra, born and bred. I love Israel. I love my parents. I'm their only child. It would be a crushing blow to them if I went to live thousands of miles away."

She knew that her fiancé of some minutes now adored her

almost perfect English, spoken with an Ivrit accent. He'd considered that the absence of a language problem would be a fantastic basis for settling down in London. Emunah had begun washing the dinner dishes and cutlery in the sink. Gary had picked up a milchich tea-towel and started wiping the crockery being stacked by his fiancée in the plastic drainer. Previously Gary had informed Emunah that he'd amazed himself at home, becoming quite the domesticated bachelor since leaving his Mum's house in Golders Green and taking a flat in nearby Hendon.

"I'm also my own mother's only child," Gary had responded after a short pause. "And please don't forget that she's a widow. How could I leave her all alone? Besides, there's my work … my legal career. It might be possible for me to get a job here as a lawyer … eventually. But there could be real problems. For a start, I would need to learn impeccable Ivrit. And there would be more exams for me to take. And then I couldn't guarantee that I'd find a firm willing to take me on, even with my professional experience. I understand there's quite a bit of competition here, not that there isn't back in England. I'm sorry, Emunah, but I don't think living in Jerusalem would work out to our benefit. And I think that, with your degree and librarian skills, you'll easily obtain an appropriate post and be able to advance your own career in London."

Emunah had put down the plate she was mopping with a dishcloth and dried herself on a hand towel that hung from a hook on the wall. After a few moments of pregnant silence, she'd turned to face the man who'd just asked her to be his wife. She'd smiled at Gary who was gazing lovingly into her eyes.

"I'm so sorry, my darling," she'd murmured. "I think we

should be doing something rather more romantic than washing dishes and debating domicile. Come on … give me a kiss."

Gary hadn't hesitated at the invitation, holding Emunah tightly in his arms and pressing his lips firmly against hers. Following several minutes in Gary's intimate embrace, Emunah had pulled away gently and announced she would make some coffee. A short while later the couple were sitting close together on the settee. Gary had placed an arm around his fiancée's shoulders and she was tenderly stroking his face.

"I love you, Gary," she'd said softly. "I love you very much. And I believe you love me too. I know it's been a whirlwind romance. Everything's been happening so fast. But I knew that one day it would be just like this. We're bayshayrt, as my mother and father would say. You've really swept me off my feet. I do want to marry you, Gary. And I will marry you."

Her fiancé opened his mouth to say something relevant but she placed a slender finger gently on his lips. "You will be my husband," Emunah continued, smiling warmly. "And I must be where my husband is. Just as Ruth promised Naomi, wherever you go, I will go and happily, my love."

Gary had nuzzled Emunah's neck. Their lips touched and the loving kiss had endured for a long time.

"I love you so much," Gary had whispered as they drew apart finally. "We'll buy a big house with a large guest room for your parents to come and stay with us on their hopefully regular visits."

Emunah had nodded, grinned and given him a demonstrative peck on the cheek.

"Perhaps one day we'll return to live in Israel," the solicitor had said reassuringly. "In the meantime you can steadily improve my dubious Ivrit. For the notoriously bad linguist that I am, I have to tell you that this is likely to take some time, patience and effort on your part as well as mine."

They'd laughed out loud as she'd grasped his hands, brought them to her mouth, brushing the digits with her soft lips, and gazed into the young man's light blue eyes.

"Please don't say any more," she'd pleaded. "Don't make any unnecessary promises now. We're just beginning this wonderful new adventure together. We'll wait and see what happens in the years to come. We've got our whole lives ahead of us. And maybe, one day, we'll have other lives to think about also. There'll be plenty of time to make such decisions. For now, and for the foreseeable future, let's just enjoy our love together … you and me."

Gary had nodded assent with a glowing pride and admiration for the wise words of his darling Emunah. Then the couple kissed again, this time more passionately than ever they'd done in the few days they'd known each other.

★ ★ ★

The wedding reception and dinner for well over a hundred guests was held in the exquisitely appointed banqueting suite of the hotel, where the tastefully landscaped and radiantly sun-lit gardens had formed the backcloth for the chupah. Emunah, looking a million dollars in her frothy white dress, and Gary, coolly stylish and debonair in a dazzling white suit, shared the top table with her parents, his mother and Uncle Alex and Auntie Stella. Isaac and Hannah had spared no expense in making the day as wonderfully memorable as they could for their loyal, dutiful and ever so deserving daughter, whom they loved so much, and for her husband Gary, who'd grown quickly in their affections and respect even though he was taking Emunah to live in England.

During the gourmet extravaganza of a seasonally light and appropriate five-course meal, accompanied by a six-piece band playing tunes from Hollywood musicals, Alex exchanged seats temporarily with Stella in order to sit beside his dear friend.

"It's all absolutely fantastic, Isaac!" he praised his neighbour with gusto. "You've done Emunah and Gary really proud, to say the very least."

"Thanks a lot, Alex. They deserve it. Personally, I'm steering well clear of one or two courses … you know how some food can play havoc with my intestines."

His good friend nodded solemnly, wrapping an arm about Isaac's shoulders and squeezing him manfully.

"Look, Isaac, I know that you and Hannah are more than a trifle upset about Emunah settling in London, so far away from you. It's partly my fault, I realise that of course. But believe me, that nephew of mine's the kindest, most honest and good-hearted of men … and I know he loves your daughter more than he could say in words."

"Don't you think we can see that, Alex? Now that we've got to know him well, Hannah and I are extremely fond of our son-in-law. But there's another thing. You see I can't help thinking about what I've lost in the past, in the war, in the camps, in the gas chambers … my parents, other close relatives, my friends, everyone I knew. And now we're losing Emunah …"

Alex was saddened to see tear globules rising in his host's

eyes on such a joyous occasion as his daughter's wedding. He rapidly broke into the increasingly emotional flow of his friend's sad reminiscence.

"But, Isaac, you shouldn't think in such terms. I can't identify with what you must be going through. But ... and it's hardly necessary for me to state this, what's happening now is a world and a dimension apart from what you remember of those horrific times more than a half-century ago. I know that you lost everyone close to you, everyone you loved, in the Shoah. And I accept that you'll never be able to forget that heart-rending period in your life. But Emunah has just got herself married to a superlative man who adores her. This is supposed to be your proudest day, Isaac. Please be glad for your daughter. She's blissfully happy with the man she loves. She'll be living in England with a husband who'll care for her as you and Hannah would wish. And London isn't the other side of the Milky Way galaxy. I've no doubt that you and Hannah realise that well enough. I know, as I'm sure you do, that Gary and Emunah will be returning to Jerusalem on a fairly regular basis. And you and Hannah can visit them in London. Emunah will continue loving you both just like she always has done. You can't ask more of her. It's her life, Isaac. I'm sure it'll be painful for her to be separated from her beloved parents and, early on I'm certain, she's likely to feel quite homesick in a new country with a rather different culture to the one she grew up in. Try not to mention your feelings to her. It will make matters uncomfortable all round. Remember, my dear friend, you can look forward to visits with a loving anticipation. And in years to come, please God, Emunah and Gary will bring your grandchildren with them to see you and Hannah. So here ends the first lesson … I'm sorry for the long speech, Isaac."

Alex's sentimental, though well-intended words caused Isaac to bite his lip and search quickly in his jacket pocket for a handkerchief. He couldn't find one and gratefully took the proffered tissues. When he'd finished clearing his eyes and had adequately regained his composure, the wedding host embraced his dearest friend. He caught his beautiful daughter smiling at him and countered with a paternal air kiss, blown from his now only slightly tremulous hand.

Fay was schmoozing with her sister-in-law as the lively orchestra began playing a selection of music from the hit show Fiddler on the Roof.

"You know, Stella, I'm really looking forward to having Emunah in London with us."

"Yes, Fay, she's a delightful and very clever young lady," Stella responded with a Mancunian dialect scarcely diluted even after several decades in the land of Israel. "Gary's got a good shidduch for himself. He's a very lucky man."

As she considered this, Fay began humming the piquant melody to Sunrise, Sunset. A crisply uniformed waitress cleared away some used crockery from the table, which boasted elegantly presented flower displays on a glitter sprinkled white, blue and pink cloth cover.

Having thought for a moment, Fay reacted snappily.

"And Emunah's not doing so badly for herself either," she crowed. "Gary has been looking for the right girl for a long time. I know he has now found her, Stella. He's a very good son to me, especially since his Dad passed away. I want my darling boy to be happy, like Sam and I were. And Gary really works hard at his law firm. Well into the night on many occasions.

Don't tell him I told you, but he's mentioned they're likely to make him a partner soon."

Stella widened her eyes then puckered her bright red lips and nodded approvingly.

"That's wonderful, Fay … Mazeltov!"

Coming up behind the two chattering women, Gary overheard the traditional Jewish congratulatory exclamation.

"What's the Mazeltov for, Auntie Stella?"

She twisted in her chair to look up at the ambitious lawyer as Fay nudged her arm warningly.

"Your Mum says you're going to be a partner in the firm. From what she tells me, you really deserve this promotion. Mazeltov, Gary!"

The young man frowned then grimaced at his mother, who was looking down guiltily at her clasped hands.

"Mum," he whispered in her ear, "I told you not to say anything yet. Nothing's been finalised."

Fay looked up and limply waved a part contrite, part dismissive hand at her hovering and apparently glowering son.

"That's his trouble," she teased, glancing at Stella. "He's too modest by half."

The white-suited bridegroom shrugged his shoulders and sighed with resignation at his irksome mother's untimely and, literally, promotional publicity.

"I don't know what I'm going to do with you, Mum!"

Gary turned away, concealing a grin, kissed a beamingly gorgeous Emunah who'd crept up on him and swung her onto the spacious dance floor. Stella touched Fay's arm.

"Listen to me seriously for a moment," she said quietly, looking around like a plotter. "Make sure that Emunah is happy in London. You know how sad and disconsolate she must feel to be leaving her parents, Jerusalem … Israel."

A short pause was occupied by Fay shaking her head and bunching her cheeks by a tightening together of her glistening lips.

"Don't be foolish, Stella. Don't you think I've got the wit to work that one out?"

"Sorry Fay, I didn't mean …"

"I realise that, honey … I really do know what it's like not to have someone dear to you near to you. I lost my precious Sam nearly four years ago now, and I still haven't quite come to terms with not having him with me."

Stella patted Fay's forearm and gave her a sympathetic nod.

"This isn't what we should be talking about now," she reprimanded, herself mostly, as the energetic and versatile group of Israeli musicians struck up a rousing arrangement of If I were a Rich Man. "We're in danger of becoming maudlin. And we're supposed to be enjoying ourselves here today!"

Closing his speech to the assembled wedding guests, Gary turned to his bride with a profound love in his smiling eyes.

"At the end of the Haggadah," he concluded, "which we read at Pesach, we're inspired every year by the hope and expectation in that ancient book's final words … Next year in Jerusalem. For my part, all my hopes, dreams and expectations have now been fulfilled … This year in Jerusalem!"

(4) Last year in Jerusalem

FAY APPLIED the trendy red baby buggy's brake and sat herself down on the wooden bench near the public lending library in Golders Green High Road. It's remarkably warm and sunny for an October morning, she thought. But then again, she ruminated, autumns in England were becoming much milder than they used to be, especially when she'd been a teenager, and the seasons weren't so well defined any more. Maybe the scientists were right about global warming. Anyway, it wasn't the pleasant weather that had caused the grandmother to abandon the thermal winter underwear she'd long favoured at this time of year. Nor was the mild climate responsible for her wearing the chic new topcoat her son and daughter-in-law had bought as a gift for her recent birthday.

The modish bubbeh kvelled at the sight of her five-month-old grandson Samuel, now fast asleep in his equally fashionable pram. Her late husband Sam would've been so proud to gaze upon his gorgeous namesake. Perhaps he was looking down on him from Heaven right now. Fay felt cosily warm as she imagined her beloved Sam doing just that. She could barely believe that it was a little more than five years since he'd passed away.

Fay reflected on what her late spouse of so many years might now be seeing of the family from on high. Well, she was sure that he'd be brimming with pride to note that his son was doing exceedingly well in the legal profession. Gary had been made a partner in the Finchley law firm he'd worked for since qualifying as a solicitor. And the successful lawyer was also happily married to Emunah. The girl from Jerusalem, introduced to Gary by his Israeli Uncle Alex, was such a sweet and caring young woman. Today, the couple lived in a very nice detached house in Hendon and were the prideful parents of the adorable little Samuel. Yes, Fay mused, Sam would be absolutely over the moon.

The widow liked sitting on this particular bench when the weather was fine. It was positioned close to the library at the end of the shopping area and a mere stone's throw from her home. Three days a week Emunah commuted into Central London to her part-time post as a university librarian while Fay looked after her grandchild. Samuel was a very good baby, no trouble at all to care for in his Mum's absence. And his Grandma was so glad to be able to help her daughter-in-law to continue the job she loved doing, working with books and people just like she'd done back in Jerusalem.

Fay had developed a close relationship with her son's wife, and in an amazingly short period of time. She didn't normally relate to people so speedily, unless there was a kind of psychological bond that her inner being mysteriously recognised. Emunah was the daughter of her brother's best friends in Israel. Alex had made aliyah many years ago with his wife Stella; and Fay often felt she would like to have seen more of them. But she'd been glad of Alex's tireless, though not always welcomed, efforts to bring the couple harmoniously together. The wedding in Jerusalem had been one of the highlights of her life; though the tears had flowed inevitably. And now, looking after baby Samuel had become for Fay a true labour of love. In fact, the new role had provided her with a fresh lease on life and, for the most part, had enabled her to shuffle off the sporadic bouts of depression that had followed her husband's death.

"Look, Mum, you've got to start living again," Gary had frequently urged on his Friday night visits with Emunah before Samuel's arrival. "Moping around will not bring Dad back and will not help you. I'm sure he'd say the same thing if he was standing right here. And besides, you're not old. You've still got years of life ahead of you. And if I may say so, you're not an unattractive woman for your age … though a bit too feisty at times. You look after your figure and your hair; and you've got an incredibly young-looking complexion. I'm certain you could still attract some company from the opposite gender."

Fay would generally wave away her son with a "You've got to be joking!" But spurred on undoubtedly by Gary and Emunah's words of encouragement, she'd made more than the usual number of trips to her hairdresser to maintain the darkish colouring. She'd also acquired a new wardrobe and joined some of the local Jewish clubs for her peer group; although she considered them too old and staid in their attitudes for her liking.

"How do I look?" a svelte, neatly coiffed and elegantly suited Fay had enquired of her daughter-in-law when the glowing grandmother had arrived to collect Samuel early one morning.

"You look really fantastic, Mum," an impressed Emunah had replied, watching her mother-in-law place a swanky mauve leather handbag on the hall's polished wood floor and, with twinkling eyes, perform a neat little pirouette or two. "And I love the new hairdo. Anyone would mistake you for Samuel's Mum!"

Fay flushed as she came to a slightly dizzy rest.

"T-That's a very kind thing to say, Emunah sweetheart … thank you," she said smiling coyly. "But I think you may be exaggerating just a teensy little lot!"

Fay gently rolled the pram to and fro as she relaxed on her favoured bench in Golders Green. She recalled being really flattered, flustered even, to receive numerous admiring glances when she'd taken her place in the synagogue on Rosh Hashanah and Yom Kippur. The glamorous granny, or so Gary had cheekily called his Mum, chortled inwardly as she shifted on the wooden seat and brought to her mind's eye the well-chosen Yomtov outfit she'd acquired in Bond Street. The purple, figure-enhancing suit and matching wide-brimmed, Ascot-style hat had been gob-smacking winners, if she said so herself. Fay sighed with the well-remembered gratification she'd experienced, whilst now vaguely absorbing the hooting rattle and trundling clatter of passing traffic and the hurrying movement of pedestrians passing along the High Road. She laughed audibly, but felt somewhat self-aware, as she recollected Samuel wearing the cutest tiny white kippah and nestling contentedly in his proud father's arms during the New Year service in their shul.

Long skirted young mothers in striking sheitls and wheeling designer prams or buggies, and equally modestly garbed elderly women in less stunning hairpieces but pushing shopping baskets on wheels, paraded past the bench. Some of them nodded approvingly at Fay and the shlaffing child. Maybe, she wondered, these ultra-religious ladies, young and old, thought she was wearing the requisite wig too and was equally Orthodox. Bearded Jewish men wearing large black hats or yarmulkes and lengthy black coats, and carrying black-covered prayer or study books, hastened resolutely along the pavement without casting a glance in Fay's direction. She knew it wasn't the done thing for these pious gentlemen to gaze upon, or glance with interest at, a woman other than their wives. Even if that woman might be quite mature in age. The Charedi, Fay felt, seemed so preoccupied, so withdrawn, so seemingly separate and unapproachable ... as if they lived in another world. Somehow these ultra-Orthodox men and women made her feel uncomfortable, a tad uneasy about her traditional Jewish ways.

She and Sam had kept a kosher home and attended synagogue, though mainly over the High Holydays and some of the minor festivals, just like most moderately religious Jews did nowadays. They'd enjoyed holidaying in Florida or on the Costa del Sol in the summer, and vacationing in the Canary Islands during the winter. Her husband had insisted that, when away from home, they eat only permissible foodstuffs, like fish with fins and scales and strictly vegetarian meals. Fay thought about her son and daughter-in-law. Gary and Emunah were becoming much more observant, notably since Samuel had arrived on the scene. His grandmother reckoned that the development had something to do with the religious environment in which they lived. Nowadays, her son also attended his shul's daily morning minyan before having his breakfast and going to the office. And she believed that Emunah was now using the mikveh. Gary had told his mother that he intended constructing a succah in the back garden for the festival of Succoth. Fay was more than glad that Gary and Emunah were happy in their newfound surge of faith. Though she was beginning to wonder, with some sad apprehension, how long it would be before they refused to eat in her house because it wasn't kosher enough for them.

A tall, slim and clean-shaven man, perhaps around her age Fay considered, stopped by Samuel's pram, stooped and peered under its canopy at the slumbering baby. She took in his dark blue overcoat and a matching trilby hat.

As Fay had effectively predicted, the man began making soft cooing noises. The anxious grandmother leaned forward.

"Shush," Fay murmured. "He's sleeping."

When the man straightened up to face her, Fay noticed very blue eyes and frizzy grey sideburns framing a benign face.

"Sorry," the man said. "But he's really lovely."

Fay beamed.

"I think so too," she said. "But then you could say I'm his biased bubbeh."

The man's features registered some surprise as he sat down beside, in his view, a rather good-looking lady.

"You're the baby's grandmother?" he quizzed, touching the brim of his hat. "I don't believe you."

Fay frowned at him.

"Why don't you believe me?"

"Forgive me, please. I don't really doubt what you're telling me. But, in all honesty, I thought you were the boy's mother."

Fay sensed her face blushing like that of a shy teenager.

"You and my daughter-in-law …" she chuckled. "Both of

you are right royal schmoozers!"

The man laughed. And such a manly laugh, Fay thought. Though the sound it made was rather musical in tone. This guy was quite a charmer, she concluded.

"Haven't we met before?" he enquired, his eyes smiling. "You look very familiar."

"That's a really ancient chat-up line, isn't it?"

The nice-looking man grinned.

"I don't wish to sound discourteous in any way, but why are you answering all my questions with other questions?"

"Because I'm Jewish, that's why," Fay replied steadfastly.

"So am I but …"

"Yes, I think I'd managed to twig that one."

The man laughed again and the reaction, Fay noted, creased his face quite agreeably.

"Banter aside," he went on, "I'm sure that I've seen you previously … and maybe on more than the odd occasion."

"It's a distinct possibility. This is a very Jewish area after all, so I suppose we're frequenting similar shops, restaurants … I also go to a few clubs round here."

The man nodded knowingly.

"By the way, my name's Phillip. What's yours?"

"Fay."

"Hello, Fay."

"Hello, Phillip. Maybe you've seen me at one of the clubs I go to …"

"Yes, I suppose that's quite likely. And please call me Phil, everyone else does. Anyway, I'm very pleased to meet you Fay."

She liked the way Phillip … Phil spoke her name, in a lulling lyrical way. Strange to note, she mused, but it made her feel like a young woman again … all funny inside. Oddly, it felt like she was sliding into the role of a female protagonist in a Mills & Boon novel. Her face flushed again. She learned over the next few minutes that Phillip had lost his wife Bertha about the same time Sam had passed away. Sympathetically, they shared each other's dreadful memories of a fathomless depression after their life-long partners had died. If it hadn't been for the continuous care and support of his daughter and son-in-law and their two teenaged sons, Phillip explained, he wasn't sure he could've coped with living any more. Fay nodded with a heartfelt understanding, eyes glazing with personal recollections of a dire period in her own life. She spoke of her son Gary and his new family; and of how she'd managed to transform herself into a sort of pensioner au pair. Fay and Phillip laughed simultaneously as Samuel, almost on cue, awoke with a splutter then a sneeze and finally burst into tears. His doting bubbeh rocked the pram soothingly and the baby calmed almost at once, dribbling profusely onto the coverlet.

"I'd better take him home now," Fay said rising from the bench.

Phillip offered his right hand and she shook it.

"P–Perhaps I could phone you?" he asked hesitantly. "M–Maybe I could treat you to some coffee and cake in one of the cafés along here?"

Fay, who was now releasing the pram's brake, appeared pensive for a few moments. She perceived that her companion of the last quarter of an hour looked disappointed, even crestfallen, at the absence of an instant reaction. Taking a firm grip of the buggy's shiny white handle, Samuel's regular but transient carer looked up into the man's kindly but now balefully expectant eyes.

"Yes, that would be very nice," Fay said. "Thank you, Phillip … sorry, Phil."

"My pleasure," he said, his features expanding into a broad grin. Amazingly efficiently, Fay thought, her newfound acquaintance withdrew a notebook and a biro from an inside pocket and began to write down her telephone number.

★ ★ ★

Fay was thoroughly enjoying her delicious dinner with Gary and Emunah in their garden succah, which they'd colourfully embellished with various fruits hanging from its roof beams and large poster landscapes of Jerusalem. The pictures, her son had confided, would hopefully offer a happy slice of nostalgia to her daughter-in-law. The weather had continued unusually but pleasingly dry and mild for the festival of Tabernacles, which Fay knew commemorated the Children of Israel's temporary shelters during their sojourn in the wilderness of Sinai. Just as well there hadn't been any rain-showers, she reflected while gazing up through the ceiling of closely entwined leaves at the slivers of starry black sky. An amount of water coming through the fragile green covering of this eight-day dwelling could literally put a dampener on evening meals.

"You've been looking particularly pleased with yourself of late, Mum," Emunah mentioned casually on serving up her hot apple strudel. "What's news then?"

"I was thinking the very same thing, darling," Gary added, taking a dish of the steaming dessert from his wife and waving a hand at his beaming mother. "You look just like the pussy cat that's found the cream!"

Fay remained irritatingly silent to the couple as she picked up her fork and spoon and started breaking down the hot crispy pastry coating to reveal the warm, juicily oozing apple pieces. But despite a half-hearted attempt, Fay was unable to prevent a shimmering smile from erupting across her cheeks.

"Come on, Mum," Gary demanded frustratingly, whilst stuffing his mouth with a tidy spoonful of Emunah's superbly tasty confection. "There's something on your mind, my dear mother … look at your face. Come on, out with it now!"

Fay shrugged, savouring the warming, flaky and apple-filled concoction her talented daughter-in-law had dished up.

"Don't speak with your mouth full, Gary!" she responded.

"Never mind my admittedly questionable eating habits, Mum," her son muttered, gulping hard. "Just tell us what's going on, smiley chops."

"Don't be disrespectful," Emunah chided her husband, albeit benignly, sitting down with her own bowl of dessert and staring questioningly across the table at her coy mother-in-law. "Mum's going to tell us all about it right now, aren't you?"

Fay swallowed a mixed morsel of scrumptious pastry and apple then replaced her cutlery on the plastic tablecloth and wiped her lips with a paper napkin.

"I've been going out with someone," she said quietly, with maybe a trace of self-reproach in her voice.

"What was that, Mum?"

Emunah kicked her husband's leg, though not too aggressively, under the table.

"Oh stop that, my lovely wife! I really didn't hear what Mum just said."

Fay leaned towards her son.

"I said that I'm being taken out by a friend … a man friend. His name's Phillip, Phil to his friends. He has been very kind to me. He's a very sympathetic and thoughtful person and a good listener. And I like him … I like him very much."

"That's absolutely wonderful!" Emunah declared.

Gary didn't say anything for a short while, that is until his head-shaking spouse tapped his ankle with her foot.

"W–Why haven't you told us before now?" he asked with a befuddled kind of delight. "This is really good news. It's obviously making you very happy. And that's great! I'm so pleased. But why didn't you say something?"

Fay breathed a deep sigh of relief and smiled with acute pleasure at her son's ready acceptance and approval. But after all's said and done, he'd suggested the possibility of her attracting a member of the opposite sex, she pondered.

"I am saying something!" she said firmly.

Emunah waved her arms in the air.

"So tell us about this Phillip, Mum. He sounds like a really pleasant guy."

Fay lowered her eyes.

"Yes, I think he's lovely," she said softly.

Eagerly she related the story of her initial meeting with this tall, handsome man in Golders Green; and how Phil had kept his promise to call her. Quite unexpectedly, she told her son and daughter-in-law, he'd phoned the very day they'd met. He'd actually invited her to dinner for the following evening at one of the best kosher restaurants in North West London. He'd picked her up at the appointed time and driven her away in his very nice car. They'd enjoyed a truly excellent three-course meal and a long chat. To reciprocate his generosity, Fay added, she'd insisted that the retired chartered accountant come for supper at her flat the next night. After eating then clearing away the dishes, which Phil had very kindly offered to help wash up, they'd sat together on the comfortable settee and talked for hours, getting to know each other really well.

"Phil didn't leave until two in the morning!" Fay disclosed with a certain amount of reluctance. "Well, the passing time just didn't seem to worry us."

"I see …" her son remarked with a knowing wink, as Emunah nudged his arm disapprovingly.

"No, no … there was nothing like that," his mother reacted instantly, feeling her cheeks heating up.

Why am I behaving like a sheepish and innocent virgin, Fay wondered?

"No, Gary … nothing like that at all. Phil's a charming, considerate, respectable and respectful gentleman. He brought me an enchanting bunch of red roses. It was so thoughtful of him. I almost burst into tears. But he's very understanding, I can't tell you. And I've known him only a very short while …"

"That must've been last Wednesday … I thought you'd gone to your club."

"Yes, it was last Wednesday, Gary."

"But I just get the feeling from the way you've been acting this evening that something's happened even more recently … Ouch!"

Emunah had reprised exercising her foot on her husband's shin.

Fay's upturned mouth playfully asked the air: "Let me think …"

Gary rolled his eyes then checked out the position of his spouse's abnormally active feet.

"Well, yesterday morning," his Mum continued, "Phil

phoned to say we'd been invited for dinner, that's last night, in his daughter's succah in Stanmore."

"That must've been very nice," Emunah said sweetly.

"Yes, it was … very nice indeed. Everyone was so welcoming. I met Phil's close family and then we all sat down for the meal, which was really good …"

Fay's current hostess nodded equivocally.

"But Sandra's cooking isn't quite up to yours, Emunah," she hastened to add with a tactful diplomacy, if not political correctness.

Gary gazed speculatively at his mother. He was beginning to harbour a strong feeling that she wasn't coughing up everything that had occurred.

"So what happened next, Mum?" he enquired evenly, forming a meditative triangle under his chin with his fingers and making his eyes as small and penetrating as possible. "I know you're dying to tell us something."

"Around nine-thirty last night it was becoming quite chilly in the succah, so the family went back into the house. Phil wanted us to stay outside for just a little longer. Chivalrously, he went inside to get our topcoats. And, rather sweetly, he mentioned how lovely I looked. Actually, I'd been to my hairdresser that day. Between the leaves in the roof of the succah we could see the stars sparkling in the blackness. It was such a beautifully clear night, you probably recall …"

There was a pause. Gary and Emunah nodded, hanging onto every word now.

"At that moment I felt like a young woman again," Fay went on, sensing her chin trembling slightly. "It made me feel a … well, you know, a bit awkward in a way … even guilty. Phil's marvellous … I think he could see in my eyes the uncertainty, the insecure sense of doing something wrong. He pulled up a chair and sat down beside me. 'It's strange,' he said, placing a hand on my arm, 'I feel exactly the same way as I know you do. I suppose it's only natural, Fay.' Then he put his arm around my shoulders. I was starting to shiver and not, I think, only from the dropping temperature. But in the instant, I felt that absolutely everything was all right. 'I'm sure that our beloved late spouses would be glad we're happy,' he whispered in my ear."

Gary and Emunah remained quiet as church mice while Fay related the last evening's events. Her son curved an arm around his wife's waist and squeezed with enthusiasm. The couple looked with a warm and loving intensity into each other's eyes and smiled. Fay removed a tissue from her handbag and dabbed her cheeks.

"What's wrong, Mum?" her son asked, disturbed by the transformation in his mother's demeanour from joyful to tearful.

"Nothing, nothing at all," she answered. "In fact, everything's as right as it could be. Phil said that, although we'd known each other for an extremely short period of time, he couldn't stop thinking about me. 'Carpe diem … I must seize the day!' he declared, adding that he wasn't getting any younger. He said that I was a beautiful person and that he loved me. Then … then, he asked me to marry him. And, guess what? I said … yes, thank you."

My Jewish Cat

"WHAT DEFINES being Jewish?" Barry asked me out of the blue a short while back. There we were, a couple of cholent paunchy, retired and thinly grey-haired men just chilling out with a few bottles of lager beer and an economy bag of potato crisps in the lounge of my best friend's detached North-East London home one fine June evening. As I recall, it was during the Wimbledon tennis fortnight; though we're not especially aficionados of the sport. Maybe I remember that event because we'd tucked into some strawberries and cream during the afternoon. It was probably a Thursday. Our darling wives had gone out together, first to shop then to eat and finally to the local cinema, a routine they invariably pursued on that day of the week.

"We can enjoy an interesting intellectual discussion about religion for a change," Barry continued. "For a start, I could refer to the Nazis' pernicious Nuremberg race laws of the 1930s and ..."

I interrupted my dear friend's flow: "And I might mention the State of Israel's Law of Return."

Barry shook his head.

"It's a tricky subject," he said thoughtfully.

"That may well be the case," I concurred. "But I'm certain of at least one thing."

"And what's that?"

"My cat's definitely Jewish."

Barry grinned from ear to ear across his roseate fleshy face and smoothed the ends of his incongruously dapper salt and pepper moustache with inelegant chubby fingers. Of course I recognised his time-honoured way of accepting a challenge, like the throwing down of a gauntlet in medieval times.

"Don't you need a Yiddishe Mama, a Jewish Mum, to be halachically Jewish, that is Jewish by Jewish law?" he queried with more than a tinge of smugness, if not sarcasm.

"Not necessarily," I countered, straight-faced and assured on my first service. "Many adherents to our faith are Jewish but they never had a Jewish mother."

Barry looked nonplussed for a moment.

"I'm thinking of converts of course," I explained. "And my feline is a convert to the Jewish religion."

I could tell that Barry sensed the game was becoming artfully serious.

"But your moggie's black," he asserted whimsically. "Are there black Jews?"

I served another strong ball.

"You're forgetting Operation Moses," I advanced.

"Operation Moses …? You mean when the Biblical Moses led the children of Israel out of Egypt?"

"Don't be clever, Barry," I sighed impatiently. "I'm sure you recall the thousands of Falashas that were smuggled out of Ethiopia to Israel some years ago now."

My old friend, duly reminded, offered me a condescending nod.

"Yeah, I recall the mission. Okay, so some Jews are black. That's great but your pussycat's a tom, isn't it?"

I could see immediately where his ball was headed.

"That's right," I replied with a crooked smile. "His name's George, as I believe you're aware."

My pal of more than thirty years folded his face into a smirk of self-satisfaction.

"Every Jewish male child must have a brit mila when eight days old, unless of course it's postponed for medical reasons, like jaundice," he advanced. "Or we have an adult convert, in which case the brit could be whenever appropriate. That's right, isn't it?"

"Absolutely," I responded flatly, "as you well know."

"So ... has George the convert been circumcised?"

I was more than ready for this vexatious smash into my court.

"Look Barry," I said in an intentionally low voice, "I don't want to go into the lurid details while we're drinking and nibbling but I can assure you that George has been well and truly, how can I put it ... snipped!"

My sceptical companion waved a dismissive hand at me and changed tack. It seemed that I'd taken the first game.

"Be that as it may," he stated haughtily, "George is hardly a Jewish sounding name, now is it?"

I easily returned my chum's weak lob.

"My answer to you is twofold, Barry. One, have you glanced down the Births' column in the Jewish Chronicle lately? And two, I just need to say Whoopi Goldberg! Believe me, my friend, there's little in a name nowadays to determine whether or not an individual's Jewish, unless of course someone's a Cohen or a Levy. But even then …"

Another game to me, I was thinking.

By now, Barry's visage had acquired a shiny veneer of frustration at the way his personally initiated debate was progressing … not. He went into the kitchen to fetch another couple of Australia's finest lagers, returned to the living room, handed one of the beers to me and collapsed back into his favourite armchair. For a few minutes, as I sucked down a few mouthfuls, my friend just sat silently contemplating the bottle he gripped tightly in his hand.

"But George doesn't go to the synagogue regularly, or indeed at all, does he?" he spouted at last while scratching his follicle challenged head, the sound of incipient triumph in his voice. I'd been planning a swingeing backhander to this kind of sly and underhand slice close to the net.

"Tell me, Barry," I invited. "How many Jews do you think attend shul more than twice a year, on Rosh Hashanah and Yom Kippur? Or save perhaps for simchas such as weddings and barmitzvahs, how many don't go at all? Don't forget, there are loads of merely cultural, even secular or nominal Jews."

Barry bunched his fulsome lips, a bit like the Italian fascist dictator Benito Mussolini used to do, and shrugged his shoulders in reluctant assent.

"So synagogue attendance, or rather the lack of it, is hardly a definite even satisfactory measure of whether a person is Jewish," I commented, calculating that the set was certainly proceeding well in my favour.

My friend quaffed from his bottle and adopted that hubristic

Duce expression again. I knew fairly confidently that his nemesis was not too far off now; though, obviously, it wouldn't involve any form of suspension from a lamppost.

"In any event, my point is academic," I went on. "In fact, George does attend synagogue … and as regular as clockwork, every Shabbat."

You should've witnessed the astonished look on Barry's face as his attitude changed rapidly from scepticism to incredulity. Believe me, it was an absolute wonder to behold. This couldn't be game, set and match already? Disconcertingly, my best mate burst into an explosion of cackling laughter, like a witch shrieking over a bubbling cauldron, and almost spilled the lager over his grey-flannelled legs.

"I readily confess that I don't go to shul often … but it's more than a little problematic for me to swallow that one. What a chutzpah!"

With the self-assurance of a player with a powerful forearm, I returned his high curving ball.

"I'm telling you, George comes to the synagogue every week without fail. His visits began around three months ago. My nephew Paul called me out from my seat a little way into the Sabbath service. You know Paul … my brother's son, the doctor. Well, he was on security duty inside the glass-fronted main entrance to the building. 'Your cat's scratching on the door,' he informed me with a wide grin as we walked through the shul hall to the lobby area. As you're aware, Barry, we live just a short walk from the synagogue. So it was quite possible, I thought, that our black furred pussy had trailed me from home that morning. Naturally, Paul had recognised fat George immediately. I removed my tallit, hung it over a chair in the hall and followed my nephew to the door. Through the glass panels I could see my cat sitting quite nonchalantly on the stone step and peering through the window into the lobby. As soon as George recognised me, he began scratching eagerly with a paw on the door. Paul opened it and the cat ambled in, purring yearningly whilst nuzzling my leg. I hauled up the plump puss and gave him a big affectionate cuddle."

Barry did that thing again with his moustache ends but I carried on with my narrative, completely unfazed by my fellow beer-drinker's amusing hand-to-mouth antics.

"I put the cat back down on the carpeted floor. 'Go home, George!' I commanded, physically positioning the cat so that he faced the direction of the pavement beyond the synagogue's flag-stoned front courtyard. Then I gave him a firm push on his ample rump. He moved onto the doorstep and we closed the entrance behind him. George turned to stare at us with such sad eyes, as if to say we shouldn't be evicting him from the shul. Then he waddled across the open space in front of the building. At the iron-grilled gate in the low brick wall, the cat halted and gazed back at us with hooded eyes. I waved at him to go on. But my chubby cat had other ideas. He adopted a comfy position on his haunches right up against the inside of the wall. I opened the door and shouted, 'Go home, George ... go home!' He didn't stir a single feline muscle, just sat there looking at me with a really supercilious expression. I gave up, thanked Paul and resumed my pew in shul. When I left the synagogue after Kiddush, George was still in the same position he'd adopted earlier. I wagged an admonitory index finger at him but he just blinked innocently at me. I can tell you, Barry, my cold heart softened like thawing ice. I bent down to stroke his glossy back, which arched under my hand. Then he followed me home licking his whiskered chops, doubtless at the thought of a delicious smoked salmon starter for Shabbat lunch."

Barry sat quietly as I rambled on. "As usual on my return home," I continued, "I touched the mezuzah on the street door jamb then kissed the tips of my fingers. Can you imagine my amazed amusement when George tried to emulate my actions? He jumped up and gently brushed the door post with his right forepaw. And believe it or believe it not, on landing he started to lick his furry digits. Tell me Barry, how can you possibly doubt that my cat's Jewish? He may not possess a kippah or a tallit but he tails me to shul every Shabbat. He isn't allowed inside, of course. But he sits silently and patiently by the wall. Coincidentally it's the western wall of the forecourt, reminiscent of the Western Wall of the Temple in Jerusalem. He just rests there, mostly with his eyes closed, until we emerge at the end of the service. If you saw him you might be forgiven for thinking that George was immersed intensely in prayerful meditation."

My friend didn't utter a word after I'd finished my lengthy anecdote. He took another swig of his beer but said nothing. Prematurely perhaps, I took this as an outward sign that he'd resigned himself to imminent defeat on the court of mysterious happenings. But I'd reserved to myself a resounding ace.

"There's another characteristic that supports my cat's Jewish credentials," I hastened to add. "Over time I've discovered by observation that George will refrain from any kind of work on the Sabbath. On weekdays we often find a small dead bird or mammal propped outside our back door. Not that we're overjoyed to receive these deceased creatures, you understand. But this is George's instinctive way of proving his love for us ... the only kind of presents a loyal, devoted and affectionate cat can give to his carers. However, we've never come across similar lifeless hunting trophies lying beside the garden door on a Shabbat. We've taken this to mean that George will not indulge in his normal operational activities on that sacred day."

Barry shook his head and threw me a very old fashioned, and possibly pitying, look.

"Furthermore," I continued, seeing that the ace up my sleeve had virtually routed my dear friend, "you know that you're not supposed to turn on a light on Shabbat. Well, George never does that during our holy day of rest. I know what you might say, Barry. But it's neither here nor there that he may be incapable of doing so in any case; or that felines generally see better than humans in the dark. What's more, my cat never watches television on the Sabbath. He's frequently glued to the screen on a weekday evening. But, from the lighting of Friday night candles until the recitation of Havdalah when Shabbat goes out, he's not to be found anywhere near the TV. It's true of course that we never switch on the box during that period of time. But let's not nitpick, Barry. To all intents and purposes, George is Shomer Shabbat!"

My now almost comatose Thursday night companion, and fellow verbal tennis player, suddenly sprang to life again. He'd obviously been struck by some fabulous idea to prop up his crumbling offensive.

"What about giving tzedakah, what about donating to charity?" He launched the ball into my court with a wry smile. "Aiding the poor and needy in the community is at the heart of our Jewish philosophy. It's incumbent on every Jew, if he or she can afford to do so, to contribute to the wellbeing of other people less fortunate. Surely George doesn't aspire to this mitzvah?"

Barry's conceited if not self-righteous smirk seemed to evidence a belief that he'd just hurled a game-transforming missile over the net. But I was more than prepared for such a strike, and ready to hit back with a firm defensive racket.

"Let me tell you something, Barry," I began. "I think that George does in fact aspire to such a good deed. I believe that he has a sensitive appreciation of the concept of voluntary giving. Please allow me to elucidate."

My friend folded his arms across a barrel chest, his head inclined at an angle signifying a radical cynicism and disbelief.

"Occasionally," I went on, unfazed by my friend's provocative posture, "a stray or lost pussy will venture through our cat flap into the house. It's inevitable that this will happen from time to time. More than once, however, I've noticed George unselfishly sharing his bowl of food with an unlucky and hungry fellow feline from the street."

Barry's reaction to this unexpected ball was one of almost predictable despondency. I felt a little sorry for him but only a tad, mind you. My regret quickly dissipated in a certain amount of self-satisfaction.

"I know you're struggling to identify an attribute of Jewish character or ethos which George doesn't or can't possess," I said sympathetically. "Well, permit me to oblige you. What about the study of Torah? I'm one hundred percent convinced that you would say this is impossible for him. For once, maybe, I could agree with such a view ..."

At that, my dear friend's face brightened considerably.

"But I would accept any such opinion only on a purely technical basis."

Barry's eyes dulled again. A monosyllabic grunt, originating from deep within his throat, burst from his bristle-topped mouth.

"Huh!"

"Let me explain," I said. "You know I'm fairly computer savvy. Well, who isn't nowadays? Okay, I'm not talking about you Barry. I'm speaking of regular people. Anyway, I bought this amazing Torah study programme on CD-Rom. It's fantastically absorbing and enlightening. Late at night, when the wife's gone to bed, you'll find me manoeuvring my little mouse. Now that may've been the first thing that attracted my clever pussycat to this particular course …"

My friend's eyebrows lifted appreciably.

"The mouse, I mean … the mouse attracted him."

"The mouse …?"

"Yeah, the mouse … Why do you think it's called a mouse? Because it has the appearance of a small rodent, with its long thin cable looking like a tail. Anyhow, one evening the cat padded into my study, jumped onto the bookcase next to my desk, spotted the mouse and leapt onto my lap. Thank heavens I hadn't yet changed into my jimjams, if you know what I mean …"

Barry grinned as, undoubtedly, he conjured up a mental picture of what would've been my unprotected area.

"My heavyweight denim trousers proved their worth that night, I can tell you. But having taken a close peek and paw prod at the mouse, George soon realised that it was a case of mistaken identity. He rubbed his head on my arm and purred softly. Then he turned to face the bright VDU and was immediately fascinated by the movements on screen. He squatted down, with his hefty rump against my body, and peered over the keyboard at the flashing words, signs and images. Whenever I run the Torah CD, and George seems to have an extra sense for anticipating this, he'll join me in the study, assume his usual place and stare intently at the monitor. You know and I know, Barry, that George will never be taking semichah. But, believe you me, if you could see his glowing face after a learning session you too might say, *There are more things in Heaven and Earth than are dreamt of in our philosophy ...*"

My friend blinked rapidly as my ace flew off the verdant court with a puff of white rising behind him, metaphorically speaking of course.

"Okay, okay ... enough already!" he conceded. "I almost surrender."

Naturally I questioned his conditional acceptance of failure.

"What do you mean, *almost*?"

With a mock-cynical air, he let fly his final, desperate assault by batting a really powerful ball.

"Well what about your cat and Kashrut, then?" he baited me, sneeringly. "What about our strict Jewish dietary laws? I'm pretty sure that pet food manufacturers aren't especially fussy about the ingredients of pussy pieces ..."

Barry's ball climbed really high before descending, but I was ready for it.

"If you knew George as well as I do, you wouldn't even dream of raising this issue," I responded pertly. "I wouldn't say our cat's fat but I've needed to enlarge the backdoor flap twice! We certainly don't over-feed him ... that wouldn't be right. But he's nearly nine years old and he loves his grub. Why? Because he's a Jewish cat and his meals are the best wholesome kosher cuisine cooked by my darling wife's own fair hands, whether it's fish, meat or poultry."

Barry shook his head and I wondered why.

"Hold on, my dear friend. Just listen to this. Maybe even more significantly, George will drink from his saucer of milk only after a meal of fish … never directly after a dish of beef, lamb, chicken or turkey."

My companion could barely stifle a giveaway chuckle.

"And did I ever mention," I went on, "that George is a great connoisseur of smoked salmon? Well, he is. And he distinctly prefers Scottish to Canadian. He gets a bit miffed if we don't get that right for him. But there's one notable food product that he craves above all others. And were the matter we're discussing still to involve even a scintilla of doubt for you, this single item will serve finally to prove that George is, without question, a Jewish cat. Any idea what it might be, Barry?"

There was a brief pause before my host sighed what constituted easily the longest, deepest and most evocative sigh that night.

"Go on then … put me out of my misery."

With a final victorious swing of my bat, I took up the ultimate challenge.

"George absolutely adores chopped liver. Game, set and match, I think?"

My close and enduring friend threw up his hands with a dire groan, giving in completely and utterly. Unconditional surrender!

Without figuratively vaulting any net, we shook hands like tennis pros, roared with laughter and drained the last of the golden liquid from our Aussie lager bottles.

"Listen Barry," I urged, after we'd taken a welcome breather from our heated debating contest. "Have I told you about my daughter's dog, Dov?"

A florid head shook questioningly and expectantly in front of me.

"Well, apparently, he has recently become an atheist …"

Stacey's Turkish Delight

"YOU'RE JEWISH aren't you, Stacey?"

"How can you tell, Ibrahim?"

The eighteen-year-old London media undergraduate had learned the guy's name, and he hers, in the hotel's crowded disco an hour or so earlier.

"It's pretty obvious really ... " the olive-complexioned young man with the slick and thick black curly hair replied, smiling appealingly and pointing to the gold talisman on a chain hanging from Stacey's neck.

Stacey had been enthralled by the language student's superb command of English, his Eastern Mediterranean accent and, perhaps more especially, his dark but sensually expressive eyes.

"Be careful, Stacey," Melanie had urged in a whisper just before her friend walked hand-in-hand with the dishy bloke from the packed dance floor to the lamp-lit terrace overlooking the moon-dappled Aegean. "I've warned you about the reputation of these young Turks."

"But he's so fantastically good-looking," Stacey had countered sotto voce as she'd brushed past her fuller-figured holiday companion into the caressingly warm and fragrantly scented night.

The slim youth was too preoccupied with leading the coolly attractive English miss with the long, silky auburn hair to catch Melanie's maybe jealous admonition or his erstwhile dancing partner's flattering but surreptitious compliment.

Moments earlier, Stacey had been undulating rhythmically to the pulsating disco music, her lissom body in its fetching little black dress splashed with the flashing fluorescence of the multicoloured strobe lighting. It hadn't been easy to keep uppermost in her mind the fact that this was only the first day of her first vacation abroad without her parents in tow. Now she inclined against the stone parapet of the terrace with the attentive student seriously close beside her.

On the romantically illuminated space they were sheltered by tall secluding palm trees, their fanning fronds sighing in the gentle breeze wafting from the silvery sea. Stacey spotted a few other couples embracing in the arboreal shadows. She had to admit to a slightly woozy feeling but not as a result of her alcohol intake; in fact she'd drunk relatively little of the delicious cocktails. Rather she'd become intoxicated with a heady and bewildering mixture of excitement and anxiety. But drifting to her ears on the sultry zephyr were the soft soothing sounds of water lapping against the rocky coastline below and the heart-pulling smooch music floating out from the disco. What a discordant combination, she thought fleetingly, an odd mixture of the natural and unnatural.

"I've seen the Star of David emblem many times before," the young man continued. "Lots of Jewish girls wear it."

Stacey raised the threadlike lines of her eyebrows.

"Oh yes …?" she said, a teasing lilt skewing her voice. "And what were those other Jewish girls like, then?"

The young man smoothly touched the short sleeve of the girl's mini-dress.

"You misunderstand me," he said, a pained look in his eyes as he ploughed long fingers through his tightly coiled hair with a vaguely distracted movement. "I've got some friends who work in the town's leather boutiques. I've told you that, during my college breaks, I have a part-time job in a café on the seafront, near to the bazaar."

The girl nodded.

"There are many tourists from Israel who love coming to this resort …"

"I know," Stacey interjected. "I've been here just one day but I've noticed loads of them around the hotel's pool …"

This time her companion intervened.

"Yes, you would do. They're encouraged by the fact that, generally speaking and apart from the odd glitch, Turkey and Israel have had quite good diplomatic and commercial relations with each other. And things are much cheaper here."

"But why are Israeli kids allowed to run amok, shouting their heads off? I could've been holidaying in Tel Aviv!"

The young man chuckled disarmingly.

"Yes," he agreed, his white silk blouson hanging loose above knee-cut denims. "They can be exceedingly noisy. But their parents make it very profitable in the leather shops. Many of the adults and children wear a golden or silver Star of David, or sometimes their names inscribed in Hebrew. Even some of my friends sport the star and speak some Ivrit … to attract the customers, you see."

Stacey did see, and smiled knowingly.

"Do you know what, Stacey … you're even more beautiful, if that's possible, when you smile like that."

The media student felt her cheeks flushing at the sudden charm offensive and was glad the colour would be veiled by the shaded moonlight. In the background, the dance music from the disco was throbbing again. The two students laughed and gazed over the balustrade into the water and the invisible crescent of bay. The Londoner turned to look at her handsome escort and noted that, all at once, he was looking rather melancholy.

"What's wrong?" she enquired, placing a hand on the linguist's shoulders and trembling slightly at the firmness beneath the sheer material of his silky shirt. "You suddenly seem quite sad."

"I've just got the feeling that you're hesitant, possibly reluctant, to be here with me," the young man reacted forlornly.

"Don't be silly," the girl chided lightly, shaking her head so that her hair fanned wispily about her face. "I don't feel at all hesitant … or reluctant. I don't know where you got all that from … I'm sure you can be trusted."

The two youngsters glanced around at the couples beneath the dark trees that stood tall and upright like guardian sentinels at the edges of the terrace.

"There must be a couple of hundred people in the disco just a few metres from this spot," Stacey observed. "I don't think you'll make any move that I can't handle. And it makes no difference to me that you're a Muslim, Ibrahim, and I'm Jewish … if that's what you're concerned about."

The young man, probably two or three years older than his fellow student, was about to mention something he felt was important when Stacey placed an upturned finger on his lips and shook her head imperiously.

"No Ibrahim, I mean it! Our different religious affiliations don't affect my attitude towards you in any way. We can dance and talk together. Why not? What's to stop us? We're both students learning about the world. We can exchange thoughts, ideas ... and try to understand one another. Why should I feel inhibited or be prevented from doing that? We're both human beings. And as members of Abrahamic faiths, there's more that unites than may divide us. I'm certainly not afraid of you."

"That was quite a speech, Stacey. But why should you be frightened of me in any event? I'm not going to attack you, you know ... and I'm not a fanatic, if that's what you're thinking."

"I do know. And no, it isn't what's in my mind ... there are extremists in many faiths. But I really don't believe that you're one of them."

"I think you should be a politician when you grow up."

The girl's forehead furrowed: "When I grow up?"

"Sorry, Stacey, I meant when you're older. My English needs polishing off."

"No, I don't want to be a politician, Ibrahim. But I would like to work on TV documentaries. Mum and Dad would like that. They're very ambitious for me."

"Interesting ... but what would your parents think about you and me being out here on our own, far from your home on a beautiful evening?"

Stacey fingered her chin

"You're funny, Ibrahim, you know that?" she sighed with amusement. "Let me see. Well, Mum would have seven fits. And my Dad ... well, Dad would probably want to kill me! But he's such a bigot, anyway. He doesn't really take to anyone unless they're Jewish. But then again, he doesn't particularly care for most Jewish people. It's either that they're too wealthy and arrogant, or too pious and narrow-minded. To tell you the truth, I don't know what to make of him. But he is my Dad, and I love him."

The teenager paused for affect. Her companion remained silent, closely watching the incipient future documentary maker.

"He'd probably have a go at you about the Middle East even though you're Turkish," Stacey went on. "Assuming you'd regained consciousness after he'd flattened you for chatting me up! Maybe he'll mellow … when he's ninety!"

The young man smiled and took the girl's soft warm hands in his grasp.

"With the greatest of respect," he said, "it does sound as if your father is a very insecure man, though understandably protective of his lovely daughter. I can appreciate that parental concern well enough. Do you happen to be an only child?"

Stacey shook her head, her fine hair cascading over slender apricot shoulders.

"No, I have a brother. He's six years older than me and a dentist. Despite the age gap, we get on very well together. I suppose that's because we share a similar philosophy of life, living and … people."

The young man's face broadened into an engaging grin.

"No matter what your parents are like, it seems they've got themselves a pair of very intelligent and sensible offspring. And, if I may be so forward as to say, an especially delightful, beautiful and charming daughter."

The media student felt her pale skin colouring again, even though the guy was probably only practicing his adjectives, and turned to meet the sound of the sea swashing against the jutting rocks below.

"Stacey!"

The girl reacted to the sound of her name being called. It was Melanie's voice. She was standing silhouetted in front of the open door to the disco.

"I won't be long, Ibrahim … don't go away," Stacey murmured before walking towards her friend.

"How are you doing?" Melanie asked with a meaningful wink.

"Okay. What about you?"

The reciprocated enquiry was met by a hugely undignified yawn that hovered over a generous body vibrating with the gaping mouth movement.

"It's just past one in the morning, Stacey." The information emerged as a disconsolate whimper. "And I've had no takers … not a single dance all night. I thought they liked girls with big boobies here. I'm fed up and going to bed."

Stacey gave her full-figured friend a caring and supportive hug.

"Better luck tomorrow …" she sort of promised, tentatively. "I'll be along to the room soon. And I'll try not to wake you up when I come in."

"Thanks. But, anyway, I'm too weary and depressed to sleep."

Melanie waved goodnight to her more romantically successful mate with a limp fleshy hand. The young man had been observing the two girls with interest; though he wasn't close enough to hear what they were saying. He smiled, blew an air kiss to the overweight one then pivoted neatly to face the darkened bay.

"Cute little toches," Melanie sighed as a parting gift to her friend. "But don't do anything that I would ... which isn't really saying very much."

Stacey watched with sympathetic eyes as Melanie arduously climbed the steep stone steps at the side of the disco entrance. These would lead her up through the hotel's lush gardens, past the expansive, heart-shaped swimming pool with its rather tacky artificial waterfalls to the main residential building.

"Don't get yourself lost on the way ... and please avoid falling into the pool!" she shouted, as her roommate vanished into the gloom beyond the dimly illuminated trees.

Stacey walked back to rejoin the dishy student posing against the parapet.

"Let's go back inside," he suggested as she came up to him. "It will begin to get quite chilly soon."

The girl nodded and allowed him to take her hand. Back in the disco, the DJ was spinning a popular Turkish love ballad. Stacey came to life again as she let her tactile partner guide her onto the packed dance floor. He held her closely around the waist and their cheeks touched. When the song ended he gently nibbled her earlobe, sending a pleasurable frisson along her spine. He led her to a miraculously vacant, small, candle-lit table in a shadowy corner of the cavernous chamber. They slid into the padded bench seat by the wall and he ordered drinks from a passing waiter. The language student wrapped an arm around Stacey's shoulders, tenderly drawing her closer to his chest. But instead of whispering sweet amorous nothings in her ear, as she'd hopefully expected, he began asking rather mundane questions about where his disco partner lived in London.

"Do you reside at home with your parents?" he asked as the

waiter returned with two exotic-looking cocktails in funnelled glasses.

Stacey clasped the drink's bendy straw and took a quick sip of the colourful concoction before replying to this unromantic enquiry.

"Yes, I do," she confirmed, disappointment clearly evident in her delivery. "And where do you live … when you're working here during the summer season?"

"Mustafa, that's my boss, permits me to stay in a tiny studio flat he owns above the café. Needless to say, it's very convenient for work, especially since I'm always oversleeping."

"I believe you, particularly if you spend most of your slumber time at these hotel discos chatting up English birds."

"But tonight is different," the young man responded, taking the girl's hand. "Tonight fortune smiles on me. I meet you, the breathtaking Stacey."

He spoke quietly now, and in a seductive way that those English lasses she'd had in mind earlier had doubtless found difficult to resist. Then he moved even closer to the student in the eye-catching black frock.

"In fact I would like to ask you to see my flat …"

Stacey wriggled out from the young man's overly lovey-dovey grasp.

"I wondered when you were going to ask me to view your etchings."

The guy looked puzzled: "My what?"

"Your etchings … mate."

"My …"

"Oh, never mind!"

"I'm sorry, Stacey, but I think that you misunderstand what

I say. I said that I would like to ask you to see my flat, not that I'm asking you actually to come and see it."

"That's a bit subtle, Ibrahim. Your tutors must be very pleased with your semantic and idiomatic fluency in the English language."

"Thank you, but you see I've met many girls here in the resort. All they want from me is ecstasy …"

Stacey threw a seriously questioning glance at the guy sitting beside her; though not so closely beside her compared with a few moments earlier.

"The pills, you understand," he went on. "You know, Ecstasy …the pills that help give you the energy to stay awake throughout the long night."

There was a pause during which Stacey weighed up whether she should immediately return to her room. She started to rise.

"Please don't go," the young man begged, taking the girl's arm and gently re-seating her. "I regret that I haven't made myself very clear. Maybe I'm not as good as you suggest at your English language. What I'm trying very hard to say is that you are different from all the others. I respect you … really I do."

Stacey made a face but sat down.

"I bet you say that to all the girls."

"No, you're quite wrong. You're the first one that I'm respecting so much … even so soon after meeting with you. And, by the way, I never do those pills."

She swallowed a little more of her multi-hued cocktail, striving to recall the origins of the current confusing exchange.

"So what are you asking me, Ibrahim?"

He held back for a second or two, his mouth slightly ajar.

"Only that I would like to ask you out on a date," he said, with the trace of an expectant smile. "Perhaps you could come with me tomorrow evening?"

"Aside from all the codswallop you've been handing me about respect and all that jazz, give me one good reason why I should accept your invitation."

The young man's eyes appeared to indicate that some profound thought process was exercising his mind. He reached behind his back and took something from a pocket in his foreshortened jeans. Then he handed the object to Stacey. She took what looked like a smallish, slim and dark blue bound book.

"What is it?" she asked, mystified by the proffered article.

"Please regard it closely," he said, his eyes dancing into the girl's.

She flicked through the pages and noted the photograph and the official stamps. Then she glanced at the cover and scrutinised the information at the beginning of the thin volume.

"You rat, Ibra ... or should I now say, Avram?"

He raised his hands, palms outwards, in a kind of simulated capitulation.

"Could I have my Israeli passport back, please?" he requested with a guilty grin. "And Stacey, I didn't say that my name is Ibrahim or that I'm Turkish. You just heard my Turkish friends from the café calling me by that name here in the disco back awhile tonight. It's a sort of affectionate nickname they've given me. I'm sorry, but you just made an incorrect assumption."

Stacey took a deep breath then exhaled a massive sigh, and looked to the world as if she might turn seriously violent at any moment.

"But why didn't you tell me your real name?" she pressed,

invisible hot daggers flying from her glowering fiery eyes. "Why didn't you say that you're an Israeli citizen … and that you're Jewish?"

Stacey glared at the young man and made to get up again. He held onto the girl's hands and implored her to stay.

"I did try to tell you a short time ago," he pleaded. "But please look at it this way. I'm Jewish but I'm not too religious. Certainly, I'm not narrow-minded. I'm a poor student and, in my humble opinion, not at all arrogant. Tell me, Stacey. Would I not stand a good chance if you introduced me to your Dad?"

The Shoah Tree

I AM the Shoah tree. My roots are iron rods buried in concrete above the mass graves. My trunk is fashioned in hard metal; my steel branches curve downwards to a lifeless earth. My leaves are engraved with the names of thousands of Hungarian Jews murdered during the Nazi Holocaust. I am planted in the grounds of the Byzantine-style Dohány utca Synagogue, the largest in Europe, on the edge of what was Budapest's wartime Jewish ghetto. My form is that of a weeping willow. When it rains the tears from heaven trickle down my branches, moisten the grooves in my leaves and fall to wet the soil that holds the bones of our people. My branches and leaves sigh for their souls when the icy wind from beyond the plains wails through the city.

★ ★ ★

"It's through there, I think."

My wife points towards the arched entrance to an alleyway tunnelled into the grey-grim, miserable-looking tenement standing on the opposite side of the road. Lunchtime approaches and we're feeling peckish as our search continues for the kosher restaurant noted in our Jewish travel guide to Eastern Europe.

"I'm hungry in Hungary!" I quip as we cross the long narrow street called Dob utca. My wife ignores the attempted pun and we reach the gaping mouth of the dismal and dank archway. We're enjoying an autumnal break in the cosmopolitan Hungarian capital before the Yomim Noraim. Each of us clutches a carrier bag containing rattling bottles of kosher Egri Welshreisling and 47 percent proof slivovitz purchased at the Jewish wine store in the nearby square known as Klauzál tér, in what had been the broken heart of the wartime ghetto.

There's an old man, possibly Jewish, standing beside the entrance. He's wearing a long shabby overcoat of indeterminate age and colour and a battered black, or maybe brown, trilby hat. The heavy greyish stubble on his face may be an indication that he hasn't bothered shaving for several days. His sunken eyes, deep within an ashen wizened face, dully follow our movements. As we pass him he holds out his right hand, palm upwards and slightly cupped; or maybe its curvature suggests a rheumatic problem. We stop for a moment, feeling sorry for the destitute soul. I take out a 500 forint note, worth about two pounds sterling, from my wallet and give it to him. I notice his creased and sallow cheeks breaking into a faint smile. He nods, touches the sleeve of my wife's jacket with the tips of what now look like bony arthritic fingers and raises them purposefully to his dry cracked lips. We're slightly discomfited by the surprising gesture of gratitude and move off hurriedly into the dim passageway through the drab and dreary premises. As we leave the old man he whispers the word Shekoach close to my ear.

His stale warm breath lingers around my nostrils.

A damp musty odour pervades the claustrophobic and cobbled passage. We quicken our step in unspoken concurrence. But our relief at finally emerging into the light again evaporates instantly. The tunnel opens onto a deserted courtyard surrounded by dingy, dilapidated housing blocks. There's certainly no kosher restaurant to be seen. Strewn about the squalid space range heaps of rubbish surrounded by scattered litter of every description: broken tables and chairs, split barrels and upturned sofas their stuffing extruding like the innards of an eviscerated fish. We're on the point of withdrawing when we hear an oddly compelling noise. I can feel my brow furrowing as I turn to my wife.

"Sounds just like a train," I intimate with some surprise because I know the station and tracks are some way from our present location.

My wife nods in agreement.

"That's strange," she says. "There isn't a railway anywhere near here."

I nod in turn and we both continue to listen intently. Together we glance in the direction of a stone staircase leading up into one of the depressing, impoverished dwellings.

"I don't understand," my spouse adds. "The din seems to be coming from somewhere inside that building."

We approach the doorway to the gloomy housing block with its horribly blackened façade eroding and crumbling to piles of detritus in the courtyard, like rock rubble at the base of a severely weathered cliff face. On reaching the stairway we exchange glances and hesitantly begin our ascent. For support on the broken stone steps we grab hold of the rusting iron handrail attached to the filth-smeared walls. Constantly we peer upwards into the murk of the upper floors. Climbing with trepidation, but urged on by a compulsive curiosity, we note the crazily split and stained plasterwork and the spreading maps of dampness above our heads. We recoil in horror at the sight of two grossly gas-inflated but thankfully dead rats, long whiskered snouts contorted by their death throes. Peculiarly undeterred by this gruesome pair of rodents, we continue our way up to the gradually amplifying volume of locomotive sound.

On the third floor there are two wooden doors, grubby and splintered and beyond need of a coat of paint. The doors face each other across a constricted landing. One is shut, the other slightly ajar. But it's whatever lies behind the closed one that seems to be the source of the weird rhythmic clamour. We approach the door and listen carefully.

"I tell you it sounds just like a train," I whisper.

At that moment an uninvited image enters my head: a steam engine belching black smoke and pulling a long line of cattle wagons. I hear the sinister clacking of iron wheels on steel rails. I shake my head but fail to lose the incursive screams of the mass of listless Jews packed like animals into those freight cars, gasping for air and water in the oppressively stifling and fetid atmosphere. Horrendously, I can hear the ghastly rattles in their parched and tortured throats. I can almost sense a terrified collective mind tormented by unimaginable agonies. My face feels clammy moist with sweat. My wife's startled voice breaks into the wakeful nightmare.

"No, it's not the chugging of a train we can hear," she says. "Do you know what I think the noise is? It's the sound of men davening."

I wipe my wet forehead, cheeks, chin and neck with a handkerchief and, bending forward, I lean as close to the fractured and dusty old door that I dare.

"Y-You're right!" I confirm in a restrained exclamation. "It definitely sounds like hundreds of men praying."

I straighten up as my spouse grabs my arm.

"Let's go now," she insists. "I'm cold and very uncomfortable."

I'm about to concur when I hear what sounds like a child sobbing. This new rumpus is coming from the other door, the one that's slightly open. Instinctively, we edge our way in the direction of an apparently weeping infant. My wife looks at me with many unanswered, maybe unanswerable, questions in her eyes. I return a similarly perplexed expression. We gesture to each other in silent consent and push the door further open. On the other side of the creaky portal we find ourselves in a tight hallway cloaked in gloom. With the dubious benefit of a faint light from the landing behind us, we can just make out peeling, nondescript paper on sodden walls exposing disintegrating plasterwork. Tentatively, and hand-in-hand, we move slowly along the narrow corridor sniffing a sweet sickly smell and hearing some unnerving scuttling that mingles bizarrely with the constant stream of crying.

At the end of the hall, and after passing two flanking closed doors, is a third door that's also shut. I make a decision. The handle turns easily in my grip. I push this last wooden barrier with a gentle shove. My wife and I gaze into a small room illuminated by a ghostly pale glow coming through the single, dirt-encrusted and curtain free window opposite us. It's obviously a bedroom and an absolutely freezing one. Against one wall stands a ramshackle wardrobe with one of its doors hanging at a crazy angle from a smashed hinge. A threadbare rug lies on stripped floorboards in front of an iron bedstead beside the window. Lying in a foetal position on its torn and stained mattress is a young girl. Slowly she raises her red-eyed, hollow-cheeked little face as we step across the threshold.

The girl looks to be around twelve years old but it's difficult to be sure in the unusual circumstances. Incongruously, she's wearing neither a pair of pyjamas nor a dressing gown but an ankle-length topcoat that might once have been red in colour. I speculate that her clothing has something to do with the icy climate in the room. Her hair is long and dark but appears horribly matted and greasy. She shifts what I guess to be a gaunt body beneath the coat, lifts and props herself against the dark wooden headboard and draws up her legs. She stares at us blankly but without any apparent fear or apprehension, just as if we didn't really exist and therefore couldn't hurt her in any way. Tears pour down the child's cheeks and sobs wrack her small and likely skeletal frame. We approach the bed circumspectly, unthreateningly with hopefully kind and compassionate faces. We're appalled by the conditions in which the girl's living. Or rather, merely existing.

"What's your name, dear?" my wife asks softly, her voice full of a mother's anxious concern for a child. "Please don't be afraid."

The kid is doing nothing more than stare curiously at us, as if she can't believe we're real people; or, maybe, because we're actually invading her home. Certainly we've got no right to be in the privacy of her bedroom, however benign our motivation. But, fortuitously, her sustained inquisitiveness about our sudden appearance seems to be having a calming influence. Her weeping diminishes as I turn to my spouse.

"I don't think she'll understand our language," I suggest.

"Oh, but I do!" the girl declares in amazingly well articulated English.

We're dumbfounded by this incredible development. It takes a long silent pause before we recover our focus. My wife dips into her handbag then gives the child a handful of clean white paper tissues. The girl looks at them oddly then, emulating my other half's display of pretend face wiping, she begins to mop her own, sopping wet cheeks.

"What's your name, sweetheart?" my wife repeats, kneeling on the floor by the bed as I hover right behind her.

"Miriam," the child replies, removing some more moisture from around her red-ringed eyes.

"Where's your mother, Miriam?" I enquire.

The young girl rolls over to face the window and points at it. "She's down there … in the square."

We stand on our toes and try to peer down through the smeared glass. Below is a large level space that looks vaguely familiar; though we're now quite disorientated, and not only geographically speaking. We can just about make out huge tapering mounds of earth, rising like pyramids from the four corners of the strangely deserted square of open ground.

"Is that Klauzál tér down there?" I ask the girl.

She nods with deliberation then starts whimpering again. I gaze at my wife.

"That's very odd, isn't it? We've just purchased these bottles of drink in a shop off the square. Why does it look so different now?"

"Perhaps it's because we're seeing it from a different angle, a bird's-eye perspective," she offers by way of an explanation.

"You may be right, but I don't remember noticing such mountains of earth."

My wife addresses the girl again.

"We can't see anyone down there, Miriam. Please don't upset yourself so … Has your mother gone out shopping?"

We can see that the child is starting to tremble, whether from the cold or fear or for some other reason we can't tell. She waves forlornly at the window.

"My mother's buried in the mass grave down there."

We're unable to grasp what she's saying. My wife sits on the edge of the bed and clasps the little girl's hands. She turns to me quickly.

"They're like tiny blocks of ice, the poor thing," she whispers, again giving her complete attention to Miriam.

"I'm sorry, sweetheart, but I didn't quite understand what you just said."

The girl looks directly into my wife's eyes.

"My mother passed away a month ago … the square's a cemetery now."

I shrug my shoulders, incapable of comprehending what Miriam is now telling us. I can see from my wife's face that she, too, doesn't know what to make of the distraught child's words.

"Where's the rest of your family, Miriam?" I ask.

The girl is clearly struggling to refrain from weeping more tears. She sighs, such a profound sigh for one of such few years.

"My father was arrested by Gestapo and Arrow Cross men a few months ago, soon after the Germans invaded our country. I don't know where he is now. My brother was forced to join a labour battalion outside Budapest somewhere. He could be in the Ukraine. I really don't know."

We're unable to grasp what the girl is saying. But at that moment we hear coughing and spluttering coming from close by. Startled, my wife and I literally jump off the bed.

"Who's that, Miriam?" we ask independently, but in unison.

I'm looking apprehensively through the bedroom's open door and along the flat's hallway; and thinking this is all so unbelievable, so uncanny.

"It's my zayder," the child answers tearfully. "He's lying in the next room. He's very ill but the hospitals are full to bursting with the sick. They can't take any more patients. He has to stay here. But it's hopeless, anyway. I love him so much but I'm afraid that h-he's … yes, h-he's dying …"

★ ★ ★

"It's through there, I think."

My wife points at the arched entrance of an alleyway tunnelled through the drab grey tenement building on the other side of the road.

"How many more times must I say it?" she reprimands me tetchily.

"No, I don't think so," I assert, struggling to recall something … someone.

She glances at her wristwatch.

"We'd better skip lunch," my spouse advises, "or we'll miss seeing the Jewish Museum. It closes at three."

I nod assent.

"Okay. We can seek out the kosher café tomorrow."

We hasten along Dob utca, swing left into Kazinczy utca, hurry past the Orthodox synagogue and the Jewish Educational Institute and then veer left again. To our right is the Temple of Heroes, dedicated to the ten thousand Jews who fell fighting for Hungary in the First World War. At the junction of Wesselényi utca and Dohány utca stands the Great Temple, Europe's biggest shul. We know that the Jewish Museum adjoins the huge synagogue and that it's built on the site of Theodor Herzl's birthplace. My wife and I turn a corner to discover the museum directly ahead. Further along the street, iron railings skirt the boundary of the wartime burial ground behind the building. Beyond the graveyard the metal fence guards the Holocaust Memorial of Budapest.

Gazing up the street in the direction of the Memorial, we spot what appears to be a very old woman stooping close against the railings. An almost magnetic impulse draws us towards her. Approaching nearer, we notice that the woman has wispy white hair protruding from a black headscarf; and that she wears a long red outdoor coat. We stop a few metres away. Through the iron bars we can see the monumental weeping willow of iron, its branches of steel and its leaves of thin metal inscribed with the names of thousands of Jews who perished at the brutal hands of the Nazi monsters.

Now we're shifting our attention back to the old woman. Her frail body is pressed tight against the railings, her right arm stretched out through the bars. The gnarled fingers of her right hand are splayed rigidly and straining, as if she needs to touch or maybe even to embrace the Memorial with her very soul. It's like she wants to become an integral part of this poignant cenotaph. We stare at her profile and note the tears trickling down a deeply lined and anguished face. And I recollect another face … and, surely, another time. I'm feeling emotionally crushed by the woman's obvious pain of grief and mourning. Perhaps someone she loved dearly, maybe passionately, is now just a name etched into a metal leaf. I glance at my wife and can tell from her glazed eyes that she's reacting exactly as I am. I think both of us want to reach out and comfort the clearly grief-stricken woman. But instead, we turn and walk away, leaving her with whatever heartrending memories are seeking to propel her bodily through the railings and into the depths of the Shoah Tree …

The Heights of Abraham

SAUL PRESSED a silver button on the walnut dashboard of his
Bentley saloon. As the lofty, iron-grilled gates of his North West
London villa swung open he just hoped and prayed that the rabbi
had gone home. The luxury motor's engine purred like a lion cub
as the olive-skinned and six foot tall 39-year-old steered slowly
between the high-mounted CCTV cameras. The electronic
entrance gates closed automatically behind the powerful, sleekly
prestigious and shiny black limo as it swashed across the inclined
gravel driveway and came to silkily smooth rest in front of the
imposingly white, and opulently detached, house.

Grabbing his leather Cardin briefcase from the front
passenger seat, the dark brown-haired businessman glanced into
the rear-view mirror, winked at his reflection and exited the
favourite of his three classy automobiles. The Mercedes coupé
was being serviced and the Porsche was parked in the treble
garage. Saul moved with an athletic agility to the arched, solid
oak front doors within a columned portico. As he approached,
they silently glided inwards at the feather touch of a tiny blip on

his gold key-fob. Entering his home's elegantly spacious, terracotta floor-tiled reception area the formally dark-suited, but boyish-looking entrepreneur tossed his case then his Armani jacket onto a marble-topped side-table. Now he walked towards the rear of the property, passing under the lofty, glass-domed atrium of the inner hall with its magnificent, curved stairway.

"I'm home, Angie darling!" he called, heading for the kitchen.

Passing under a Moorish archway, Saul negotiated the bar salon. Behind its long, brass-railed mahogany counter, mirror-backed shelves were lined with myriad bottles of spirits and liqueurs of every description. En route, he patted each of the six, black-leather covered barstools before bursting through batwing doors into the extensive kitchen area. His healthily tanned wife Angela was propped against the impressive central island chatting with Maggie, the couple's matronly and highly capable and efficient, live-in cook-housekeeper.

Saul almost leapt across the white Provençal tiles to embrace his wife of fifteen years. He lifted her willowy body, planted a kiss on her lips and twirled her round three times like he was a human funfair ride.

"Love you, Angie baby!" he proclaimed, finally replacing her on terra firma.

"Likewise, I'm sure," she said, endeavouring to steady herself after the unexpected carousel trip. "First time you've swept me off my feet since you proposed."

Saul grinned, like a schoolboy let loose in the tuck shop, loosened the red and yellow striped tie from the collar of his blue Savile Row tailored shirt and stepped towards his wife. But she backed off, running stunningly manicured fingers through the blaze of her copper-burnished hair and clearly reluctant to be subjected to another roundabout flight.

"Can I take it from this outlandish and dizzying display that you've had good news from Daniel?" she enquired, her midriff bare between a Chanel knitted black crop-top and white Versace trousers, whilst edging towards her buxom and middle-aged factotum standing by the Aga.

"Your brother's a genius!" Saul announced jubilantly. "I would say he's just about the best chartered accountant in the City … no, correction, in the entire country if not the world!"

He danced around his wife then pecked Maggie on an ample rosy cheek. The well-rounded family retainer blushed crimson, sighed with resignation and brushed her employer away like she would an annoying bluebottle. Smoothing down her fresh white apron she huffed audibly and gathered up some dishes to distract herself.

"Danny says the businesses are doing fabulously," Saul went on gleefully.

Despite her husband's many successful ventures over the years, Angela thought to herself, he always displayed the same jingle-jangle, positively upbeat effects of an adrenalin rush whenever he received excellent financial news.

"He tells me that if profits this year meet our expectations, we can get that fantastic duplex apartment in Cap Ferrat and the handsome, Italian-designed yacht you fell in love with at Puerto Banus. Not bad going, eh darling?"

His wife's exquisitely complexioned features presented a glowing pride in the latest of Saul's marvellous corporate achievements. She stretched on tiptoe, held a now fashionable, all-day stubbly face in the flat palms of her hands and pressed her lips tightly against her husband's.

"I couldn't have done any of this without you," he murmured holding Angela really close. "You're absolutely great, darling. And I love you very much."

"You're not so bad yourself," she cooed in his ear.

"Don't mind me!" Maggie groaned as she carried a tray-load of crockery and cutlery towards the dining room. "Why don't you do it here, in the kitchen ... right in front of me?"

Saul smiled and blew her a big air kiss.

"But you know I love you, too," he said with feeling.

Maggie shrugged and rolled her eyes. She muttered something under her breath and disappeared.

"Careful Saul," Angela warned. "Maggie was brought up a strict Catholic. We'd never get another one like her."

"Don't be ridiculous, she loves it."

"I don't think so. And keep your voice down, you idiot. She'll hear you."

"Just to change the subject, my darling wife, where is everybody?"

The couple perched themselves on two of the kitchen's short-backed highchairs.

"Well, Françoise has taken the girls to the park. And Ben's still in the study learning his barmitzvah parashah with the rabbi."

The triumphant businessman's jaw dropped. Once again, he felt that familiar pang of conscience. He'd hoped the rabbi would've left the house by now. Saul knew very well that he ought to put in some appearances at the synagogue on Shabbos. His son's big day was only a few months away. Saul rubbed the back of his neck, a sure sign, at least to his wife, that he was sorely troubled. He knew that she knew precisely what her husband was thinking. They'd often talked about it but he'd insisted on the need to go into the office on a Saturday morning. Besides, as he'd mentioned more than once, Ben didn't seem so keen on attending shul anyway. Now that further self-justification, even excuse, was rattling around his head again. All of the lad's enthusiasm these days seemed to be channelled into football, football and more football. But, as the boy's father considered guiltily, he'd hardly encouraged Ben to think about attending the synagogue. On the rare occasions Saul bumped into the community's minister, the rabbi had hinted heavily at the appropriateness of regular shul attendance, especially bearing in mind the proximity of Ben's barmitzvah.

"I think maybe you should start taking Ben to shul, Saul," Angela recommended circumspectly, fully aware of her husband's business preoccupations. "After all, his barmitzvah is in three months. Why not take him next Shabbos?"

"It's very difficult for me, Angie. Raymond's coming to the office Saturday morning with plans for the new showroom. I need to be there, as you know."

At that instant and sporting the full Tottenham kit a gangly Ben mock-dribbled an imaginary football into the kitchen. Annexed by a clip to the top of his tufted fair hair was a small blue and white cupple.

"Hi, Dad!" he chirped, slapping his father's raised palm in a High Five.

"Has Rabbi Gold finished with you now?" his mother enquired.

The boy tugged at the door of the massive copper-tinted fridge.

"Yeah, Mum," he answered absently whilst scanning the

packed shelves. "He's just going. But I think he wants a word with you before he leaves. Got anything to nosh? Hebrew singing makes me so hungry!"

Saul decided to take a diplomatic dip in the indoor pool before dinner. But his wife had other ideas for his immediate future. Firmly, she grasped her husband's arm and conducted him, surprisingly without any resistance, through the house in search of Ben's religion teacher. It was at the foot of the staircase in the main hall that they found him, a middle-aged man short of stature but long on presence, bearded, bespectacled and wearing a black suit with a broad-brimmed black hat. He usually waited here while his pupil ran to tell his mother that the minister was about to depart. All three adults nodded politely. As Rabbi Gold held out his hand to Ben's Dad, Angela clandestinely prodded Saul in the lower back with a bunched fist. They'd been married long enough for her husband to receive his wife's message loud and clear.

"How's Ben getting on with his portion, rabbi?" Saul asked dutifully as, reverently, he took the older man's hand.

The community's learned and much respected minister straightened his head gear over a peeping black yarmulke, rocked his head a little like one of those plastic dogs some motorists have in their cars then scratched his hirsute chin.

"Ben's doing okay," he replied, slightly expanding his cheeks and patting Saul's arm reassuringly. "Your son's got a very sweet soprano voice, kin-a-hora. But I have to say that his Hebrew pronunciation could be a bit better."

The teacher could see from their expressions that Ben's parents appeared concerned about the brief but rather mixed review of his student's efforts.

"Please don't worry," Rabbi Gold exhorted with a kindly smile, as he fanned the air with his arms in a gesture inviting Heavenly willingness. "He'll be fine on the day … I can guarantee that. We've still got some time remaining to hone and polish."

Saul and Angela tentatively acknowledged the reassurance. Next came a topic that at least one half of the husband and wife team was dreading being raised by the personable minister.

"It would be a great pleasure to see you and Ben in shul," he said, his eyes glinting through thick lenses and directed unwaveringly at Saul.

The boy's father opened his mouth to say something that his mind had been working on in the previous few seconds, whilst mentally kicking himself for returning home earlier than normal that day. But the rabbi continued speaking.

"Ben tells me he'd really like to attend the Shabbos morning service."

Looks of astonishment mingled with doubt spread across parental faces. The teacher adjusted the angle of his spectacles, buttoned his suit jacket and carried on speaking despite the disparate reaction to his information.

"He's a good boy, very intelligent for his age. Do you know what he told me this afternoon? Ben said that he believes in the Almighty. Regrettably these days, I seldom hear such words of Divine faith volunteered by a 12-year-old. Don't worry … I'll see myself out as usual."

The rabbi puffed his cheeks again. He could see that Ben's Mum and Dad seemed dumbstruck at his report of their son's declared expression of belief. He left them staring after him, a veneer of incredulity stuck to their faces, walked across the hall and opened the door to the outside world.

"Could you give me a hand with my homework tonight, Dad?" Ben asked pleadingly across the dinner table that evening. His younger twin sisters, seated opposite him, tittered playfully alongside their French au pair.

"Well son, I've got to go out for a while to see an important customer …"

Angela pulled a flinty face at her recalcitrant husband. Saul saw his wife's menacing frown as lucidly as he might see the man in the moon on a brilliantly clear night. But her face, however, was much too close to him for comfort.

"But I should be back to give you an hour before bedtime. Is that okay, Ben?"

The boy gave his father a double thumbs-up sign.

"What's the subject, Ben?" his Dad queried, passing a big bowl of steaming roast potatoes to his now beamingly vindicated wife.

"We've got to write an essay about the solar system," Ben replied. "I've got most of the info. I just need to ask you a few questions."

Saul picked up a dish of mixed vegetables as Maggie brought in more steaming hot food from the kitchen.

"Fine, son … we'll meet up later, then."

At nine-thirty that night father and son were seated at the boy's desk in his bedroom. On its walls hung big posters of soccer heroes, football match action shots, team photos and club pennants. To one side was set up Ben's computer, monitor, keyboard, printer and mouse. In front of them was a pile of books on astronomy, the sun and its planets. Above and behind the desk was a large window its roller blind not yet pulled down to blot out the cloudless night sky. Ben finished writing a note in his school exercise book and gazed up through the glass at the thousands of twinkling stars. Then he turned to face his father.

"Dad …?"

"Yes Ben?"

"Do you ever look up at the night sky?"

Saul pondered the question for a few moments.

"Sometimes," he said, leaning back in his chair.

Ben adopted a mien earnest beyond his years.

"I mean, do you look really hard at the heavens … at the distant stars?" the boy quizzed, the thrill of excitement in his voice.

Saul thought about this.

"Well …" he began, but Ben interrupted.

"Sorry Dad, but I do … often. Do you know that there are billions of stars like the sun in our galaxy, which is called the Milky Way?"

Before Saul could say a word, his son blurted: "And there are billions of galaxies in the universe … each with billions of stars. We can't even imagine the number of planets orbiting these suns!"

Ben stared at his father who observed, with a cosily pleasurable feeling, the eagerness and wonder in his son's light blue eyes.

"Do you ever think about the universe, Dad?"

Saul sighed.

"Frankly son, I just don't have the time these days … you know how it is with me."

Ben nodded with a look that again belied his inexperience of life. Then he glanced through the window again.

"But haven't you ever wondered how it all began, Dad? The universe, I mean."

Saul was pensive for a second or two before reacting.

"Don't the scientists say that there was a big bang, or something, that exploded the universe into existence?"

Ben wildly worked his head up and down and grabbed a book from his desk.

"Yeah Dad, that's right … and this author said on TV that one day we might discover exactly how the universe began."

Saul was more than a little impressed by Ben's knowledge and mature, philosophical viewpoint. He grinned with pride and approval and gave his son a few gentle pats on the back.

"But he also said," Ben went on, "that we'll never know why the universe came into being because that would mean knowing the Mind of the Almighty."

Saul placed an arm around his son's shoulders. Unexpectedly, he felt his eyes watering.

"After your lesson today and before he left, Rabbi Gold told your Mum and me that you've expressed to him a strong belief in God."

"Do you have a strong faith, Dad?"

Saul tenderly lifted his son's chin and looked into his handsomely wondrous face

"To be honest with you Ben, I really don't know."

Ben held onto one of his father's hands.

"You know Dad," he remarked, eyes widening. "I really don't think the universe came into being all by itself. I believe what the Torah tells us in Genesis … that the Almighty created it. I read somewhere about one scientist's theory that all it needed to create the universe was gravity. But you know what I would ask that scientist: Who created gravity? The astronomers say that the universe is expanding all the time. But my question is: Expanding into what?"

Emotionally moved by his son's handholding gesture, Saul offered: "Into space?"

"Okay Dad. But does space go on for ever and ever? And if not, what's beyond space?"

Saul withdrew his hand from Ben's warm little grasp and shook his head.

"I really don't know, Ben."

Again, the boy gazed up through the window.

"But I think I do, Dad," he said in a low voice, his eyelids beginning to droop significantly. "Whenever I look up at the night sky, I know that the Almighty exists ... here, there, everywhere and beyond. And I know that He created this marvellous universe. There can't be any other sensible explanation."

Saul kissed his now yawning son goodnight and tiptoed quietly out of the bedroom. He went downstairs immersed in meaningful contemplation. He walked into the bar salon, mixed himself a generously alcoholic gin and tonic in a highball glass and settled onto a stool by the counter. For a few minutes he stared meditatively at his reflection in the mirrored wall. The dynamic entrepreneur's BlackBerry lay on the bar top a few centimetres away. He reached out to grab it but reconsidered and withdrew his hand. He gulped down a third of his drink in one huge swallow, shivered momentarily like someone had proverbially just walked over his grave then went for the mobile again. This time he picked up the black smart phone and lightly touched its glowing screen.

"Raymond ... is that you? Hi! Yeah, it's Saul ... Look Ray, I'm really sorry but I can't make it to the office on Saturday morning. We'll have to postpone the meeting till one day next week. What's that …? I know it's urgent, Ray. What did you say …? Well, I'll tell you precisely why I can't make it. You see, Ray, on Saturday mornings now I'm going to be taking my son to our synagogue …"

Glossary

Adon Olam *The final prayer, usually sung joyfully by the entire congregation, generally at the end of the Jewish Sabbath morning service*

Aliyah *Literally, a going up; a call to the reading of the Torah; settling in Israel*

Aron Ha'Kodesh *The Ark or cupboard in a synagogue holding the Sifrei Torah*

Ayn Komochah *The prayer recited before the removal of a Sefer Torah from the Aron Ha'Kodesh*

Barmitzvah *Jewish boy's coming of age on reaching thirteen*

Batmitzvah *Jewish girl's coming of age on reaching twelve*

Bayshayrt *Preordained*

Becher *A drinking cup, usually made of silver, for wine*

Beth Chayim *Literally, House of Life; a cemetery*

Bimah *Raised platform in a synagogue from which the service is conducted*

Broiges *A longstanding row, generally resulting in those involved not speaking to each other*

Bracha *Blessing*
Brit/Brit mila *Circumcision ceremony for a Jewish male child eight days old*
Bubbeh *Grandmother*

Challah *Plaited loaf of bread eaten on the Jewish Sabbath and festivals*
Chanucah *Jewish festival of lights celebrating an ancient miracle*
Chanuciah *Candelabra used during the Jewish festival of Chanucah*
Charedi *Ultra-Orthodox Jews*
Chazan *Cantor; one who sings liturgical music and leads prayers in a synagogue*
Chazanut *Cantorial/liturgical music*
Cheder *Religion school for Jewish children*
Chessed *Loving kindness*
Cholent *Jewish stew originating in Eastern Europe, eaten on Shabbat*
Chupah *Canopy under which a marriage ceremony is conducted in the synagogue; the actual marriage ceremony itself*
Chutzpah *Cheekiness; impertinence*
Cupple *Skull cap*

Davening *Praying*
Der Heim *Literally, The Homeland; usually taken to refer to Russia and the countries in Eastern Europe where Jews lived in the 19th century*

Falashas *Black Jews originating in Ethiopia*
Fleishich *Meaty*
Frum/Frummer *Very Orthodox; very Orthodox Jew*
Gelt *Money*
Gutte neshomah *Literally, a good soul; a good person*

Glossary

Haftorah *Weekly reading in the synagogue from the Prophets*

Haggadah *The book relating the story of the Children of Israel's Exodus from Egypt*

Halachah *The body of Jewish laws*

Hashem *The Almighty*

Havdalah *The ceremony in the synagogue, or in the home, to mark the end of the Jewish Sabbath*

Heimische *Amiable, informal, warm, cosy Jewish atmosphere; Jewish ethos*

High Holydays *Rosh Hashanah and Yom Kippur*

Ivrit *Modern Hebrew, as created and spoken in the State of Israel*

Judaica *Items generally of Jewish religious significance*

Judenfrei *Free of Jews*

Kaddish *Memorial prayer recited by a mourner*

Kashrut *Jewish dietary laws that dictate whether particular food or drink is kosher*

Kedushah *The holiest part of a particular Jewish prayer in the synagogue when congregants must stand*

Kehillah *A Jewish community*

Kiddush *Blessing recited over wine and bread on the Jewish Sabbath and festivals*

Kin-a-hora *An expression used to ward off evil/the evil eye*

Kippah *Skull cap*

Kishkes *Guts or innards*

Kneidlach *Matzah balls served in chicken soup, often with lokshen*

Kosher *Food and drink that can be consumed under Kashrut (Jewish dietary laws); (colloquial) genuine, legitimate, above board*

Krenker *Literally, a person who is ill; a person who complains or moans about his or her ailments*

Kvell *Brim with pride, usually at the success of children or grandchildren*

L'Chaim! *Literally, To Life; a toast*

Levoyah *Funeral*

Leyning *Reading aloud from the Torah, generally but not necessarily by a rabbi*

Lokshen *Thin noodles, usually served in chicken soup*

Luftmensch/Luftmenschen (pl) *Person whose head is in the clouds; a person who is not too good at practical matters*

Maftir *The final portion of the weekly reading from the Sefer Torah*

Magen David *Star of David; literally, Shield of David*

Matzah *Unleavened bread required to be eaten during Pesach/Passover*

Mazeltov *A wish for good fortune; an expression of congratulation*

Mensch *A good individual; one who does the right thing by his fellow man*

Mezuzah *The prayer container fixed to the doorposts of Jewish homes/buildings*

Mikveh *Ritual bath*

Milchich *Milky*

Minyan *The quorum of ten Jewish men required for prayer*

Mishegass *Madness/stupidity*

Mitzvah *Good deed*

Mussaf *Literally, additional; the final section of prayers for a Sabbath or festival morning service, commemorative of the communal offerings in the Temple on days of particular holiness*

Glossary

Nebbish *A pitiable person (the word is virtually indefinable)*
Noch *Also*
Nussach *The cantor's special intonation of Jewish prayers in the synagogue*
Nuchus *The parental feeling of pride at the success (usually) of children*

Parashah *Portion of Torah reading*
Parve *Relating to food comprising neither fleishich nor milchich products*
Pesach/Passover *Jewish festival commemorating the Children of Israel's Biblical Exodus from Egypt*

Rabbi/Rabbonim (pl) *Jewish religious leader and teacher*
Rebbe *Rabbi*
Rebbetzin *The wife of a rabbi*
Rimonim *The silver bells that decorate a dressed Sefer Torah*
Rosh Hashanah *The Jewish New Year*

Sabra *A person born in Israel*
Semichah *The qualification required to become a rabbi*
Schmoozer *A person who chit-chats and gossips; a flatterer*
Sedra *The weekly reading from the Sefer Torah*
Sefer Torah/Sifrei Torah (pl) *The scroll containing the Five Books of Moses*
Shabbat/Shabbos *The Jewish Sabbath*
Shabbat shalom *Sabbath greeting*
Shacharis *Morning prayer*
Shadchen *Go-between for an arranged marriage*
Shalom *Peace*

Shayner madel *A lovely girl*

Shekoach *Literally, strength; usually said to a person who has performed an aliyah*

Shema *A prayer acknowledging the sovereignty and Oneness of the Almighty*

Shidduch *An arranged marriage*

Shlaff/Shlaffing *Sleep; sleeping*

Shlep *To carry a (usually heavy) load; (colloquial) to journey inconveniently*

Shoah *The Nazi Holocaust of six million Jews*

Shomer Shabbat/Shomer Shabbos *Keeping all the laws of the Jewish Sabbath*

Shtetl *Jewish village or township in the Eastern Europe and Russia of yesteryear*

Shtiebl *Small shul*

Shul *Synagogue*

Simcha *Joyous celebration, such as a wedding, barmitzvah or batmitzvah*

Simchat Torah *Literally, Rejoicing of the Law; joyous Jewish festival celebrating the end and the beginning of the annual cycle of readings from the Torah*

Succah *The historic temporary dwelling used during the Jewish festival of Succoth*

Succoth/Succos/Succot *Jewish festival of Tabernacles commemorating the wandering of the Jews in the wilderness of Sinai before reaching the Promised Land*

Synagogue *Building used specifically for Jewish worship*

Tallit/Tallis/Tallisim (pl) *Prayer shawl with fringes, and usually white with black stripes, generally worn during services in the synagogue*

Glossary

Torah *The Five Books of Moses: Genesis, Exodus, Leviticus, Numbers and Deuteronomy*

Toches *Buttocks*

Tzedakah *The giving to charity; charitable donation*

Yad *Pointer, usually made of silver, used for reading from a Sefer Torah scroll*

Yarmulke *Skull cap*

Yahrzeit *Literally, time of year; anniversary of the death of a close relative*

Yeshivah *Advanced religion college for Jewish men*

Yeshivah bocha *Student at a yeshivah*

Yiddish *A language (basically German with words added mainly from Hebrew) originated by Central and East European Jews*

Yiddishe *Generally related to Jewishness*

Yiddishkeit *Traditional Jewishness*

Yomim Noraim *Literally, Days of Awe; Rosh Hashanah and Yom Kippur*

Yom Kippur *Day of Atonement, the holiest day of the Jewish calendar*

Yomtov/Yomtovim (pl) *A Jewish Holy day or festival*

Zayder *Grandfather*